LITTLE APPLE

LITTLE APPLE
Leo Perutz

TRANSLATED FROM THE GERMAN BY

John Brownjohn

ARCADE PUBLISHING · NEW YORK

LITTLE, BROWN AND COMPANY

First North American Edition 1992

First published in Germany in 1928 under the title
Wohin Rollst Du, Äpfelchen

The characters and events in this book are fictitious. Any similarity to real
persons, living or dead, is coincidental and not intended by the author.

Library of Congress Cataloging-in-Publication Data
Perutz, Leo, 1882–1957.
   [Wohin rollst du, Äpfelchen? English]
   Little apple / Leo Perutz ; translated from the
German by John Brownjohn. — 1st North American ed.
     p. cm.
   Translation of: Wohin rollst du, Äpfelchen?
   ISBN 1-55970-169-2
   I. Title.
PT 2631.E5W6413   1992
833' .912 — dc20   91-41877

Published in the United States by Arcade Publishing, Inc., New York, a
Little, Brown company, by arrangement with HarperCollins Publishers

10 9 8 7 6 5 4 3 2 1

RRD–VA

Published simultaneously in Canada by
Little, Brown & Company (Canada) Limited

Printed in the United States of America

CONTENTS

Where are you rolling, little apple . . .

Russian marching song

THE PLEDGE

There had been an unforeseen roll-call in the railway station's big medical centre, but that was the last piece of excitement. From Moscow onwards the journey proceeded without incident. When Kohout produced the dog-eared pack of cards from his pocket and suggested a game of pontoon, insisting that they owed him a chance to get even, they all joined in, including Feuerstein, who had fainted on the platform while their names were being called.

Emperger, who was in charge of the communal purse, got out at Tula and bought some bread, eggs, and hot water for tea. He even rustled up two bars of chocolate. His return was accompanied by the announcement that he had bidden Russia a final farewell and shaken its dust off his feet for ever more. He was now on neutral soil, he said, because he couldn't regard the hospital train as Russian territory.

Vittorin's face darkened. Was Emperger implying that he wouldn't return to Russia under any circumstances? What if the choice fell on him? Was there some ulterior motive behind his remark? Was he hedging his bets after all – was he subtly and unobtrusively hinting that he didn't feel bound by their agreement?

He looked up from his cards but could detect nothing in Emperger's face, with its prominent, utterly expressionless eyes, that might have confirmed his suspicions.

It was impossible! They had all made a solemn pledge. "I swear, as an officer and a man of honour . . ." – that was the form of words they'd used. There could be no going back, not now. Perhaps Emperger had been unaware of the implication

9

of his remark – perhaps he'd simply spoken without thinking. If so, it would be quite in order to deliver a friendly rebuke.

Vittorin laid aside his cards and buttoned his tunic, but he was still debating what to say when Lieutenant Kohout forestalled him.

"Sounds to me like you're trying to duck out," he said. "One of us will have to go back, you know that. What's to say it won't be you?"

"You misunderstood me, Kohout," Emperger told him. "Of course one of us will go back, but this is the last time Mother Russia will see me as a prisoner of war. If I do return, I'll be a free man. There's a difference, you have to admit."

"I've made a mental note of the name Selyukov," said Feuerstein. "I'll never forget it as long as I live. You can count on me."

"The whole thing's settled," Professor Junker protested from his window seat. "Why rake it up again? Here we are, enjoying a nice trip in a nice, clean, almost European-standard railway carriage. Why spoil it by reminding us of that man?"

Vittorin shut his eyes. There's no question of entrusting Emperger with a mission of such importance, he told himself. Emperger's a mummy's boy: soft, spoilt, and thoroughly unreliable. A good comrade, though, and a nice enough fellow in other respects. Plucky too, perhaps – after all, he did win the Silver Medal Second Class – but what a womanizer! The man thinks of nothing but his amours. Lisa, Magda, Frieda from the skating club – I've had to listen to his amatory reminiscences a hundred times. Night after night, when we'd finished our game of chess, off he would go: "Ah, those were the days!" That was his invariable prelude. Then it was Eva or the civil servant's luscious wife or Lilli from the Kaiser Bar, who always nibbled his lips. He thinks he's irresistible. Anyway, he isn't all that plucky in spite of his Second-Class Silver. He wasn't keen to come with us at first. "You'll see," he kept telling us, day and night, "we'll never get beyond Omsk – we'll get stuck there." Now that we're actually on board the hospital train, he's putting on airs and playing the train commandant. No,

I'll make sure Emperger doesn't win the vote. The Professor is equally out of the question – he wasn't an officer. "Indispensable to the world of scholarship" – that's what I'll say if someone suggests him. Kohout? With his stiff arm? That only leaves Feuerstein. I'll have him to reckon with, admittedly. He's a cunning devil – a born survivor. Whatever he wants, he gets. That fainting fit at the station was an act, you bet. He doesn't have any papers – not even a medical certificate. I doubt if he'll stand aside for me without an argument. He's got money, too – in fact he's supposed to be really well-off, an industrialist or something. Still, that could count against him, his money and his occupation. I'll point out that anyone who takes on a job like this should have no ties. Feuerstein would spend the whole time thinking of his factory and the business he might be missing. No, I'd better not say that or he may . . . After all, he's supposed to be putting up the money. We need Feuerstein, so I mustn't offend him. Kohout is bound to vote for me. I can depend on Kohout . . .

"What the devil's the matter with this train? Are we going to be stuck here for ever?" Kohout exclaimed. "Hey, where's Emperger? Can't you shut the window, Professor? There's a howling draught."

The Professor was whiling away the time by calling out "*Dosvidanya*" – "*Au revoir*" – to the peasant women lining the platform. Emperger returned with news.

"A minor mechanical fault, that's all – nothing serious. They should have it repaired in half an hour. Do you know who the old gentleman in the next compartment is? A Tsarist court official – a grand duke's son-in-law who escaped from St Petersburg by the skin of his teeth. He possesses nothing but the clothes he stands up in – the Bolsheviks robbed him of everything else, or so I was told by the lieutenant attached to the Danish Red Cross. Anyone care for a beer or some cigarettes? Another hour and we'll be in Ukrainian territory. We're all entitled to five weeks' leave, the lieutenant says. We have to put in a request at the depot."

"Of course we'll get some leave," Kohout growled. "We

don't need your lieutenant to tell us that. Let's get on with the game. Who's bank?"

"Yes," Emperger pursued, "but first we have to spend three weeks in quarantine at some rotten little hole in Podolia. It's no mere formality – can't be avoided. How about that for a nice surprise, Professor?"

Professor Junker shrugged. Kohout shuffled the pack, waited for someone to cut, and dealt.

"Your girl-friends will simply have to do without you for another three weeks," he said. "Meantime, you may as well sit down."

"When did you say we cross the border?" asked Vittorin.

"An hour from now at most."

"Kohout, time to sort out our things."

Kohout rose, reached for the luggage rack, and got down the wooden army suitcase containing his and Vittorin's belongings.

"All right, split 'em up," he said, shifting from foot to foot and wringing his hands in his characteristic way. "Straight down the middle, no more sharing."

Vittorin opened the suitcase and deposited his things on the seat: toilet articles and underclothes, a Russian smock, a fur coat with an astrakhan collar, and a pair of calf-length felt boots – unwearable at home, but a pleasant memento of his time in Siberia. Then came a skilfully woven horsehair necklace strung with four Chinese silver coins. Next, letters from his father and sisters. Vally was an infrequent correspondent, but Lola, the elder, had written punctually on the first and fifteenth of every month. Franzi Kroneis's letters were bundled together and tied up with string. "My Dear Boy . . ." They all began like that – he had no need to look at them. The ill-written letter on the top was from his brother Oskar. He unfolded this missive and proceeded to reread it.

"Dear Brother, it's ages since I wrote to you, my dear Brother, but please don't be angry with me for being so inconsiderate. Now for some news of my doings. For some

12

time now I've been taking lessons in German, shorthand, correspondence and French from a teacher at the business school. That's four lessons a week at two kronen the lesson. I also have homework to do and practise the piano in my spare time, not that I get much. Let's hope this everlasting war ends soon, and that you, dear Brother, will be able to come home. We received your dear letter dated January 16th, and were very concerned to hear of the poor conditions you're living in. Another thing: I go to the theatre and even attended some of my fellow students' parties during Carnival. Now that this letter has brought you so much news and set your mind at rest, my dear Brother, I shall close with affectionate regards. Your loving brother Oskar."

Vittorin smiled. His little brother, who had still been playing cowboys and Indians when the war broke out, would soon be a grown man himself.

Next, the red exercise book containing his Russian vocabulary lists. Several issues of the mimeographed camp newspaper. A pad of colourful Chinese writing paper. A leather waistcoat, an English grammar, a Tungus cap. A wooden ashtray carved by a fellow prisoner in the dragoons. A packet of cigarettes, and, carefully stowed away at the very bottom, the two faience vases with bird's-head handles, the white dragon on a blue ground, and the glazed green china bowl. He had acquired these pieces for next to nothing, but Emperger, who knew about such things, said they probably dated from the Ming period and were all extremely valuable. The china bowl alone was worth at least fifteen hundred roubles.

Vittorin bundled everything up in his fur coat and secured this makeshift bedding-roll with a strap. Then he lit a cigarette.

The train got under way again. Professor Junker waved his handkerchief and called "*Dosvidanya!*" Feuerstein confessed that he hadn't really believed in the mechanical fault. He'd been convinced that a telegram had arrived from Moscow, and that he would be plucked off the train at the last moment. The past half-hour had given him a nasty turn. Had anyone noticed?

"I did," Kohout told him. "You were as white as a sheet."

Emperger proceeded to do his accounts. No more joint expenditure being foreseen, he was delighted to announce that, thanks to his careful husbanding of the communal exchequer, he was in a position to reimburse each contributor to the extent of seventeen-and-a-half roubles. No receipt would be required.

Now, however, the solemn moment had come. Vittorin produced a notebook and requested the travelling companions who had for two years been his room-mates at Chernavyensk Camp to give him their addresses.

Emperger, as he already knew, lived in Prinz-Eugen-Strasse – naturally, since it was Vienna's most elegant quarter. He was also in the telephone directory. Kohout, wringing his hands, declared that he had no fixed abode at the present time, but that a letter addressed to the Café Splendide in Praterstrasse would always reach him. That was his regular Viennese haunt, and he looked in there once or twice a day.

Vittorin inscribed the four names in his notebook, and beside them their owners' military rank, civilian occupation, street and house number. Beneath them, in big, bold capitals, he wrote: "Mikhail Mikhailovich Selyukov, Staff Captain, Semyonov Regiment."

That completed the first step: everything was down in black and white. Mikhail Mikhailovich Selyukov had now to contend with a close-knit organization, a league of five men who had defined their objective and were prepared to make any sacrifice in order to attain it. The matter would have to take its course.

The train pulled into Ryekhovo, its final destination. Two Bolshevik officers, their peaked caps adorned with the Soviet star, were pacing up and down between tall stacks of timber. Standing beside the water tower on the other side of the station was an Austrian sentry with rifle at the slope and bayonet fixed. A big brown dog was roaming among the freight cars and two peasants were hauling a hen-house ladder across the tracks. The door of the station commandant's office was open.

A Honved major with pepper-and-salt side whiskers emerged, and the lieutenant from the hospital train stepped forward to present his report.

While waiting for the Vienna express in the station buffet at Cracow, Vittorin caught sight of a lieutenant at the counter wearing the aiguillette and black velvet revers of a dragoon regiment. The lieutenant gave him a friendly, familiar wave. By the time Vittorin responded, which he did in a rather stiff and hesitant fashion, the dragoon officer had come over to his table.

"Well?" he demanded, and Vittorin saw that it was Emperger. "Surely you don't expect me to introduce myself? Fancy staring at me like that! Couldn't place me, eh? Seems you only know me when I'm trudging around in a *rubashka* and felt boots; when I look like a human being, you don't. Ah no, my dear fellow, my eskimo period is over and done with, thank God. And you, what are you up to? How are you? Back from the depot already?"

Instead of waiting for Vittorin to reply, he promptly launched into an account of his own doings.

"In my case everything went off in double-quick time – *I* saw to that. Five days under observation at Brest-Litovsk, a new set of kit, and off to Vienna. Now I'm on my way to the reserve battalion – in other words, on leave. Vienna's quite a sight – you'll get a shock when you see the place, it's awful. Influenza raging, pitch-black streets at night, nothing to eat in the restaurants, not even the better ones, people queueing up for a morsel of beef . . . Yes, my friend, it's a far cry from the old days, when I used to dine on stuffed grouse and wild duck braised in red wine at the Weide in Hietzing. It doesn't bear thinking of. The opera – that's the only thing left. Care for a decent cigarette? Cercle du Bosphore, first-class brand – I bought them off a carpet dealer who got back from Constantinople last week. The word in Vienna is, the whole of the Bulgarian army has gone over to the Entente. Some allies, eh? How true it is, I don't know."

A Red Cross nurse nodded to Emperger as she left the station buffet on the arm of a hussar captain. He clicked his heels and bowed.

"That's Vicky Fröhlich," he whispered to Vittorin. "You know, the coal magnate's niece – she's nursing at Neusandec. I wonder how Captain Nadherny managed to latch on to her. Do you know the man? He's got a glass eye – spends every morning in the Café Fenstergucker."

The stationmaster appeared in the doorway and announced the arrival of the train for Neusandec, Gorlice and Sanok.

"Seen any of our friends yet?" Vittorin asked.

Emperger was still staring after the Red Cross nurse.

"Should I put a bit of a spoke in Nadherny's wheel, I wonder?" he mused. "That girl's far too good for him. I'd stand a fair chance with her."

"The others," Vittorin insisted, "– have you heard anything from them?"

"The Professor's back in Vienna already," Emperger replied. "It was in all the papers: 'Professor Junker returns from a Russian POW camp.' He's lucky, of course, to have been a civilian internee – no reporting to any regimental depot for him. Kohout I bumped into at the quartermaster's stores in Brest-Litovsk. Impossible fellow, Kohout – downright suspicious, the way he fraternizes with the rank and file. He'll come to a bad end, you mark my words."

"What about Feuerstein?"

"Feuerstein's brother was waiting for him at Kiev with some discharge papers in his pocket. My own affairs are shaping nicely too. As soon as the war's over I'm joining the Credit Bank as a legal adviser. They're keeping the job open for me."

Vittorin listened with only half an ear. He had been waiting on tenterhooks for Emperger to broach the subject that preoccupied him so unceasingly, day and night, but the man confined himself to matters of supreme unimportance. Was it a deliberate ploy, an attempt to trivialize the Chernavyensk agreement? Vittorin decided to clarify the situation once and for all.

16

"Is there any news of a certain subject?" he asked point-blank. "Did you discuss it with Kohout?"

"Discuss what?"

"Discuss *what*?" Vittorin repeated angrily. "Why, Selyukov, of course."

"Selyukov? What news would there be? There's nothing to be done for the moment. I haven't given a thought to Selyukov, quite frankly, nor to Chernavyensk. It's as if I'd never been there. You'll feel just the same once you're back in Vienna. The first day, when I woke up in my own bed at home, I looked at the time: five forty-five! God Almighty, I thought, five forty-five, I'd better get up quickly, reveille will be sounding any minute! And then of course, as you can imagine, I lay back and wallowed in an indescribable sense of bliss, and as I lay there I recalled Camp Regulations, Paragraph 2: 'When reveille sounds, all prisoners of war will get up, make their beds, wash, and clean their huts. Tea may be drunk until 0800. Well, I told myself, all bad things come to an end. Now I can drink tea any time I feel like it.'"

Vittorin glanced at the clock, summoned the waiter, and paid. The Vienna express was due in five minutes' time. Emperger insisted on accompanying his friend and former room-mate out on to the platform. Here he hurriedly imparted a few more useful tips on life in Vienna.

"You can go around in civvies if you like – nobody cares. If you want to buy something to eat, try the North-West Station. You can get everything there: meat, butter, eggs, flour – you know, from the men on leave from Galicia. They make you pay through the nose, of course, but still. Coffee-houses? Don't touch the stuff they call mocca. If you fancy a real mocca, go to the Café Pucher and mention my name to the waiter. They still serve genuine Turkish coffee there, but only to special customers."

"I think we'll hold our first meeting around Christmas," Vittorin said. "We'll have to fit it in with our leave, so we're all in Vienna at the same time."

"We'll all be on leave soon, if you ask me," said Emperger.

17

"There are rumours to that effect. So long, Vittorin. Take care of yourself."

The train was crowded. Vittorin sat huddled beside his bedding-roll in the dimly-lit corridor and tried to sleep, but a hateful voice kept jolting him awake.

"*Sdravstvuyte* – welcome," it said in melodious tones, and Vittorin sat up with a start, transfixed by a fleeting vision of the strangely chiselled profile, the domed, rather bulbous forehead, the slightly parted lips with their hint of arrogance, the cigarette between the slender, tanned fingers. Had he ever seen Mikhail Mikhailovich Selyukov without a cigarette? Yes, once, when that drunken Cossack struck the Austrian captain from Przemysl with his *nagaika* and Selyukov came to the prisoners' hut to apologize in person, his full-dress uniform adorned with the Order of Vladimir and the Cross of St George. "The fellow will be dealt with most severely. You know what penalty Russian military law prescribes for a Cossack, a peasant. Believe me, Captain, I couldn't be more sorry." And then, with an inclination of the head, he had shaken hands with his prisoner and brother officer. Oh yes, Mikhail Mikhailovich Selyukov knew his manners. He was no peasant, no Cossack – he could be charming when he chose, and all the worse for that.

The train stopped. Vittorin went to the window and peered out. He had once spent a holiday near here, twelve – no, fourteen years ago. His uncle had still owned the mill in those days. Now he toured the villages selling threshing machines.

Fourteen years. How quickly time went by, yet tonight seemed endless, absolutely endless. Only a quarter to one. Tomorrow he would be in Vienna. Had they received his telegram? Who would be at the station? His father, his sisters – Franzi too, perhaps. If only he could sleep . . .

He closed his eyes, but sleep was ousted by a vision from the past, a memory that haunted him relentlessly. He was back in Chernavyensk, standing outside the camp commandant's office. He had a request to make. Selyukov could be gracious

18

as well as sadistic. "Submit your request, Lieutenant," he would say, "I'm listening. Whatever I can do for my prisoners of war" he would continue in French, "I do . . ."

Vittorin's fingers were numb with cold. The *starshi*, the Russian NCO who was escorting him, brushed the snow off his greatcoat, stamped his feet, adjusted his cap, and knocked.

Staff Captain Selyukov was seated at his desk. He didn't look up; he continued to leaf through a book, smoking and making notes as he did so. He had an elegant, nonchalant way of holding his cigarette left-handed while writing: he compressed it between the tip of his little finger and his ring finger. The desk was littered with military manuals, miscellaneous printed matter, French novels.

Grisha, Selyukov's orderly, put his head round the door, saw that his master was busy, and withdrew. The room was filled with a faint, subtle aroma of Chinese tobacco. There was something else in the air as well: a whiff of some exotic scent. Of course, Selyukov occasionally received women visitors. If she was in the room, the woman whose name no one in the camp knew – if she was there, the thin-faced young woman with the apprehensive, darting eyes, she could only be concealed behind the screen. Vittorin strained his ears for the sound of her breathing.

Five minutes went by, and still Selyukov didn't look up. Every now and then, as he wrote, his tongue would emerge from between his teeth, caress his upper lip, and disappear again. Vittorin watched this silent proceeding with a peculiar relish for which he could find no explanation. Eight minutes. The white enamel cross on the yellow ribbon was the Cross of St George. Selyukov also had the Order of Vladimir and St George's Sabre, but those he wore on special occasions only.

He completed his work at last. The NCO, standing at attention with his hands on his trouser seams, said a few words in Russian.

Mikhail Mikhailovich Selyukov propped his head on his hand and stared straight through Vittorin with half-closed eyes.

"You must submit your request to the non-commissioned officer of the day," he drawled, as though addressing the coat hanging on the wall behind Vittorin. "It's not my job to listen to complaints from prisoners of war. You know the rules here. You're breaking camp regulations. This is the third time you've pestered me with requests and complaints."

Vittorin flushed scarlet and stared at the screen.

"Your conduct is unbecoming to an officer," Selyukov went on. "In France they call it *bochisme*. To teach you respect for Russian military law, you're confined to quarters for ten days. You may go."

Vittorin, eager to justify himself, stood his ground and put what he had to say into French. Selyukov must be made to see that he was dealing with an educated, cultivated person who was fluent in the language of diplomacy. "It's cruel, sir," he said in that language. "It's quite inhuman to stop our letters for three weeks, just because two lights were still on at eleven. My comrades . . ."

Vittorin couldn't get another word out – he was unequal to the situation. Selyukov tapped the ash off his cigarette. Then he nodded to the NCO.

"Pashol."

He said it very quietly – so quietly that it sounded as if it meant "One moment" or "Wait a minute", not plain "Out!" *Pashol!* The NCO turned about, grabbed Vittorin by the shoulder, and hustled him out of the office.

The Tyrolean lance-corporal in the other ranks' camp across the way caught hold of the Russian medical officer who had slapped his face and strangled him with his bare hands – yes, and was executed by firing squad the next day without turning a hair. And I? What of me?

Very well, Mikhail Mikhailovich Selyukov, so you chose to treat me *à la canaille. Pashol!* Very well. The French call it *bochisme*, do they? As you wish, but every dog has his day. We'll discuss it in due course, Mikhail Mikhailovich Selyukov. You think I'll forget? You're mistaken, Captain. There are some things one never forgets. Conduct unbecoming to an officer, did you say? The French call it *bochisme*? Just you wait, Captain. The day of reckoning will come. I won't forget.

Pashol . . . Had she heard that, the woman behind the screen? A Frenchwoman, so it was said in camp – a landowner's child bride who travelled four hours by sleigh each time she came to see Selyukov. *Pashol* . . . Had she understood? Oh yes, of course she had. Perhaps it had amused her – perhaps she'd laughed, perhaps she'd chuckled to herself, silently and inaudibly, in her hiding place behind the screen.

Vittorin bit his lip. Shame and anger brought the blood to his cheeks, and he clamped his forehead against the cold windowpane. He hadn't said a word to his comrades about what had happened in Selyukov's office, but the memory of that ignominious encounter ate its way into his distraught soul like some corrosive poison.

He wasn't alone. His friends, too, had a score to settle with Selyukov. They were bound by a pledge, an oath solemnly sworn over the open grave of one of their comrades.

Vittorin straightened up. Determination flooded through him.

We'll get down to business as soon as the war's over and we're all back in Vienna again. The Professor, being the eldest, can preside over our deliberations. Feuerstein will put up the money and I'll be given the job of returning to Russia. It's mine by right, and I won't let anyone dispute it.

Here I am, Captain, don't you remember me? Lieutenant Vittorin of Hut 4, Chernavyensk Camp. That's right, the French call it *bochisme*. Why so pale, Your Excellency? You weren't expecting me? You thought I'd forget? Oh no, I haven't forgotten. What did you say? *Pashol?* No, Captain, I'm staying – I want a word with you. Remember the air force lieutenant you deprived of officer status because his papers weren't in order? Think for a moment, take your time. When he refused to work in the other ranks' kitchen you locked him up in a cellar. He was sick – recurrent fever, chronic malaria – but you left him lying on a plank bed in that filthy cellar until . . . You claimed he was malingering. 'The camp medical office has got better things to do than cope with prisoners' vagaries,' you said. 'He's putting it on, pretending he's ill. There's nothing wrong with him at all.' The day he was buried we swore an oath, the five of us, and now, as you see, the day of reckoning has come. You don't remember? But you do remember me, don't you? Conduct unbecoming to an officer, the French call it . . . There, take that! That's for *bochisme*, and that's for impounding our mail, and that's – stop, what are you looking for? Your revolver? That'll do you no good, Captain. Ah, here's Grisha. *Sdravstvuy*, Grisha. Tell your orderly, Captain, that I'll shoot him if he so much as lifts a finger. Yes indeed, I've come prepared. You challenge me to a duel? Very well, that sounds reasonable. The choice of weapons is yours. My seconds will . . .

The conductor, coming down the train with a lantern in his hand, was suddenly confronted by an infantry lieutenant standing in the middle of the corridor, pale as death, with one clenched fist extended. He walked on, shaking his head, turned to look back when he reached the communicating door, shrugged, and disappeared into the next carriage. Vittorin retired to his corner feeling faintly annoyed and sheepish.

One-thirty . . . I really must try to get some sleep. What on earth can that fool of a conductor have thought? I'm dog-tired. Why did he stare at me like that? Damned impertinence! Grisha – that was the name of Selyukov's orderly: Grigory Osipovich Kedrin or Kadrin from Staromyena in the Government of Kharkov – he dictated his letters to the Professor often enough. I'll write it down just in case . . .

He pulled out his notebook and wrote the following under Selyukov's name:

"Grisha, Selyukov's orderly. Grigory Osipovich Kedrin (Kadrin?) from the village of Staromyena, Glavyask Railway Station, Government of Kharkov."

LIMBO

From the carriage window he caught sight of his sisters, Lola and Vally, in the waiting throng. So they had both come. Vally had developed into a pretty girl. A child no longer, she was a slender nineteen-year-old with lustrous eyes and airy, graceful movements. Three years was a long time. And there was his father, too, still erect and every inch the retired army officer, but a little older-looking for all that.

Vittorin stepped down on to the platform. He was relieved of his bedding-roll by a young man with angular, unfamiliar features, a minuscule moustache and brown kid gloves: his brother Oskar. Three years ago Oskar had still been wearing blue sailor suits. The friendly but formal way in which he shook his elder brother's hand conveyed an emphatic and unmistakable request to be treated like a fully-fledged adult.

Innumerable questions: how had he stood up to the journey, was Moscow cold at this time of year, had he seen anything of the Revolution, was he glad to be back in Vienna again? "Let's take a look at you, Georg. Hm, not bad, a bit thin in the face, though." – "Franzi Kroneis has been dropping in every day to ask for news, and yesterday she'd only just left when your telegram arrived." – "What are we standing here for? *Avanti, avanti!* Let's go." Was he hungry, was he tired, did he still feel his leg wound sometimes? "That man Lenin must be a fantastic person," said Oskar, offering his brother a home-rolled cigarette. "I find him tremendously impressive."

They slowly neared the barrier, and there stood Franzi Kroneis, beaming, excited, and flushed after her brisk walk to the station.

"You haven't changed a scrap," she said. "Not a scrap."

Then, as if it were the most natural thing in the world, she took his arm. Quite a change from the old days. Three years ago they had kept their understanding a secret from everyone else.

Georg Vittorin had often pictured the moment of arrival, which had once seemed so unattainably remote, during his endless peregrinations through Siberia and Transbaikalia. It was associated with a vision of himself nonchalantly lolling back in an open cab as he rode home through bustling streets on a fine, warm day in late summer. This mental picture had been particularly vivid at the station in Manchuria, when they were trudging along the shell-torn platform and over the makeshift wooden bridge. Now that the coveted moment had come at last, they took a tram.

Franzi said au revoir at the tram stop. She had taken half an hour off from the office to welcome him at the station, but now she had to get back. She drew him aside. Would he care to collect her from the office that evening? 17 Seilerstrasse. "That's right, the same old place. No, I don't suppose you'll be going out again today – you must be tired. Till tomorrow, then. You can always phone me. Sleep well, and don't dream too much about – what are the girls in Russia called? Sonya? Natasha? Marfa?"

"Anyuta, Sofya, Yelena," said Vittorin.

"You knew as many as that? All right, see you at seven tomorrow. Did you think of me a little sometimes?"

Nobody spoke much in the tram. Lola, hoping to please her brother, remarked that Franzi was a charming girl – so affectionate, too. Oskar insisted on buying his own ticket. Herr Vittorin produced a stubby meerschaum pipe from his pocket. The war would soon be over, he said – it couldn't last much longer. The decisive battle would probably take place in the West, in Champagne. Morale there was as high as it was elsewhere. A lieutenant just back from the Piave front had told him that morale was good there too. He filled his pipe with

24

tobacco to which he had added woodruff and marinated pump-kin leaves to make it go further.

"It's not a bad smoke," he said. "According to a newspaper article by some medical expert – I've forgotten his name – this mixture has a very stimulating effect on the lungs. Mind you, the chief accountant in our office still smokes his Trabuco. Where does he get the money? Hm, 'nough said!"

Vittorin's father suggested a game of chess after supper, but his sisters jibbed. No chess tonight, they said – they could play another time. Georg must tell them about himself.

"All right," said Lola, "begin at the beginning, the day they took you prisoner on the Dunajec. That much I do know, because you wrote us about it, but not the details. How did you feel when the Cossacks dumped you in that cart? When did they first dress your wound? Ella's brother was wounded too, in the lung, but he's still in the hospital. Which reminds me: I saw the chief clerk from your office a couple of weeks ago, quite by chance, in the street – you know, the one with freckles. He was arm in arm with a very tall red-head – not his wife. He'd have asked after you if he'd been on his own, I'm sure."

"You must go and look him up," said Herr Vittorin. "It's only proper – he may be offended if you don't put in an appear-ance. He's bound to hear you're back in Vienna. Word soon gets around."

"If you feel like going to the theatre next week," said Oskar, "I can get you some complimentary tickets. I mix with a lot of theatrical types these days."

Georg Vittorin experienced a kind of malaise, almost as if he were sickening for some fell disease. His secret preyed on his mind. It was clear from every word his father and his sisters uttered how glad they were that he would soon be readapting himself to his old, uneventful, well-ordered way of life. Should he shatter their illusions on his very first day home? Who could he confide in? His father? Yes, perhaps. Father had been an army officer in his youth, a lieutenant in the regulars. His sword and the faded group photograph that showed him surrounded by his brother officers still hung on the wall below Mother's portrait. Should he get up and take him aside? "May I have a word, Father? I've something to tell you." No. For the past seventeen years Father had been a civil servant in the audit office of the Finance Ministry. Off to work at nine every morning, lunch at three-thirty sharp, then the newspaper, then the daily constitutional, the "big one" out to Dornbach on Sundays, the "little one" through town on weekdays, and finally, when evening came, a hand of cards or a glass of beer across the street – such had been Father's world and way of life for seventeen long years. No, he couldn't tell Father.

The doorbell rang. Lola looked up from her embroidery and listened intently. Vally hurried out, came back, stuck her head round the door and pulled a face.

"Lucky old Lola!" she whispered. "Ugh, it's Herr Ebenseder."

"Ah, Herr Ebenseder!" exclaimed Vittorin's father. "So he's honouring us with his presence again, is he? Come in, come in, Herr Ebenseder!"

Oskar rose, buttoning his jacket, and turned to Georg. He was awfully sorry – he would so much have liked to stay awhile, but unfortunately he had to rush – he'd arranged to meet some friends.

"A colleague from the office," Herr Vittorin explained. "The only one who's really on my side. The others are an ambitious, scheming bunch. Ebenseder's a most intelligent fellow – you'll like him. He's a keen collector, incidentally – buys anything connected with the theatre. He can afford it, too – he owns four houses. Ebenseder collects actors' portraits, play scripts, set designs, old playbills, views of the Ring Theatre and the Kärntnertor Theatre, even cloakroom tickets . . . Ah, good evening, Herr Ebenseder! Permit me to introduce my long-lost son Georg, just back from Siberia. Georg, meet Herr Ebenseder."

"Delighted to make the acquaintance of another member of

this esteemed family. I've heard a lot about you. So you only got back today, eh? Delighted, truly delighted."

Herr Ebenseder, a short, stout gentleman with a goatee beard, a big bald patch and pudgy fingers, went over to Lola and ceremoniously, reverently, kissed her hand.

"My respects, Fräulein Lola. Your humble servant. Diligent as ever, I see. What nimble little fingers you have! Never idle for a moment, eh? It's a pleasure to watch you."

Herr Vittorin fetched a bottle of wine and poured his guest a glass of Gumpoldskirchner. Herr Ebenseder, as etiquette prescribed, staged a show of reluctance.

"Why go to such trouble on my account, Herr Vittorin? It really isn't necessary in these hard times. I never say no to a cup of tea – everyone brings their own sugar nowadays – but a genuine Gumpoldskirchner! Ah well, if you insist. Your very good health! A 'seventeen, isn't it? I could tell at once. What a year! Quite superb!"

He smacked his lips so loudly that Lola gave a little jump. Then he produced a shiny black skullcap from his pocket, clapped it on his bald pate – it paid to be careful of drafts – and drew his chair up to Lola's.

Vally's meaningful glance at her brother signalled that she was going over to the attack.

"Is it really true, Herr Ebenseder," she inquired with an air of innocence, "that you're one of the few people still alive who were personally acquainted with Nestroy?"

"What nonsense, Vally!" cried Ebenseder. He gave a fat, contented chuckle. "There you go again! Nestroy? How could I possibly have known Nestroy? He died in the eighteen-sixties! I did see Matras, though. I saw him at the Carl Theatre when I was a boy – Matras and Knaack and Katharina Herzog, who was in the original cast of *Der Verschwender*."

"Since when have you addressed me by my first name, Herr Ebenseder? I don't remember inviting you to do so."

"There's a first time for everything," Herr Ebenseder replied archly.

"And that time hasn't come," Vally retorted. "Nor will it."

Her father glared at her and changed the subject. He'd recently seen a watercolour in the window of Feldmayer's Bookshop. It depicted Charlotte Wolter in gipsy costume conversing with an elderly man who was looking at her through his lorgnette. He thought it might be something for his esteemed colleague's collection.

Herr Ebenseder pricked up his ears at once.

"The man with the lorgnette must be Laube, the director of the Burg Theatre," he said. "Of course I'd be interested in the picture – very interested indeed. Feldmayer's Bookshop, eh? I'll pop in there tomorrow. Wolter in gipsy costume . . . I wonder which play it could have been."

He proceeded to count on his fingers. He'd seen the great Burg Theatre actress as Phaedra, as Mary Queen of Scots, as Lady Milford, as Sappho, as Medea, as Iphigenia, in a modern play whose name escaped him, and lastly, a year before she died, as Adelheid in *Götz von Berlichingen*.

"Ah, Charlotte Wolter!" he said to Lola. "I pity the modern audiences who never saw her. There'll never be another like her – never! May I?"

Sighing, he poured himself another glass of wine.

Georg Vittorin sat there with half-closed eyes. Herr Ebenseder's droning voice sounded very remote. He wrestled with the snug sense of security that had descended on him. The objects in the room reached out and held him fast as if he were their property. The ticking of the clock on the wall, the muted glow of the lamp, the discreet clink of glasses, the haze of bluish smoke from his father's meerschaum pipe, his sisters' noiseless movements – all were calculated to lull him and induce him to abandon his grand design. He felt that the impending battle would decide matters once and for all; it had to be waged without delay.

His desire for solitude became overwhelming. He rose with something of an effort, saying that he was tired and wanted to go to bed, and the moment he did so the battle was won. The surrounding objects had lost their hold over him. The clock on the wall ticked mournfully on, the smoke rings from

28

his father's pipe drifted to the ceiling in melancholy silence.

He left the room.

Lola followed him out. She found him on his knees in the cramped little box-room whose barred window overlooked the air well, unbuckling the strap around his bedding-roll.

"Oskar doesn't like him either," she said after a while. "He only comes because of me. I'm glad you're back, Georg. I think he's already spoken to Father."

"Herr Ebenseder, you mean?"

"Yes, but I'd sooner drown myself. He's already been married twice. His first wife died young – he bullied her into the grave – and the other one ran off. They were both in vaudeville. What does he want with me, the repulsive brute? I'm not an equestrienne – I can't jump through a hoop."

Vittorin had opened his bedding-roll.

"This is some Chinese writing paper, and here are the envelopes to match. See how prettily painted it is?"

"It's very pretty – very stylish, really. There's something I've been meaning to tell you, but you mustn't be angry. You'll have to share this room with Oskar for the next few days. Your room – I wrote and told you we'd taken a lodger, didn't I?"

"I don't remember. No, I don't think so."

"I'm sure I did. A nice, respectable fellow – we've been really lucky from that point of view, one never sees or hears him during the day. He's paying a hundred and eighty kronen, and that's a very useful contribution to the family budget, believe me. Have you any idea what everything costs these days? Prices have been creeping up all the time. Of course, I told the gentleman he'd have to move out as soon as you were back in Vienna."

"That won't be necessary," Vittorin said. "He's welcome to keep the room. I'm not staying."

"But Father says the war will soon be over."

Vittorin rose slowly to his feet.

"When it is, I'm going back to Russia."

"Back to Russia? Are you serious?"

"Keep your voice down, the others mustn't know yet. This is just between the two of us. Yes, I have to go back."

"For long?" asked Lola, staring at him fixedly.

"I don't know."

"Did you promise her you'd come back? Why didn't you bring her with you – wasn't it possible?"

Vittorin evaded the question.

"The cigarettes are for Oskar," he said. "Be a dear and dish out the other things for me. The leather waistcoat is for Father, the Chinese porcelain –"

"But Georg, what about Franzi? What ever will Franzi say, poor thing? Do you have a photo of her – the other girl, I mean?"

"The bowl's for your china cabinet – it's supposed to be a very rare old piece. The two vases are for Franzi. You're wrong, by the way. It's nothing to do with a girl."

Two weeks later, when Vienna was in the throes of revolution, Vittorin got news of Chernavyensk from a repatriated ex-prisoner who had spent the last part of his journey from Siberia on the running board of an overcrowded railway carriage. The place had been occupied by Czech legionnaires and Staff Captain Selyukov was camp commandant no longer. He had set off as soon as the Czechs marched in, presumably for Moscow, to offer his services to the Red Army, which was short of experienced officers. The former prisoner had caught a final glimpse of him at a small station on the Siberian border not far from Krasnoyarsk.

There could be no doubt that Selyukov's flight was a development of far-reaching importance. For the time being, Vittorin decided to inform no one but Emperger of this change in the status quo. A two-man steering committee, they would confer in private before taking the others into their confidence. They must await further reports and seek confirmation of the news. A station not far from Krasnoyarsk . . . Everything suggested that Moscow was Selyukov's final destination. This'll make Feuerstein sit up, Vittorin told himself. "You mean you're still in touch with Chernavyensk?" – "Of course I am, Feuerstein, what did you think? Naturally I've kept in touch with the camp – I took care of that. I hear everything that goes on there!" Even so, certain preliminary steps would have be taken without delay. It would be best if Feuerstein made some cash available at once. Then there was the matter of the passport and entry permit for Russia.

The revolution was a worrying feature. *Were* there any government departments in the present chaotic situation, and which one issued exit visas? He couldn't travel without a passport. Had railway traffic with Russia been maintained?

Vienna buzzed with the wildest rumours. Czech forces were planning to occupy the capital and the whole of Lower Austria. The Emperor had been arrested by revolutionary troops while trying to cross the Hungarian border. Wöllersdorf and Wiener Neustadt were in flames. A demented army driver raced through the streets in his car, urging people to go home and lock their doors. Fourteen thousand Serbs and Russians from the Siegmundsherberg POW camp were marching on Vienna, he yelled. Anyone in possession of firearms was to report to police headquarters.

The established facts were no less alarming. An assemblage of officers and other ranks had elected a nine-man soviet "to do away with the hidebound bureaucracy and regimentation, cowardice and malevolence of the ruling classes". A captain in the Stockerau Rifles proposed the formation of a Red Guard but was shouted down; a corporal who couched the same demand in stronger language was applauded and hoisted shoulder-high. Gangs of coal-heavers and deserters looting warehouses and wagons at the Nordbahn freight yard seized an entire military supply train. Two hundred convicts took advantage of the general confusion to break out of Wöllersdorf Prison, and jewellers boarded up their window displays in a trice. A Czech battalion about to be disarmed at the Brigittenau marshalling yard offered resistance and attacked the station guard with hand grenades and machine-guns.

Tobacco and army blankets, knapsacks and shoe leather,

cleaning materials and mess tins – all these commodities, of which unlimited supplies were obtainable from discharged soldiers, went down in price. By contrast, the cost of a small loaf of bread soared to fifteen kronen. The Food Office announced that the meat ration of a quarter-pound of meat per head per week could not be sustained because Czechoslovakia had imposed a ban on the export of foodstuffs. In street and tavern, people sang new words to an old tune:

> Who's to govern the poor Viennese
> now that Austria's down on her knees?
> The Czechs know how best
> to feather their nest,
> and to hell with the poor Viennese!

Bogus military police patrols stopped soldiers and relieved them of their food and personal belongings, and gunfights broke out when they clashed with detachments of the Vienna garrison. It was nonetheless possible to discern isolated signs of an undiminished will to survive and faith in the future. A film poster advertising "The Princess of Berania, a Hymn to Love and Sorrow" rubbed shoulders with an official announcement stating that the 11th Class Lottery would be in no way affected by "recent events", and newsboys still hawked special editions containing communiqués from the Western Front: "Brisk artillery fire on both banks of the Meuse. Strong American forces have been brought to a standstill in the woods north of Boval."

Dr Emperger was busy sorting through his civilian wardrobe when Vittorin called on him. Dinner jacket, morning coat, fashionable pin-striped trousers, neckties, coloured shirts, an overcoat, a short fur sports jacket, and a brocaded silk waistcoat lay strewn around in picturesque confusion on the sofa and chairs. The room was filled with a penetrating stench of camphor and naphthalene. Arrayed on the desk in order of battle were oxfords, riding boots, pumps, lace-up boots, and galoshes.

32

Emperger greeted his former fellow prisoner of war with a badly crumpled officer's cap in his hand.

"Take a look at that!" he said. "There's gratitude for you. Two years in the trenches, two years in Siberia, and yesterday they repaid me by cutting the rosette off my cap. Callow youths, apprentices, budding clerks. Ah well, good riddance, no use crying over spilt milk. Have a seat, Vittorin – if you can find one, that is. You can see the state of this place. What shall I do with my greatcoat and uniform tunic? Do you think a costumier's would buy them off me? I'll throw in my Second-Class Silver. Who knows, some day it may be the height of fashion to go to a fancy-dress ball as an Austrian officer vintage nineteen-eighteen. Yes, my friend, this is a historic moment. Frau Wessely, when are you going to tidy up? I can't leave everything scattered around like this, for God's sake! Frau Wessely! She hasn't heard again, the old bitch. Do sit down, Vittorin. What brings you here?"

"I've had some important news," Vittorin said. "I wanted to discuss it privately first and sound you out before I officially inform the others. Listen to this: Selyukov isn't at Chernavyensk any longer. All the reports I've received in the last few days indicate that he's . . . what is it? Where are you off to?"

Emperger had scuttled out of the room.

"What's the matter with you, Frau Wessely?" Vittorin heard him shouting. "Why don't you come when I call you? When are you going to tidy up in there? The place is an absolute pigsty, and it's half-past five already. Let's see what you've brought. Is that all? Sardines, I told you, and liver pâté. Surely you could have drummed up a slice or two of salami? I can't offer my guests turnip jam, for heaven's sake. Two bottles of curaçao and one of anisette, I said. Lump sugar, salami, sardines – yes, Portuguese will do, any kind you like as long as they're edible. Money? What, again? It's scandalous! I gave you some only this morning. What do you do with it all, chuck it out of the window?"

He returned out of breath.

"You must forgive me, Vittorin, I don't know whether I'm

33

on my head or my heels. The apartment hasn't been aired yet, and I'm expecting guests this evening. I have to see to everything myself. Well, what about Selyukov? Let's have it."

Vittorin was thoroughly put out. He'd lost the urge to confide in one for whom news of Selyukov took second place to curaçao, lump sugar and sardines.

"I've received certain reports," he said curtly. "We must fix a meeting for tomorrow or the day after, no later – the matter's urgent. Kindly make the necessary arrangements."

"Tomorrow or the day after?" Emperger exclaimed. "Impossible! I'm dining with my boss tomorrow night, and the night after that I've got tickets for the opera. Days are no good – I don't have a moment to spare now I'm settling in at the bank. Maybe you'll have to do without me this time – no, wait a minute! Of course, that's the simplest solution! Feuerstein and the Professor are coming tonight. You must come too – you'll meet a few nice people. That's settled: half-past eight, quarter to nine. I'll look forward to seeing you then. We can sit on for a bit afterwards and discuss the matter. Sorry it never occurred to me to invite you in the first place."

"Fine," said Vittorin. "I'll come, and I'll also make it my business to let Kohout know."

Emperger seemed anything but pleasantly impressed by this suggestion.

"Kohout?" he said. "You intend to bring Kohout too? Well, if you think it's . . . Oh, all right, just as you please, I don't mind."

Vittorin rang Emperger's doorbell at a quarter to nine and was admitted by a manservant who worked by day as a cashier at the bank. Emperger greeted him in the hall.

"Ah, there you are," he said. "I told the others you were coming. It's only a small party, but a mixed one. Kohout's already here. A rum fellow, Kohout. He's brought some friend of his who spends the whole time swearing at the bourgeoisie – embarrassing, isn't it? I don't know what to do with the man. He uses the familiar form of address to Feuerstein, either because he's taken to him or as a mark of contempt. Hurry up and get your coat off. Heaven knows what's going on in there – they may be at each other's throats by now."

Vittorin entered the room with a vague premonition that he wouldn't cut a very elegant figure in his pre-war frock coat. There were at least a few familiar faces in sight, thank God. The Professor shook his hand. Feuerstein, sweating profusely in a cutaway far too tight for him, vainly endeavoured to rise. Kohout, who seemed thoroughly at home amid the tea things, sandwiches, and assorted liqueurs, delivered a species of military salute. Emperger made the introductions.

"Lieutenant Vittorin, another comrade from Chernavyensk. Vittorin, meet Fräulein Edith Hoffmann, who volunteered to play hostess but is, I regret to say, neglecting her duties. Ditti, kindly stop flirting with the Professor and look after my guests. The Financial Consultant's glass is empty and my friend Vittorin would like a cup of tea."

"I told you I was taking a break," the girl said petulantly. "Irene's standing in for me."

"Fräulein Irene Hamburger," Emperger pursued, introducing Vittorin to the girl in question. "Irene isn't making much of an effort either. What a trial these female helpmates are!" He moved on. "And this is Fräulein Bella Roth, an ornament to her sex, a connoisseur's delight. Stop scowling at me like that, Bella. You don't love me any more, I know – your heart belongs to another, don't deny it, and I can guess who the lucky man is. He came, he saw, he conquered, c'est tout. Dear God, this cigarette smoke! Shouldn't we open the window for a while? There, that's better. The rest of you can introduce yourselves, can't you?"

Two young men rose and stated their names: Glaser, civil engineer, and Simitsch, fine arts student. The clean-shaven, elderly gentleman who was holding Bella Roth's hand – on the pretext of reading her palm – turned out to be the aforesaid financial consultant. Kohout's friend was wearing breeches, puttees, army boots, and a green woollen sweater under his uniform tunic.

35

"Comrade Blaschek, since yesterday a member of the Soldiers' Council," Kohout announced in a respectful tone. "Elected by a majority of one hundred and twenty-four votes. He's right in the thick of the Movement."

"Join us, Vittorin," called Feuerstein. "It's a regular treat to see you again." He turned to the fine arts student. "We were cell mates, so to speak, in a Siberian prison camp."

The soldiers' councillor leaned across the table. "How much time d'you do?" he demanded.

"I'm sorry?"

"I asked how long you were in the pokey."

"Comrade Blaschek wants to know how long you spent in the prison camp," Kohout interpreted.

"Two years, if it's any business of yours," Feuerstein replied curtly.

"Two years, eh? Congratulations! They really put one over on you, the Russians did. Serves you right. Why d'you get yourself captured?"

"What a charming fellow," said Fräulein Hamburger. "Really sympathetic."

Kohout laughed. Feuerstein, who was essentially good-natured and eager to live in peace with everyone, rebutted the charge of cowardice in very moderate language.

"In the first place, esteemed comrade, I didn't 'get myself captured', as you put it. That's point one. Point two, I don't see why I should have to tolerate your –"

"Not captured?" cried the newly-elected soldiers' councillor. "Not captured? Go on! Did the Russians win you in a lottery or something?"

"That was a direct hit," the Professor observed admiringly. "Feuerstein, you're beaten. Lay down your arms."

"I can see something very interesting here," said the financial consultant, who still had hold of his lady companion's hand. "This line, with its numerous ramifications, is indicative of musical talent. The small indentation on the right suggests that you have an exceptionally passionate temperament. You're still trying to suppress it, but in vain: human nature will out.

You're going into light opera, I can tell you that here and now. Your training will be financed by a gentleman friend."

"And you can tell all that from my hand?" asked Fräulein Roth.

"Partly from my own as well," the financial consultant assured her in a meaningful undertone.

Vittorin beckoned to his host.

"A word with you, Emperger," he murmured. "You know I only came here to pass on some vital information. Arrange it so we can have a few minutes' quiet chat."

"Yes, but how?" Emperger whispered nervously. "I'd like nothing better than to break them up. Fur's bound to fly in the end, you mark my words. Feuerstein won't tolerate that fellow's impertinence for ever."

"Why did you invite the others – the financial consultant, for instance?"

"The financial consultant . . ." mused Emperger. "Yes, I'm beginning to ask myself the same thing. Have you seen the way he operates? He's making a play for little Bella. He may be a conceited old fool, but he's getting places. See how she's falling for his line of patter?"

"Were you in the army too, Professor?" the civil engineer inquired from the other end of the table.

"Oh no, it never came to that with me. I was simply arrested. The Russians hauled me out of bed and detained me. It was my misfortune to be on a sabbatical in Southern Turkestan when the war broke out."

"Turkestan?" Fräulein Hamburger exclaimed delightedly. "What's your special field of study, oriental art?"

"Far from it, my dear. I lecture on grasses and seeds at the Agricultural College. Not a subject to appeal to young ladies."

"This may interest you, Professor," said the civil engineer. "Just before the outbreak of war my firm marketed a manure spreader and grain drill – a brand-new model capable of sowing all types of seeds in precisely measurable quantities."

He asked for a pencil and paper and demonstrated with the

aid of a small diagram how the machine could be converted into a manure spreader by removing the seed hopper.

The Professor, having taken the diagram and examined it, raised his eyebrows and nodded several times. The financial consultant proceeded to deplore the workers' exorbitant wage demands. God alone knew where they would lead, he said. Feuerstein, on the other hand, took a highly optimistic view of the future and declared that money was to be made out of anything termed merchandise. He planned to concentrate exclusively on the import-export business and had no intention of manufacturing anything. He expounded his ideas to the financial consultant with great eloquence, the word "merchandise" taking on a note of quasi religious fervour whenever it escaped his lips. The Professor continued to examine the sketch of the manure spreader. The ladies, who could muster little interest in the current discussion, demanded to know when they would at last be able to obtain fresh supplies of Swiss chocolate, fine silks, French fashion magazines, and English bath soap.

Vittorin stared furiously into his empty teacup, driven to distraction by this never-ending flow of verbiage. Feuerstein and the financial consultant might almost have been in league against him. They talked incessantly of tariff concessions, foreign tenders, export markets and stock market quotations as if deliberately intent on keeping the subject of Selyukov at bay. As for the women with their inane chatter and their stupid, fatuous laughter, they were quite intolerable. Vittorin wondered why he'd come at all. He signalled covertly to Emperger, but his host affected not to notice.

Kohout's friend was meanwhile outlining a programme for future implementation by the Workers' and Soldiers' Councils. Ensconced at the far end of the table, he held forth in a stentorian voice and brandished his glass in an alarming fashion.

"Comrades," he cried, "this is it! It's our turn now. We've stood there long enough – shut up and let me speak, Kohout, or I'll scramble your brains! – we've stood there long enough

38

and taken it on the chin. Now it's our turn to call the tune. First we'll take the exploiters of the masses and their girlfriends and flay their profiteering hides for fun. Then we'll confiscate all the cars. Everyone'll go by shanks's pony in the new Republic."

"Forgive me for saying so," Feuerstein broke in, "but you're jumping the gun. To the best of my knowledge, no final decision has yet been taken about our future system of government. For the present, we're still living in a monarchy."

Blaschek was prepared to concede this point.

"Call it what you like," he said. "Afterwards, we'll ride around in the cars and search folks' homes. All the stuff they've hoarded – all the coal and flour and fat – will be given to the working classes."

"And the people you've taken it from can starve, eh?" interjected the financial consultant.

"When did you ever ask *us* if we had enough to eat?" Blaschek bellowed.

"Gentlemen, gentlemen, why get so heated?" Emperger looked thoroughly dismayed. "Calm yourselves, please! Comrade Blaschek, you're absolutely right – any reasonable person can see that – but the ladies want no talk of politics tonight, they want to dance. You'll dance too, comrade, won't you?"

"You bet," said the tribune of the people.

"There you are, then. Choose yourself a partner. What shall I play, ladies and gentlemen, a waltz or something more *à la mode*? A one-step? A foxtrot?"

"A foxtrot, a foxtrot! You're driving me crazy!" cried Fräulein Hamburger, this being the title of a current hit, not a reproach.

The civil engineer favoured "Au Revoir, Sweetheart" and Fräulein Hoffman requested a boston entitled "The Skirt with the Brown Stripes". Bella Roth declared that, if she couldn't have a tango, she'd rather not dance at all. They finally settled on a waltz.

Dancing took place in the room next door. The financial consultant and the fine arts student, who formed the "island" around which the couples rotated, exchanged muttered comments on the aesthetic merits of the ladies present. The soldiers' councillor addressed Fräulein Hamburger as "comrade" and proved to be an adept at reversing.

Vittorin, who had remained behind at the tea table with Feuerstein and the Professor, saw his chance at last. He got up and closed the door.

"There," he said, "let's hope we won't be disturbed. I've waited long enough, God knows."

The Professor looked surprised.

"Bored, Vittorin?" he inquired. "Why? I'm quite enjoying myself. The only one who gets on my nerves is the engineer and his tiresome manure spreader. I'm not the least bit interested in removable seed hoppers. I didn't come here to –"

"Aren't you interested in knowing why *I'm* here?" Vittorin cut in angrily. "Do you really think I don't have anything better to do than sit around all evening with a bunch of . . ."

He groped in vain for a word that would fully express his contempt for this type of social function.

"You're a trifle hard to please, Vittorin," said the Professor. "What sort of entertainment were you expecting? The Indian rope trick? An aria for coloratura? A belly-dancer, perhaps? Personally, I'm having a whale of a time. Feuerstein, you should have seen the look on your face when our comrade from Hernals went to work on you. It was a scream!"

"I didn't find it half as amusing," Feuerstein said testily. "The cheek of the fellow! Who does he think he is, talking to me like that?"

The Professor chuckled. "To a man of a people, there must be something provocative about your smooth, rosy, well-fed face. These are hard times for the fuller figure, Feuerstein."

"Please, please don't let me interrupt," said Vittorin, suppressing his fury with an effort. "I've got something to tell you, that's why I came, but finish your conversation first by all means. I can wait."

The Professor stared at him.

"You sound positively acrimonious, Vittorin. What's wrong?"

"What's wrong?" said Vittorin with feigned indifference. "Nothing, except that I've just had some news from Russia: Selyukov's in Moscow."

Having lobbed this announcement at the others like a hand grenade, he lit a cigarette to hide his agitation and waited for it to take effect.

"Really?" said the Professor. "So Selyukov's in Moscow, eh? Interesting – very interesting. Tell me, old friend, are you really still obsessed with the man?"

Vittorin took a short, sharp pull at his cigarette.

"What do you mean, Professor? I don't understand."

"You don't understand? Very well, cast your mind back for a moment. Chernavyensk, the camp, homesickness, fits of depression, the monotony of the passing days, the ban on mail, no news from home, the knowledge that we were at the mercy of the commandant's every whim. It knocked us sideways when that poor devil of an air force lieutenant died of malaria. We not only felt sick, Vittorin, we *were* sick – mentally sick. We took refuge in the typical prisoner's pipe-dream: some day we would return and settle the score. It was a very therapeutic idea, to be sure – it helped us over some difficult times – but a symptom of mental disorder just the same. Hasn't that dawned on you yet?"

Vittorin had tossed his cigarette away and sprung to his feet. He glared at the Professor in silence.

Comrade Blaschek emerged from the room next door, where dancing was still in progress. He wiped the sweat from his brow and stripped off his woollen sweater.

"It's stinking hot in there," he said. "'Scuse me, folks, I'm on my way again."

He left the the door open. The waltz came to an end, and Kohout, accompanied on the mouth organ by Blaschek, took advantage of the ensuing interval to warble some marching songs in a maudlin tenor.

41

> Who'll mourn me when trouble and strife
> have finally ended my life?
> Glass, bottle and plate,
> Wine and beer by the crate,
> and the landlord's embraceable wife . . .

"It was a severe psychosis," the Professor went on. "Not a normal condition, that's for sure, but one has to get over it some time. You're back home again – it's all behind you. Get down to work, start from scratch, forget about the war – that's the answer now. Damn Kohout and his sentimental ditties, one can't hear oneself speak! We've got to forget about the war and everything we went through – erase it from our memories. Siberia was just a bad dream and Chernavyensk a nightmare. Why the hell should you give damn about Selyukov now? Wherever he is, Moscow or some other place, leave him be."

"Have you finished?" Vittorin asked.

A medley of sounds drifted in from the room next door: laughter, the clink of glasses, the wail of the mouth organ, and Kohout's voice.

> What things on my grave will they lay,
> and what on my stone will it say?
> A sausage, a loaf,
> and: "Here lies a poor oaf
> of a soldier who drank all his pay . . ."

"If you're through, Professor," Vittorin blurted out, pale with fury, "I'll tell you something. I find it deplorable – yes, I'll say it to your face: shabby and deplorable of you to begin by joining in and giving your word of honour and God knows what else, and then to back out on the grounds that we were suffering from a psychosis or whatever you choose to call it. You ought to be ashamed of yourself, that's all I can say. You're a coward – you're scared, that's the truth of the matter. All this talk of psychoses and symptoms and starting again from scratch – there's nothing behind it but fear. It's sad that people like you should exist, but at least I know you for what you are. At least I know – "

"Attention, comrades!" roared Blaschek. "Now for something really up-to-the-minute! Carry on, Kohout!"

"Ready when you are," said Kohout, and he launched, with mouth organ accompaniment, into:

And who will now sweep the streets clean,
and who will now sweep the streets clean?
Gentlefolk of the best
with stars on their chest:
they're the ones who'll now sweep the streets clean.

"Bravo!" cried the financial consultant, whose war service had consisted of two months' desk work. "Bravo!" he repeated in high delight. "And so they damn well should. Let them earn a crust like the rest of us!"

"At least I know where I stand with you and how much your word of honour is worth," said Vittorin, whose anger had given way to profound depression.

The Professor strove to make light of it.

"I realize, of course, that I've lost all claim to your respect," he said, "but what can I do? I shall have to live with the thought as best I can. My one consolation is that in two months you'll feel just as I do. By the way, do you really think it'll be as simple as all that, getting back into Russia at this of all times?"

Vittorin fixed him with a hostile, contemptuous gaze.

"Simple or not, that's my concern," he said. "You've no need to worry about it, not now. Anything's possible if one wants it enough. Determination is the sole requirement, not that someone of your kind would understand that. Believe me, I'll deal with Selyukov even if you all let me down – even if I have to beg my way to Moscow on foot!"

"Say no more, Vittorin," the Professor broke in. "You've just revealed the true nature of your hatred. It's an obsession, that's what it is. I strongly advise you to –"

43

"Hey, Kohout!" yelled Blaschek. "Whassa matter with you? Aren't we going to grease the guillotines tonight?"

"Patience, comrade," said Kohout. "All in good time, all in good time."

He went to the piano and picked out the tune of the executioner's song with his left hand. Blaschek joined in at the top of his voice.

> Grease the guillotines,
> grease the guillotines,
> grease the guillotines with princes' fat!
> Seize the –

"For God's sake stop, comrade!" Emperger cried desperately. "What are you thinking of? This really won't do. There's a senior civil servant living upstairs. He'll come and complain – he's already banged on the floor twice."

"Let him come, the reactionary swine!" roared Blaschek. "Let him come, if he's got the guts – I'll knock him into the middle of next week! Come on, comrades, all together now: 'Seize the concubines, seize the concubines . . .'"

The three girls withdrew to the outer room, arm in arm. Fräulein Hamburger shut the door behind her.

"There's no holding them," she said. "Poor Rudi, he'll have some explaining to do tomorrow. Personally, I've had enough of it."

Vittorin turned to Feuerstein.

"What about you?" he demanded. "Are you backing out too?"

Feuerstein, who had once, not so long ago, declared that he could be relied on to the hilt, shrugged his shoulders and said nothing.

"So be it," Vittorin growled. "I wash my hands of you both. There's nothing more to be said."

Fräulein Hoffmann sidled up with an inquisitive air.

"Have you had an argument?" she asked. "It almost looks that way. What was it about?"

44

The Professor sat back in his chair, smiling. He exhaled a plume of cigarette smoke.

"Oh, nothing much," he said. "It's just that my friend here insists on going to Moscow and killing a Russian officer."

A prey to the three girls' vacuous, uproarious laughter, his face convulsed with anger, shame and dismay, Vittorin strode from the room. He had been betrayed and derided. There was no point in his remaining a moment longer.

Outside in the hall, while the manservant was helping him on with his coat, which was still soaking wet, he had a brief conversation with Kohout.

"It was bound to happen, my friend, I could have told you that in the first place," said Kohout, shifting from foot to foot. "The middle classes have no self-respect, no guts. Didn't you notice how Feuerstein and the Professor made themselves scarce when we were singing those revolutionary songs? What a crew!"

Lola opened the box-room door an inch or two and peered in. Her brother was lying on his bed half-dressed, leafing through a notebook with a red cover. She went in.

"So you're awake," she said. "If I'd known you weren't asleep I'd have come much earlier. Do you know what time it is? Quarter to eleven. You didn't come home till one, Father heard you. Did you have a nice time? Good morning, by the way. Like me to bring you some breakfast?"

Georg Vittorin shut the notebook.

"No thanks, I'll be out in a minute. I've been awake for ages. Just revising a bit of Russian, a few words and phrases – the kind of stuff you need to make yourself understood. Did I have a nice time? Depends on your point of view. It was an instructive evening, anyway. Something bothering you, Lola?"

The subject she wanted to raise with him was very close to her heart. Herr Bamberger, the lodger, for whom she cherished the highest regard, had expressed an interest in her brother and wanted to meet him. It might prove an extremely useful contact, but she decided to start by speaking of matters to which she attached less importance.

"Franzi dropped in first thing this morning," she said. "She wondered if you'd meet her for lunch at the Domcafé. She's working right through, but she plans to take half an hour off around one, just for a snack. Why not join her? You haven't made a sign of life all week. She was going on about it like anything."

"I've been busy, she knows that perfectly well," Vittorin grumbled. "Interviews and appointments all day long – here, there and everywhere. Take yesterday afternoon: I had an important meeting in the 4th District. Half an hour later I had to be at the Café Splendide in Praterstrasse, then home to change and back to Prinz-Eugen-Strasse for yet another appointment – one long rush! Then there's the time I have to spend at the railway stations, standing there for hours on the lookout for POW trains. I need certain information. I have to make inquiries, and it's a job I can't leave to anyone else. Franzi knows that, so why does she keep pestering me?"

Lola was at a loss for an answer.

"Anyway, things are going to be different from now on," Vittorin pursued. "I won't have to hang around the stations any more. I've already found out what I wanted to know, and I've completed my preliminary discussions. Now I've got to work and earn some money. Is it really quarter to eleven already? High time I got dressed and went out – I've been lying here far too long. I mustn't fritter away another whole morning like this."

"You can afford to take it easy for another few days," Lola told him. "You needn't go back to work till the fifteenth, Father says."

"Back to the office and bang away at a typewriter?" Vittorin exclaimed. "I wouldn't dream of it. A hundred and eighty kronen a month, maybe two hundred next year if I'm lucky – you call that good money? I'd make more playing the violin in a cinema. Have you any idea how much people are earning these days?"

46

Lola perched on the edge of his bed.

"Listen, Georg," she said. "I meant to tell you this yester-day, but I hardly saw you. That cinema idea – you can't be serious. It's no kind of a job for people like us. I could sing for a living myself – my voice is good enough for a suburban music hall – and maybe I will, too. I'd sooner do that than marry Ebenseder." Her face darkened. "There was another row this morning, Georg. Father got terribly worked up – he's been so worried and irritable lately. I think they want to pen-sion him off, you see, and he's only done seventeen years. It's awfully unfair, but don't let him know I've told you. He doesn't want it mentioned."

Herr Vittorin had been completely unbalanced by the nation's defeat, the collapse of the army, the overthrow of the monarchy and the disintegration of the Austro-Hungarian Empire. Unable to come to terms with the way things were going, he had become dogmatic, argumentative, and con-vinced that everyone was persecuting him. Devoid of legal training and incapable of grasping the nature of complex fiscal regulations, he had committed numerous blunders and applied incorrect scales of charges when working out the tax demands for which his department was responsible. When hauled over the coals, he had jumped to the conclusion that he was the victim of political intrigue and defended himself in a manner that only aggravated his position: he submitted a memor-andum to higher authority in which he heaped his immediate superior with grave accusations. He not only called the man a schemer, an incompetent ignoramus, and an embezzler of government funds, but charged him with corruption, moral turpitude, and conduct unworthy of a public servant. The authorities promptly launched an inquiry which found that these charges were wholly unjustified. Herr Vittorin was urged to take early retirement, but insisted that he had no grounds for so doing. "I shall fight to the bitter end. What's right is right and nothing can change it."

Accordingly, he was suspended from duty and the final decision on his case referred to a disciplinary tribunal. At home he strove to maintain the pretence that nothing untoward had happened. He continued to leave home at nine each morning, complete with briefcase, and returned on the stroke of half-past three. The intervening hours he spent in small, secluded coffee houses, where he read the newspapers and adorned any passages that aroused his displeasure with exclamation and interrogation marks in blue pencil. Having read the papers from end to end, he engaged in muttered soliloquies or drafted interminable pleas for submission to the disciplinary tribunal.

"Pension Father off?" said Vittorin. "Ridiculous, Lola, you're always looking on the dark side. How old is he? Only fifty-four last summer, right? Anyway, what was this row about?"

"Oh, Ebenseder, as usual. Father shouted at me, didn't you hear? 'It's outrageous, the way you treat that man – I don't know what you think you're playing at! It's a miracle he still sets foot in this house. A decent, dependable, respectable man like that, and you don't appreciate him! That's the way you've always been: silly and inconsiderate and vain and irresponsible. You just can't go on like this!' I burst into tears and ran out of the room – my eyes are all puffy, can't you see? I do feel so sorry for Father all the same. When you came home, Georg, I thought at least *you* would back me up . . ."

"You'll have to be patient, Lola," Vittorin said, looking harassed. "Of course you can count on me. Herr Ebenseder isn't my cup of tea either, but you know I've got to go. I won't be so preoccupied when I get back, which will probably be in four or five weeks' time. I'll go to Father and have it out with him. 'Lola wants nothing to do with Herr Ebenseder,' I'll say. 'Either he stops coming here or we both move out, Lola and I.' And if he refuses to give way . . ."

Lola smiled. "You mean well, Georg, I know, but the situation isn't as simple as you think. We can't just walk out on Father, not now. That wasn't what I meant to talk about, though – I don't know how I got on to the subject. I had something quite different to tell you. The night before last, when I was sitting alone in the living-room and thinking of

48

going to bed, someone knocked at the door. It was Herr Bamberger, our lodger. He wondered if I could spare him a minute. Of course, I told him. Well, the long and the short of it is, he's heard that you're fluent in French and Italian, and that you know all about customs regulations and the freight business, and he thinks you may be just the man he's looking for."

"Who told him I speak French and Italian? It strikes me as odd that he should be so well-informed about me – I've hardly exchanged a word with the man. Do you know him well?"

"I see him now and again, of course, because I clean his room. Herr Bamberger is a nice, quiet, retiring person. He seems to have taken a great shine to Vally – she chats to him sometimes. Perhaps it was she who told him about you."

"All right, go on. Where do I come in?"

"He has a lot of commercial dealings with foreigners – Italians and people from the Balkans. Up to now he's had to transact all his business in coffee-houses, but he'll have his own office from the first of next month. He's very keen to have a private word with you. He'd get plenty of applicants, of course, but in your case he knows who you are. He couldn't pay you much to start with, he says, because his own resources are very modest, but he's sure he'll make a success of things, and later on he'll offer you a partnership."

"Ah, I knew there'd be a catch! He wants me to work my fingers to the bone but he doesn't want to pay me anything. It's always the same old story: promises come cheap. How naïve you are, Lola!"

"All the same, George, you ought to have a word with him some time. I'm not trying to talk you into it, of course – these things are a closed book to me – but if you're really set on giving up your job . . . Herr Bamberger makes a good impression, believe me. He looks like a man who knows exactly what he wants."

"Good heavens, it's gone eleven, I must dash! All right, I'll give your Herr Bamberger the once-over, but I'm pinning no hopes on him and I don't fall for empty promises. Human beings are unscrupulous swine, all of them, I know that now. One lives and learns, Lola dear, one lives and learns."

They were sitting side by side in a window alcove in the Dom-café. Franzi, who had finished her lunch, asked for a cigarette. Vittorin opened his case and held it out.

"I've still got a few Russian left – help yourself. They're the ones with the mouthpiece. Go on, take one. It's Crimean tobacco. In Siberia we also smoked Chinese tobacco. There was a very high-grade, expensive kind with an unusual aroma, but that was unobtainable. I only knew one man who smoked it."

Vittorin fell silent. He endeavoured to hold his cigarette in a special way, clamped between his ring finger and the tip of his little finger, but he couldn't do it properly and gave up.

"I must be back in the office by one," Franzi said, "but I've got a lot to tell you first. Do you know the latest? That young man from Agram got in touch again!"

Vittorin was drifting away from her, she could tell. She was no longer at the centre of his thoughts, she sensed that more and more distinctly every day and was frightened of losing him for good. Vaguely aware that some strange, hostile force was luring him away, she was determined not to give him up without a fight. Hoping to hold him and rekindle his waning love, she had boasted of imaginary flirtations and pretended that various men were ardently pursuing her. One of her most successful inventions, and the one she employed most often, was a Croatian medical student who tried to woo her in Viennese dialect. He had almost become flesh and blood, and she made him show up in Vienna as often as required. In addition to the Croatian student there was a sentimental giant, a courier from the Swedish Legation who sang superbly to the guitar, and a shameless young baron who wanted to install Franzi in an apartment and take her travelling with him.

"The young man from Agram?" Vittorin said absently. "The medical student, you mean? Is he back in Vienna?"

"Yes, just imagine, he called me at the office two days ago, even though I'd already forbidden him to do so twice – I told you, remember? I don't like being rung up by all and sundry, my boss might disapprove. Anyway, I said to myself, just wait, you Croatian pest, today you're going to get a flea in your ear, but he was so nice and amusing on the phone I hadn't the heart. 'Hello there, sweetheart,' he said, 'I can't wait to see you again. How are you, and how's that old scoundrel of a boss of yours?' He's terribly familiar on the phone, you see, because he knows I can't really tell him off."

Franzi paused for a moment. She searched Vittorin's face but failed to find what she sought. He was listening with an air of complete indifference.

"Well," she went on, "now for a little fun, I thought to myself, so I asked him, all innocent, 'Are you staying here long, Herr Milosh? Will you still be in Vienna on the first of December?' I haven't told you this, but my parents are planning a week-end trip to the country at the end of the month – you know, to visit my uncle, the one with the farm at Gloggnitz – and they're looking forward to it immensely. They leave on Saturday and they won't be back till Monday. I'm giving our old maidservant the day off and sending her home to her family, which means I'll have the apartment all to myself. I didn't say that to the young man from Agram – naturally not, because he might have got the wrong idea. And now comes the worst part. Guess what the fellow said?"

"Well?"

"He laughed and said, 'Of course I'll still be in Vienna on the first of December, sweetheart, why do you ask? Will you be all on your lonesome, by any chance? That would be terrific – I could pay you a visit.' Well, I was flabbergasted to think he'd figured it out so quickly. And then it occurred to me how nice it would be if *you* could spend the Sunday with me, Georg. You could simply tell your family you were going away for the day, and if the young man from Agram rang the bell you could go to the door and ask what he wanted, and he'd have to clear off. Wouldn't that be a laugh?"

51

Vittorin, looking at her, detected a timid plea and an unspoken promise in her eyes.

"We'd be together for a whole day, all by ourselves," she said softly. "We've never been that lucky before, Georg."

He put his arm around her shoulders and hugged her to him. She didn't resist, and for a while they sat snuggled up together.

"Of course I'll come," he whispered, "— that's definite. You've no idea how much I'll look forward to it."

"Ssh, Georg, the waiter's looking. So it's settled, then. You'll keep the day free?"

"It's a date. By the way, Franzi, have you heard from your Baron again?"

Franzi brushed the Baron aside with a dismissive gesture; she didn't need him any more.

"Oh, him," she said. "Yes, he wrote to me, but I sent his letter back — unopened, of course. I know perfectly well what he's after. Goodness, I must get a move on, the boss will be grumbling already. What about you, though? You haven't told me a thing. Are you going back to your old job?"

Impatiently, Vittorin stubbed out the remains of his cigarette in the ashtray.

"Back to the old routine?" he said. "No fear! You don't think I want to sit behind a typewriter from morning to night for a hundred and eighty kronen a month, do you? That's all over — I'm worth more than that. I'm not going back at all. They can think what they like, they've seen the last of me."

Franzi shook her head.

"Surely you won't just fail to turn up, Georg? That would be crazy of you. You'll get three months' salary if you give them proper notice — it's standard practice in all big firms these days. Three months, let's see . . . You'd be making them a present of over five hundred kronen. Very generous of you, I must say!"

He stared at her, nonplussed. That way of acquiring the money he needed had never occurred to him.

"You're absolutely right, of course," he said. "Five hundred and forty kronen aren't to be sneezed at. Yes, you're right, I won't pass up the money – I'll go and see them today."

Some rapid mental arithmetic told him that half the sum in question would get him to the Russian border. Vienna-Radkersburg-Belgrade-Bucharest-Galatz, and from Galatz across the frontier to Tiraspol. It made sense.

He rose.

"You're absolutely right," he repeated. "I'd better call them right away and ask if the managing director's still there. Where's the phone?"

"Over in the billiard room, third door on the right," Franzi told him. "Hold on, I'll come with you – I can just spare another two or three minutes."

Once inside the phone booth she let him kiss her and kissed him back while billiard balls clicked and dominoes clattered and waiters bustled from table to table with midday editions still inky from the press. Then she stood there for a moment, smiling happily as if her kiss had permanently vanquished the dark, alien, mysterious force that aspired to deprive her of her beloved.

"Mundus Incorporated, International Forwarding and Ware-housing Agents for Danubian and Overseas Freight" was housed in an unlovely building with dismal little windows and mortar and plaster flaking off its dirty grey walls. It had always looked that way, the management never having set any store by outward appearances. Although nothing had changed, Vittorin felt like a stranger as he entered the premises from which he had last emerged at the outbreak of war, a youthful figure attired in the uniform of an officer cadet.

A strange porter sleepily reached for his cap. Coke was being loaded in the yard. On the stairs and in the gas-lit corridors Vittorin passed young men with unfamiliar faces. One of them stopped him and politely inquired which department he wanted – Reception was on the second floor. He mumbled an inaudible reply and walked on.

At last he saw a face he knew: that of the managing director's old clerk, who might have been mistaken for a retired judge when playing billiards after office hours in the little coffee-house across the street. He greeted Vittorin like a friend from happier times.

"Why, if it isn't Herr Vittorin! What a nice surprise! So you're back already. How long has it been? Let me see, you joined up in 'fifteen – no, 'fourteen, just after the ultimatum. Who would have thought it would end this way? Tragic, really tragic. All those youngsters gone, and for what, I ask you? Still, it's a real pleasure to see you again, Herr Vittorin. If you'd come next week you wouldn't have found me here. I'm retiring – yes indeed, retiring after forty years with the firm."

"I expect you're quite glad to be retiring after forty years," said Vittorin. "Will you be staying in Vienna?"

"Glad?" the old man replied, continuing to sort and tidy the files on his little desk. "Yes and no. The place just isn't what it was. Nothing but new people and new faces – doctors of law wherever you look, and I can't get all their names into my head. As for staying in Vienna, not me – not with this inflation. I've got no children, so there's nothing to keep me here. I'm going to my wife's relatives in Vorarlberg. You get more for your money in the country. I've got a bit put by – enough for a cottage and maybe a patch of garden as well. Another week, and then it's goodbye to Vienna."

Vittorin inquired if the managing director was free. The old clerk shook both his hands again with a touch of emotion before padding off silently into the inner sanctum to announce him.

The managing director gave Vittorin a kindly, cordial reception. He congratulated him on his safe return *"post tot discrimina rerum"*, as he eruditely phrased it, and expressed satisfaction that the firm should have regained the services of such a valued employee. Vittorin was given no time to reply. They must bestir themselves, said the managing director. Diligence was the order of the day. There was plenty of work to be done now that international trade links had been restored, albeit not in full measure. Austria's economic war wounds must be healed. The new era had brought new problems in its wake;

54

that was why everyone, irrespective of status, must pull his weight. Vittorin would be temporarily assigned to the accounts department, his erstwhile post as assistant French-language correspondence clerk having unavoidably and understandably been filled by someone else.

The managing director spoke in a quiet, courteous tone, accompanying his remarks with economical but expressive gestures. Vittorin, standing stiffly at attention, stared through him and heard nothing. A peculiar thing had happened to him. He had flirted with an idea: he had tried to imagine – just for a moment, purely to pass the time – that he was standing in another office far away, and that the shadow on the wall was Selyukov's. The notion became too strong to suppress – he couldn't shake it off. Snow was drifting down outside, Grisha polishing the samovar behind the door, the stove flickering fitfully. Books littered the desk, uppermost among them a French novel whose frontispiece depicted a naked woman playing with a tiger cub. Over in Hut 4, his comrades would be waiting for news. Selyukov looked up with his tongue caressing his upper lip and the lamplight falling on his slender, tanned hand. And then:

"Conduct unbecoming to an officer – the French call it *boch-isme*. You may go. *Pashol*."

The bastard, humiliating me like that! Why did I stand for it? I should have slapped him in the face and braved a firing squad. If only I'd slapped him in the face! Too late – it's too late now . . .

"You seem unpleasantly surprised," said the managing director. "Don't misunderstand me: it's only a temporary arrangement. You mustn't think . . ."

Vittorin came to. The past was releasing its hold on him. No, he told himself, it isn't too late. It's simply a question of money, of a few hundred kronen. One I get them – once I manage to raise them – we'll speak again, Mikhail Mikhailovich Selyukov.

"You mustn't think," the managing director went on, "that the firm intends to dispense permanently with your knowledge of foreign languages and your practical experience in the correspondence department. That isn't so, I can assure you. We shall bear you very much in mind. Meantime, report to your new head of department, Herr Schödl, tomorrow or the day after, and leave the rest to me."

Vittorin stared at the green silk shade of the managing director's desk lamp with a sheepish, helpless smile on his face. The interview had taken a course bewilderingly at odds with his preconceived plan. He had felt certain that he would meet with a cool, casual, businesslike reception. He would then have found it easy to decline the managing director's offer of a steady job and demand his terminal grant – the money he needed – as of right. The fact that the managing director had spoken to him in such a benevolent, even friendly manner, and had commended his knowledge of foreign languages, was an unforeseen hurdle. Could he summarily give notice under such circumstances? Yes, he had to have that money. The managing director was looking impatient and drumming on the leather blotter with his pencil.

"Please excuse me," Vittorin said with sudden decision. "I apologize for taking up a little more of your valuable time, but I've no choice. This isn't easy for me, you understand . . ."

He faltered. It wasn't so simple to find the right words. He tried again.

"I'm in an embarrassing position. I don't know how you'll take this, sir, but circumstances compel me to . . ."

The managing director sat back and looked at him over the top of his glasses.

"Yes, well, I think I've a rough idea of what's troubling you," he said. "It's odd, but all you gentlemen back from the war suffer from the same problem. None of you seems to have managed to accumulate any assets while on active service. Never mind. Pursuant to a directive issued on August 17th of the current year, the management is empowered to grant all ex-servicemen employees with families to support a one-time ex gratia payment equivalent to three months' salary. Are you married?"

"No – that's to say, I intend –"

The managing director brushed this aside.

"No hurry," he said, "there's plenty of time. You aren't a breadwinner, so I can only authorize a quarter's advance on salary to be repaid in monthly instalments from January 1st onwards. Go and see Herr Weber on the second floor."

The telephone rang. He picked up the receiver.

"Yes, speaking . . . Good afternoon, Herr Nussbaum . . . Yes indeed, I have the file in front of me . . . No, I'm afraid I don't share your point of view, we've met you more than half-way . . . What? Out of the question. We like to be accommodating, but . . . It's a matter of . . . Kindly allow me to speak . . . Exactly, it's a matter of . . . Please think it over. I'll give you until tomorrow to reconsider my proposal . . . I should regret that too . . . What did you say? Do so by all means, Herr Nussbaum. I shall await the outcome of the hearing with an easy mind. And the same to you, sir. Goodbye."

Vittorin seized the opportunity to demonstrate his professional enthusiasm and knowledge of the firm's clientele.

"Adolf Nussbaum & Co., No. 15 Praterstrasse," he said. "Soaps and fats. Telegraphic address: Fettbaum, Vienna. That was the boss himself, if I'm not much mistaken."

"Quite right, Herr Nussbaum in person. Have you had dealings with the firm?"

"Of course, they're one of our oldest customers. They export mainly to the Balkan States and the Levant. Herr Adolf Nussbaum is a very quick-tempered gentleman. He threatens to sue at the drop of a hat."

"Good," said the managing director. "I can see you won't take long to get back into the swing. About that advance: apply to Herr Weber in Personnel, as I said – tell him to submit the cash voucher for my signature. Oh yes, and while you're here, take this folder and drop it in at the forwarding department on your way out."

Kohout had volunteered to obtain the passport and visas required for the journey. He felt quite competent to undertake this far from easy task because he had seen and learnt a great deal during his two weeks in Dr Sigismund Eichkatz's law office, where he had been engaged as a kind of confidential clerk.

Dr Eichkatz owed his brisk flow of business to a capacity for observing and, at the same time, circumventing the laws and ordinances that hampered his clients' entrepreneurial activites. He respected those laws because, having been devised by the human brain, they betrayed their provenance all too clearly in their flaws and imperfections, and he despised them because they clothed themselves in an aura of infallibility. He never permitted himself to infringe them because he knew that their rigid immutability was no match for a nimble mind. They crushed the fools who broke them and gave free rein to the sagacious souls who paid them the respect they demanded.

Dr Eichkatz was an expert in the outflanking manoeuvres peculiar to guerrilla warfare. His name was uttered with reverence in certain quarters of Vienna, and his address circulated in the coffee-houses where dealers traded in jute, cattle, barley, or artificial silk. In October 1918, when it became clear that his office staff, which comprised a typist and a receptionist, was no longer equal to the demands of his expanding practice, Dr Eichkatz augmented it by one. Kohout, with whom he had become acquainted in the billiard room of the Café Élite, was employed to keep the filing system up to date and rake in outstanding fees from tardy payers.

Vittorin, having telephoned his friend to expect him, was greeted with the long-suffering air of a man whose shoulders bore the full brunt of a responsible job.

"You'll have to wait awhile," Kohout told him. "I've got to deal with the people in the waiting-room first. Sit down and listen for a bit – it's quite entertaining sometimes. I'll be through in half an hour, then we can discuss things in peace. The boss won't disturb us if I tell him I've got a visitor." He broke off. "Fräulein Gusti, that's the Doctor's bell. He wants you!"

The typist scurried into the inner office, only to reappear a moment later.

"Herr Kohout, quick, the Spannagel file!"

Dr Eichkatz's irritable voice, resonant as a pipe-organ, came drifting through the open door.

"You expect too much of me, Herr Spannagel. I'm a lawyer, not a prophet. I've no idea how your case will turn out. If I were a clairvoyant I wouldn't practise law, I'd go on the stage with you, Herr Spannagel."

"For heaven's sake shut the door, Herr Kohout," Fräulein Gusti called from her typewriter. "He's playing the fool again today."

Kohout shut the door of the inner office and turned to Vittorin.

"It's like that all the time here. I'm not going to be able to stand it for long, believe me. I mean, did you see those people outside in the waiting-room? Some clients, eh? What faces! If you sentenced them all to three years' hard labour you wouldn't be doing them an injustice. All right, here we go. Fräulein Gusti, give that typewriter a bit of a rest, would you? I can't hear myself speak."

He extracted a folder from the stack of files on his desk and raised his voice in a stentorian bellow.

"Herr Jonas Eiermann, if you please!"

Out of the waiting-room came a short, stout, bearded man in a raincoat rather too small for him. He deposited his hat on Kohout's desk, bowed, washed his hands with imaginary soap, turned to Vittorin, said "Eiermann", and sat down.

"Herr Eiermann," Kohout began, "I gather you wish to be sued for the repayment of a debt of fourteen kronen in the district court at Innsbruck. May I ask you for something on account?"

"Why, don't you think my credit's good?" Herr Eiermann demanded.

"Good or bad, it makes no difference," Kohout told him. "We don't give credit and we make no exceptions. Money in advance, that's our rule. You fork out, we sue. I'm not lifting

59

a finger till I see a hundred and sixty kronen on this desk in hard cash."

"I can't run to a hundred and sixty," Herr Eiermann replied after a pause for thought.

"All right, I'm prepared to accommodate you. How much *can* you run to?"

"A hundred at the outside."

"Very well, make it a hundred. Fräulein Gusti, give Herr Eiermann a receipt for –"

"But I can't raise the hundred for another three weeks."

"Three weeks?" Kohout exclaimed. "Out of the question. How much can you raise right away, today?"

Herr Eiermann grimaced as if he had swallowed something nasty. He was obviously in the throes of some internal convulsion.

"I might be able to manage sixty."

"Fräulein, give Herr Eiermann a receipt for sixty kronen and let's get this settled."

"But I don't have the sixty kronen on me," said Herr Eiermann.

"You don't have them on you? I guessed as much. You decline to pay, in other words?"

"I never said that!" Herr Eiermann protested, sounding hurt.

"I see, so you *are* prepared to pay. How much do you actually have on you, if I may make so bold?"

"I'm not sure. Thirty, maybe."

"A pleasure to do business with you," Kohout said wearily. "All right, for God's sake pay your thirty kronen and get it over."

Herr Eiermann produced a leather briefcase of indeterminate colour, rummaged in the various compartments, and brought out three crumpled banknotes.

Kohout took them between finger and thumb and dropped them into his open desk drawer. Then he ushered Herr Eiermann into Dr Eichkatz's office.

Dr Eichkatz, seemingly exhausted, was seated at the desk with his eyes shut and his massive bald head propped on his hairy fists. The Virginia cigarette that dangled from his flaccid lips had gone out. His gaunt frame came to life as Herr Eiermann walked in.

"Herr Jonas Eiermann," Kohout announced. "Entry permit for Innsbruck, Tyrol."

"So you want to go to Innsbruck, do you?" said Dr Eichkatz. "What's your nationality, Herr Eiermann?"

"I'm not Austrian," Eiermann replied.

"I didn't ask what you aren't, I asked what you are," the lawyer boomed. "You aren't an Eskimo either, or a member of the African race, or a Mohammedan, or a cowboy, or an English viscount, or a Hindu dancing girl. You're none of those things, I realize that. Now kindly tell me what you are."

"I'm a Polish citizen," Herr Eiermann replied, utterly intimidated.

"At last, God be praised! So you're a Polish citizen who wants to go to Innsbruck. That'll be all, Herr Kohout," said Dr Eichkatz, and Kohout withdrew.

The typist, who had finished her work, was single-mindedly devouring a cheese sandwich. Vittorin had risen and was striding up and down the room.

"Some clients, eh?" sighed Kohout. "Haggling with Herr Eiermann was no fun. 'Pick 'em clean!' – that's what Dr Eichkatz keeps telling me, but it's easier said than done. Extracting money from a man like that is like getting blood out of a stone."

It dawned on Kohout that Vittorin was growing impatient.

"Now to business," he went on. "The folks outside can wait." He glanced at Fräulein Gusti and lowered his voice. "If only that creature would push off and leave us to talk in peace. She's usually out of here like a shot at half-past five. She's got a railwayman boyfriend – he waits for her downstairs. They're engaged, more or less, but he'll never marry her."

"Tell me something," said Vittorin. "You stayed on for a while at Emperger's the other night. Was any more said about the matter?"

"You bet. They all poked fun at you." Kohout shifted from foot to foot and wrung his hands. "That knucklehead

Emperger claimed you'd become infatuated with a Russian officer – those were his very words. The Professor said you were going to Russia to increase the sum of human suffering – you know what he's like, always trying to impress people with his philosophical turns of phrase. As for Feuerstein, he called the whole idea plain stupid."

Vittorin chewed his lip and stared into space.

"A thing can be stupid and necessary just the same," he said.

"Of course," said Kohout. "Have you got the money?"

"Yes, six hundred kronen."

"You must change them into dollars right away. Your best bet is to go to the Café Élite, buttonhole one of the foreign exchange racketeers in the back room, and say you want some American noodles – that's their slang term for dollar bills. Mind you don't pick a con artist, though – perhaps I'd better go with you. As for a Russian visa, you won't get one through normal channels, I've made careful inquiries. The Russian Red Cross mission in Vienna issues visas, but they can take months to come through. We'll have to handle this another way, and I know how: Galatz – that's where you're going."

"Galatz? Won't I need a Rumanian visa?"

"Yes, the Rumanian military mission will issue you with one. That won't be easy either, but money talks. Getting across the Russian border will be no problem once you're in Galatz. You can go on foot, by road, or, if you really want to play it safe, there are passport factories all over Rumania–Braila, Focshani, Bottoshani, Galatz itself. It'll cost you two hundred kronen – a tidy sum, admittedly, but you'll have to allow for that. Herr Eiermann's problem is far simpler. He only wants to go to the Tyrol, not Russia."

"Herr Eiermann?" said Vittorin. "You mean he's also after an entry permit?"

"Of course, didn't you hoist that in? The provincial authorities in the Tyrol won't let anyone domiciled in Galicia across the border. Herr Eiermann has urgent business in Innsbruck, so what does he do? He gets us to sue him in the local district court for non-payment of some trivial sum – fourteen kronen or whatever – and produces his summons at the checkpoint. All in order, nothing to be done. They have to let him across."

Vittorin was horrified.

"And that's the sort of sharp practice you engage in here?"

"My dear fellow, what do you expect? Transactions like these are relatively kosher. People come to us with the most outrageous requests and proposals, you've no idea! I sometimes wonder why I ever studied law for four terms – a course in picking pockets would have been more to the point, but never mind, I ought to be grateful that Eichkatz took me on. I wouldn't find another job too easily, not with this arm of mine. As for home . . . My father's remarried and I don't get on with my stepmother – she makes some spiteful remark every time she puts a bite of food in front of me. If only I could go back to university and get my degree, but no: I've got to earn, earn, earn! Isn't it enough to turn you into a Bolshevik, the lousy, rotten, putrid society we're living in today?"

Vittorin rose. "You ought to come to Russia with me," he said.

"Yes," said Kohout, "I'd thought of that too."

On Kohout's advice Vittorin sold everything of value he possessed: his bicycle, two gold rings, the classics and deluxe editions in his bookcase, the Goertz binoculars he'd bought before the war and paid for by monthly instalments, a Kodak camera, a walking stick with an ivory handle, a tie-pin set with two small sapphires – a birthday present from his father – and, last but not least, a Domb oboe and a pair of Halifax skates. His sisters failed to notice the gradual disappearance of these articles, the proceeds of which, added to his existing nest egg, were sufficient to cover his travelling expenses. Now that nothing humanly foreseeable could prevent him from putting his plan into effect, Vittorin regained his peace of mind and emotional poise. The phantom that had taken possession of his brain granted him a brief spell of relaxation before plunging him into a world of adventure.

63

He had resolved to give no further thought to his mission, as he termed it, until that mission summoned him away. He was on leave, so to speak, but there were obligations to fulfil even now. He wanted to devote his remaining days of freedom to the people who had a claim on him: his father, his sisters, his employer, and the girl who loved him. He would give none of them cause for complaint.

He was first in the office at eight each morning. Having still to be assigned specific duties, he helped out wherever he was needed. In an effort to make himself useful and pull his weight, he performed all kinds of menial work. He answered the telephone, added up long columns of figures, and typed letters dictated to him by junior colleagues. At home he was always ready to look through his brother's French exercises, fetch books and sheet music from the lending library for his sisters, or play a game of chess with his taciturn, pipe-smoking, careworn father, who had retired into his shell. When plans for the coming week – a visit to friends, for instance, or a Sunday afternoon outing – were under discussion in the family circle, he would listen in silence with an indulgent, almost imperceptible smile that gave no inkling of how remote he felt from all such concerns.

The evenings he spent with Franzi, who would emerge from her office to find him waiting at the end of the street in his old army tunic. They frequented cinemas, wine cellars, or small suburban inns, but wherever they went there were people. Never alone with him for a moment, Franzi grew tired of waiting. She would happily have shared a small bed-sitter with him as his wife or mistress, no matter which, but she realized that this wouldn't happen overnight. There were too many hurdles to surmount. Franzi became doubly impatient for the day when they would be all by themselves. She made cryptic allusions to that day, the first of December, without betraying any of the little surprises she had prepared for their assignation in her parents' apartment. She had borrowed a gramophone and some of the latest dance records from a girl at the office. Her other acquisitions included a small supply of wood and coal, a bottle of brandy, and the ingredients for a bowl of punch: rum, lemons and sugar – all of them things that had long possessed rarity value.

Two glasses of wine were enough to make Franzi frolicsome and exuberant. She would begin to take an interest in the other male customers and throw them flirtatious glances, and when these evoked a response – when someone covertly raised his glass to her or made some jocular remark – she would turn to Vittorin with a look of helpless bewilderment, as if to ask him what the man was after. Later, her high spirits abruptly gave way to dejection. She would rest her head on Vittorin's shoulder and sob till the tears streamed down her cheeks. She never omitted to explain the reason for her fit of the blues: she was crying because of the dismal autumn weather, or because her boss had shouted at her during the day, or because her mother wouldn't allow her to keep a canary, or simply because life was so sad and wonderful and short.

After walking her home, Vittorin often looked in at the Café Élite, where Kohout would interrupt his game of billiards to report progress. Things were shaping nicely. The Rumanian route had been abandoned because East Galicia was far more accessible: to obtain an entry permit you had only to feign a wish to visit the grave of a brother killed in action there. Once in East Galicia, Kohout declared, you were home and dry. All that remained was to get through the Red Army's lines, but for that no papers were needed. The new Russia was devoid of bureaucracy. Personal courage, resourcefulness and self-assurance – all would depend on those alone.

It was now taken for granted that Kohout would accompany Vittorin to Russia. However, his father must know nothing of this decision until confronted with it at the last minute, so extreme discretion was the order of the day. Kohout looked around for potential eavesdroppers – he claimed to have enemies and rivals everywhere – and his voice sank to a whisper.

"He won't let me go without a fight, that's for sure," he said, wringing his hands. "You mustn't breathe a word to anyone, you hear? In Moscow I'll have prospects – reliable comrades and intellectuals are at a premium there. Here? Here I've been chucked on the scrapheap. The money for the trip'll be forthcoming when I need it, never fear. I'll get it all right. How? Leave that to me. And now, please excuse me, my opponent's getting fidgety. It's my only form of amusement, an occasional game of billiards in the evening."

Vittorin's interview with Herr Bamberger took place one day toward the end of November. Lola, who had engineered it, lingered in the room for a while, patting cushions and straightening chairs. She gave her brother an encouraging look – he was standing there rather forlornly – before going out and shutting the door quietly behind her.

"Do sit down, Herr Vittorin."

Herr Bamberger, his shoulders hunched against the cold, was pacing to and fro in the confined space between his desk and the stove. Short and slight, he had a pallid, sickly face alight with intelligence. He did not seem to attach much importance to clothes. He wore an ill-fitting suit, obviously bought off the peg, and an old-fashioned knitted tie. His dainty patent leather shoes struck the only note of almost foppish elegance.

"I don't propose to beat about the bush," he said, "and you yourself would doubtless prefer us to get to the point right away. I have a position to fill, as you know. Your sister was kind enough to inform me of your qualifications and experience. You're familiar with customs regulations and the freight business. You write French and Italian –"

"I speak Russian too," Vittorin put in, settling himself on the sofa.

Herr Bamberger registered this information with an appreciative nod.

"Russian too, excellent. Most important of all from my point of view, you're also acquainted with standard practices in the various stock and commodity exchanges. Can you by any chance tell me the terms governing transactions in tin on the pre-war London market?"

"Tin?" said Vittorin. "Let me see. One moment, please . . ."

The question had whetted his ambition. His memory was functioning perfectly: he could show off his paces. If only Selyukov had asked him such a question, but no. Out with him – *pashol!*

"Tin," he repeated. "For delivery as follows: Class A, Singapore tin, Penang tin, Australian tin, English refined tin. Class B, ordinary tin of recognized quality, at least 99 per cent pure. Available in bars, slabs and ingots. Payment: net cash on receipt of contract. Further terms in conformity with the Rules and Regulations of the London Metal Exchange. Minimum quantity: five tons or a multiple thereof. The discount on Class B –"

"Stop!" exclaimed Herr Bamberger. "That's enough, that's enough. My knowledge of such matters is nil, to be frank, but this much I can tell: you're just the man for the job I mentioned."

"What kind of job is it?" Vittorin inquired.

"Personal assistant to myself," Bamberger replied without interrupting his tour of the room. "You'd have to be available whenever I'm doing business – in other words, at any hour of the day. In the evenings too, sometimes – even at midnight if need be."

"Evenings would be fine," Vittorin told him, gratified by Bamberger's tribute to his expertise, "but I couldn't manage the daytime. As you may or may not be aware, I'm already employed by the Mundus Corporation. I've every prospect of promotion to deputy head of department in two or three years' time."

Herr Bamberger came to a halt, thrust his hands into his trouser pockets, and looked Vittorin in the eye.

"Deputy head of department, eh? Congratulations. Five hundred kronen a month and a full pension after thirty-five years' service. Very nice. The prospects I can offer you are of a different order. I intend to go places within the next six months and take you with me."

"I don't understand," Vittorin said. "Take me where?"

"Where? What an odd question. To the *table d'hôte* of life, Herr Vittorin. Or, to be more precise: to the Riviera in my limousine, if you prefer."

As if the thought of the Riviera had reminded him just how cold the room was, Herr Bamberger went over to the stove and warmed his hands at it. Vittorin laughed aloud.

"Bravo!" he said. "I'm your man. Menton, Cannes, Monte Carlo – I wouldn't mind that. How soon do we leave?"

Bamberger seemed deaf to the derision in his voice.

"I've one or two things to attend to first," he said without looking round. "As I told you, I aim to make my fortune in the next six months – a fortune sufficient for my needs."

"In Monte Carlo, I suppose," said Vittorin.

"No, the risk factor in Monte Carlo is too great," Bamberger replied as earnestly and matter-of-factly as ever.

"But getting rich in Vienna is a dead certainty, eh?" Vittorin sneered.

"For someone who can foresee how things will develop in the next few months, yes."

"Really? Then perhaps you'd tell me how you plan to get to – what was it? – the *table d'hôte* of life?"

Bamberger tossed two briquettes of compressed wood shavings and sawdust into the dying embers. Then he straightened up.

"Far be it from me to resent your sceptical reaction to my proposal," he said. "I never expected us to agree terms right away. My position in regard to you is anything but easy. I'm asking you to give up a modest but reasonably secure job, just like that. The only security I can offer you in return is an assurance that I've weighed up my chances of success with the utmost care, and that I'm fully aware of my responsibility toward you."

He paused to inspect the stove, which had now gone out completely, and resumed his pacing of the room.

"It's possible, Herr Vittorin, that you underrate yourself and your abilities. I can't believe that a person of your education would be content with the humdrum existence of a glorified clerk. You're still a young man."

"I'm twenty-nine years old."

"Two years my senior, in other words. Does a 'steady job', so called, really represent the pinnacle of your ambitions?"

"I'm not worried about my steady job," said Vittorin. "There's even a chance that something may happen in the near future to make me give it up, but that's only by-the-by – I'd rather not go into it now. In any case, it's only one aspect of the matter. The other, if you'll pardon my saying so, is that you're asking me to hitch my wagon to a virtual stranger. May I be absolutely frank? I've no idea what form your commercial objectives take. I don't know the extent of your business or how sound it is, nor do I know whether or where you've been in business previously. I should have to be clear on all those points before reaching a decision, surely you can see that?"

"Of course I can," Bamberger replied. "Perhaps it's time I told you a bit about myself. I went to university, but the subject I studied bears no relevance to the matter in hand. I've never been actively engaged in business. I inherited a small income that enabled me to watch and wait for the ideal moment to embark on my operations. As I see it, that moment has come. I've obtained orders from a number of major foreign firms and I'm currently negotiating the bank loans I require."

"You could be right," Vittorin said. "Now that frontiers are opening up again and international trade links have been restored – "

Bamberger raised his hand.

"Say no more!" he exclaimed. "International trade links, forsooth! Open frontiers have always existed. I know Austrians who exported timber to Italy during the war. During the war, mark you! In return we got – I can't recall exactly what our Italian enemies sent us in return, but no matter. International trade links? No, I have totally different grounds for believing that the ideal moment has arrived. We've just had a successful revolution, and hard on its heels will come – as it has throughout history – bad money. All revolutions are born

69

in blood and expire in a sea of paper. Hamstrung by a gigantic deficit, the government will try to print its way out of trouble. I don't know if our new banknotes will be adorned with the Goddess of Liberty. The only certainty is that this flood of new money will sweep away long-established fortunes and destroy existing rights of ownership. All the possessions we now covet will become ownerless assets ripe for acquisition by those with a proper sense of timing. The war may appear to be over, Herr Vittorin, but with us it's only just beginning. It'll be a merciless war – a war of each against all. Speaking for myself, I intend to win it."

He paused and glanced at the clock.

"Forgive me," he said, "I still have two letters to post. We'll talk again tomorrow or some other time. I must hurry or they'll slam the window in my face."

THE SUMMONS

Vittorin's sisters were sitting in the living-room on the afternoon of November 30th, Vally pretending to read a book from the lending library, Lola plying her needle. The autumn weather was damp and chill. Outside, street lamps floated in a sea of mist and raindrops trickled down the windowpanes; inside, all that broke the silence was the gentle hiss of the gas lamp and the ticking of the clock on the wall.

Georg Vittorin was so remote from the world around him that the oppressive hush did not impinge on his consciousness. He was getting ready to go out. Standing in front of the mirror, he knotted his tie with care. There was plenty of time. Franzi, who had still to complete her preparations at home, wanted him to find the table laid and the room warm and snug. They had arranged that he would turn up at seven, not a minute before, and tap discreetly on the door of the apartment. "Don't ring the bell," she had impressed on him. "I'll hear you all right, and there's no need for the neighbours to know I've got company . . ."

The clock struck six. Vally went to the window and looked down into the street. Everything was glistening wet with mist and rain: kiosks, shop signs, cars, pavements, tram lines. Figures hurried past, emerged from the shadow of buildings into the glow of the gas lamps, acquired faces – weary and indifferent, morose or carefree – and vanished into the darkness again. From the end of the street came a honking of horns and the raucous cries of newspaper sellers.

"By the way," said Vittorin as he parted his hair and slicked it down with a wet brush, "you mustn't worry if I don't come home tonight. The friend I'm dining with lives right out at Hietzing – well, Ober-St-Veit, actually. I'll probably beg a bed off him. He isn't on a tram route, and the thought of walking home in this weather . . ."

He thought he detected a half-indulgent, half-mocking smile on Lola's face, unaware that she wasn't listening to him at all. His elaborate excuse for staying overnight seemed suddenly threadbare and implausible. It annoyed him that he hadn't concocted something better.

"It's pointless, going out in this lousy weather," he improvised, "but since I said I would . . . Besides, this is my last free evening. From Monday onwards my time belongs to Herr Bamberger. *Tu l'a voulu*, Lola dear. What'll come of it remains to be seen."

"There they are at last!" Vally called from the window.

Lola looked up from her embroidery. A flicker of suspense and apprehension crossed her face, but she suppressed it.

"Thank God," she said quietly. "Waiting, that's the worst part."

"They came by cab," Vally reported. "I only caught a glimpse of Father – he went straight in. Herr Ebenseder's still down there, talking to the cabbie."

"What's the matter?" Vittorin asked.

Lola didn't reply. Vally glanced at her hesitantly, uncertain whether to tell him or not.

"What is this?" Vittorin demanded impatiently. "A secret? All right, keep it to yourselves."

"I think," said Vally, "– that's to say, Lola thinks that the decision on Father's retirement came through today."

Vittorin was in no mood to take much interest in anything that obtruded on his own concerns.

"You think, Lola thinks!" he exclaimed, glancing at the clock, which now said a quarter to seven. "Don't be so silly, Father would have told me."

"You know Father – he didn't say anything to me either," Lola retorted. "But Ebenseder was here twice yesterday. They closeted themselves in the study and talked for ages – didn't you notice? – and this morning Father got a registered letter. He took it and . . ."

There was the sound of the front door closing. Voices could be heard in the hall.

"Do me a favour, Georg: don't ask any questions," Lola said in a hurried whisper. "Pretend you know nothing. He'll come out with it himself soon enough if things went the right way." And she bent over her needlework again with an unaffectedly casual air.

Preceded by the corpulent figure of Herr Ebenseder, who was somewhat out of breath after hurrying up the stairs, Herr Vittorin strode in wearing an expression from which it seemed clear that he was pleased with himself. He saluted with his walking stick, sword-drill fashion, and cried *"Servitore!"* Herr Vittorin had always, ever since his army days in Trieste, favoured the use of certain Italian phrases. He would say *"Ecco mi pronto"* when answering the telephone, herald his departure with an *"Avanti"* or an *"Andemo"*, and enjoin someone to drop an unwelcome subject with a curt, incisive *"Basta cosi"*.

No sooner had he entered the room than he filled it with noise and bustle. Pacing up and down in a stiffly military manner, he requested Vally to fetch his smoking jacket and an easy chair from the bedroom for Herr Ebenseder, Lola to brew some tea, "extra hot and strong and laced with rum if there is any; if not, slivovitz will do", Georg to inform him of his brother Oskar's whereabouts – "The young scamp is probably sauntering down the corso with his friends again – you really ought to take him in hand a little" – and everyone present to look cheerful.

"You'll stay to supper, won't you?" he said, turning to Herr Ebenseder. "It's no trouble, I assure you. Only potluck, of course – a couple of sausages and a glass of beer. Vally, don't slouch! Where's Lola? Lola!" he called in the direction of the kitchen. "Forget about the tea, there's no point, we'll be having supper soon. Well, everyone, in case you didn't know, today was the day."

Satisfied that his words had sunk in, he calmly lit his pipe while Herr Ebenseder, fidgeting around on his chair, endeavoured to attract the girls' attention by winking and signalling in a variety of other ways.

"The committee took the form of a tribunal," Herr Vittorin went on. "There were three of them, with an undersecretary from the ministry in the chair. The undersecretary was a charming fellow, incidentally – a gentleman to his fingertips. 'Please speak quite freely,' he told me. 'That's why we're here, to listen.' Well, I'd come prepared. I said my piece at long last, and I didn't mince matters either, believe me."

He turned to Herr Ebenseder in quest of confirmation and approval. Ebenseder, who had abruptly stiffened, gave several vigorous nods.

"'Gentlemen,' I told them, 'mistakes do happen, I grant you. Far be it from me to paint myself in rosier colours than I deserve, but gentlemen, don't forget the most important thing of all: integrity! What do I mean by that? Well I've already given you a frank and uncompromising picture of the state of affairs prevailing in our department. For a start . . .'"

He drew himself up, took a deep breath, and treated himself to the pleasure of repeating his speech for the prosecution to an admiring audience.

"'For a start, take the chief accountant – my superior, admittedly, and entitled to due respect. His personal circumstances are no concern of mine, but gentlemen, note this salient fact: he cycles to and from the office every livelong day, and who can afford to buy tyres on a chief accountant's salary these days? He has no private means – on the contrary, he's in debt, yet his wife waltzes around in silk stockings and expensive gowns and lord knows what else. Where does he get the money, I venture to ask? Another thing: he hasn't taken a day off since the outbreak of war. Why not? Because he's such an exceptionally conscientious public servant? Oh no! The chief accountant alone knows why he never lets anyone peek at his books. Enough said – you gentlemen must draw your own conclusions.' That sank in! The undersecretary took my point – he was entirely on my side, I could tell – not, of course, that

74

he could say so straight out, being the chairman. Absolute impartiality, that's the rule, but you should have heard how he asked me to send in the chief accountant for questioning! The man was as white as a sheet when I passed him on the way out. I wouldn't have been in his shoes for anything."

"Well, what was the outcome?" Vittorin asked. "How did the chief accountant get on?"

Herr Ebenseder, who had donned his silk skullcap, shrugged and knit his brow to indicate that he had his own opinion of the outcome.

"It's still in the air, I'm afraid," Herr Vittorin said. "Today's session was purely informative, the undersecretary told me. I don't suppose they'll reach a decision before Monday . . . Wasn't that the doorbell? Who can it be at this hour? Oskar has his own key. Perhaps it's someone from the office. No, Vally, don't bother, I'll go myself."

He hurried out. The two girls gazed anxiously at Herr Ebenseder, who was lolling back in his chair, contemplating the ceiling and shaking his head.

"He hasn't the first idea," he said. "The whole thing was a farce, a mere formality. The decision to retire him had been taken in advance."

There was silence for a moment. Vally looked at Lola, who had turned pale. Ebenseder stroked his chin with a meditative air.

"We're all very sorry," he went on, "– especially yours truly. I tried to talk him out of it, but in vain. Forty per cent of his present salary if he's lucky – that's the most he can expect. No, it won't be easy. Fräulein Vally may have to deign to take a job as a secretary or shorthand typist. Then she can contribute something to household expenses instead of lounging around all day."

Georg Vittorin looked up sharply.

"I don't recall asking for your advice, Herr Ebenseder," he snapped. "How we manage from now on is our business. I'm here too, after all."

"Delighted to hear it," Ebenseder retorted. "Up to now,

I've always had to help out when your father couldn't make ends meet at the end of the month."

Vittorin flinched as if Ebenseder had struck him in the face. He looked at his sisters. Vally had flushed and was staring at the patterned wallpaper. Lola, without looking up from her embroidery, gave an almost imperceptible nod.

"It won't happen again, Herr Ebenseder," Vittorin said bitterly, "you can depend on that. How much does my father owe you?"

He pulled out his wallet. In it, wrapped in tissue paper, was the money he had amassed for his journey to Russia. Herr Ebenseder glanced nervously at the door and tried to dodge the question.

"No, honestly, it doesn't matter," he said. "There's plenty of time. I didn't mean it like that. I'm in no hurry, I assure you."

"I asked how much my father owes you," Vittorin repeated.

As if the scales had suddenly fallen from his eyes, it dawned on him that the little world which formed a part of his existence – his home – was in danger of collapsing under the onset of dreary, dismal everyday life. He forgot all about Selyukov and his adventurous journey into the blue. With the profound sense of relief that stems from the knowledge of a duty fulfilled, he mentally shouldered the burden of care to which his father and his sisters had proved unequal.

But he bore that burden for a moment only.

His father reappeared, quite unaware of the significance of the message which fate had destined him to transmit.

"Georg," he said, "there's a Herr Ferdinand Kohout outside. He'd like a word with you."

Kohout was sitting on the hall bench, pale and agitated in the extreme. He was so nervous that he had kneaded his white felt hat completely out of shape, and his lips were in constant, silent motion. He rose, took a step toward Vittorin, and drew a hand across his brow.

"Thank God I've found you," he said. "I thought you

76

mightn't be at home – I was in despair. I phoned your office innumerable times, but there was no reply, so I went there. No one around, just the janitor and the cleaning women."

"The office shuts at two on Saturdays, surely you knew that? What's up?"

"What's up? You're joking! Here's your passport, your visa, your ticket and reservation. Quite a job, I can tell you! Anyone else would have given up days ago. I've jotted down what you owe me on this piece of paper. Better hurry up and get ready, our train leaves at half-past eleven."

"Half-past eleven?" Vittorin repeated mechanically. Kohout thrust the various items into his hand. He took them, striving to collect his thoughts.

"Yes, this is it at last," Kohout said. "We leave at half-past eleven, but you'd be wise to get there an hour before. We've got reserved seats, well and good, but I wouldn't depend on them. Better safe than sorry."

"Not tonight, though, surely?" Vittorin protested in dismay. "You can't be serious!"

Kohout stepped back and looked him up and down with a mixture of anger and contempt.

"What's this?" he demanded. "Changed your mind after all, have you? Lost your nerve? Of course, I should have known! First you talk big, and then, when it comes to the pinch –"

"Nonsense!" Vittorin exclaimed. "Of course I'll go, but not tonight. For God's sake, I can't just breeze in there and say, 'So long, folks, take care of yourselves, I'm off to Russia tonight.' I simply can't, surely you can see that?"

Kohout dismissed this objection with a scornful, supercilious gesture.

"A typically bourgeois attitude," he said, shifting from foot to foot and wringing his hands. "You should have thought of that sooner. I only got the visas at ten this morning. The trains are chock-a-block – there were only two seats left, so I had to decide on the spot. Now it's your turn to decide. Are you coming or not?"

"It's no use," Vittorin replied. "I can't leave before Monday."

"Very well," said Kohout, "stay if you must, but in that case you can kiss the whole idea goodbye. There are only two trains a week, and you can't board them without a reservation. Even if you managed to wangle a reservation – I say 'if' because it isn't easy, believe me; it takes some doing – your visa would have run out. No, get this straight: either you go tonight or you'll never go at all."

Vittorin stared at the floor in silence.

"Well," said Kohout, turning to go, "suit yourself, I'm off anyway. You won't mind if I give Selyukov your regards, will you?"

Vittorin straightened up with a jerk. Selyukov! He hadn't heard the name uttered for so long that it overwhelmed him and shook his resolve. Family ties meant nothing compared to that one word. He couldn't understand why he'd wavered in the first place.

"You're right," he said, "there's no time to lose. We've waited far too long as it is – we don't even know if Selyukov's still in Moscow. Of course I'm coming. I'll be at the station at ten-thirty sharp. Have you let Emperger know?"

Kohout frowned. He seemed taken aback.

"Emperger? Why on earth? What's he got to do with it?"

"Emperger must be told," Vittorin said. "I insist. He's the only one of our former comrades who's behaved with a modicum of decency."

"Like hell he has," Kohout protested angrily. "You're dead wrong there. He's always poking fun at you behind your back."

"So now he'll see I'm serious. I'm going to telephone him."

Kohout saw that further resistance would be futile.

"All right, if it means so much to you, but kindly leave me out of it. Promise you won't let him know I'm going too, word of honour? I don't want anything to do with the man – I've got my reasons. That's settled, then: ten-thirty sharp at the Nordbahnhof."

78

They shook hands.

Vittorin lingered in the hall for a full minute after Kohout had gone, thinking hard. Then he switched off the light and returned to the living-room.

His father, his sisters and Herr Ebenseder had already started supper. He went slowly over to his father, searching for the first, all-important turn of phrase. Lola, seeing her brother's distraught expression, could tell at a glance that he had come to say goodbye.

Vittorin knocked on the door very quietly, as arranged. He heard her approaching footsteps. Then the door opened. She took his hand and drew him into the darkened hall.

"So late!" she hissed. "Why so late? The neighbours didn't spot you, did they? Shut the door and I'll put the light on. No, let's stand here in the dark a moment longer, like this. Your hands are frozen, sweetheart, are you cold? It's nice and warm inside. I've got the stove going a treat – it's red-hot. I've been waiting so long."

He shivered a little at the thought of what lay ahead. He'd meant to tell her at once that he couldn't stay – that he had to go away, far away, this very night, and that time and life had come between them. Now, however, as he stood there with her body so close to his, he couldn't get a word out. He kissed her – her lips were as cool as a spring breeze – and while he kissed her he let his knapsack slide to the floor and thrust it silently into a corner with his foot. Franzi noticed nothing. She tilted her head back and laid his hand on her brow.

"We've never been really alone before, Georg. There's always been someone around, watching us. No, there was one time, but it's so long ago you won't remember. Do you ever think of that summer at Dürnstein? I can still see the room I slept in. We played hide-and-seek in the woods once, and the two of us had to hide while the rest came looking for us. One of the girls kept calling, 'Come out, come out, wherever you are!' Her name was Berta, and she was tall and fair-haired and freckled and wore glasses – I still see her sometimes in the street, but she doesn't recognize me. Anyway, she kept calling us and we let her call, and we sat there in the middle of the blackberry bushes and watched the ants. We were silly little kids then – no, you were a big boy already. You wanted to be a swimming champion – at least, that's what you told me while we were hiding in the brambles, remember?"

Vittorin remembered nothing of the kind.

"Yes, and we've never been alone again since. But today we're well and truly hidden – no one'll ever find us. Berta wears pince-nez these days, but they don't suit her any better. Tell me, wouldn't your family let you go out? I mean, you're so late. Those sisters of yours . . . Vally's nice, but I'm a bit scared of Lola, she looks so stern. You haven't said a word – have I offended you? You're cold, poor darling. Fancy me keeping you standing out here in the freezing hall! The trouble is, this is the only place where we can be really alone. There are two gentlemen inside. I've got visitors, you see. You'll be disappointed, I expect. I didn't invite them, but what can I do now they're here? Don't pull a face. Take your coat off and come in. They're a nice couple – I'll introduce you to them."

Two motionless figures were seated on the sofa in the overheated living-room. Ingeniously constructed of cushions and cast-off clothes, they were dummies got up to look like visitors engaged in an animated conversation. One of them, which looked almost lifelike at a distance, was leaning forward with its arms resting on an old umbrella.

Franzi was hugely delighted.

"You nodded to them," she cried. "You actually nodded to them when you walked in – I saw you, so don't deny it! You fell for it, you silly boy! Did you really think I'd let anyone in tonight? I made them to pass the time – I was bored, you kept me waiting so long. Allow me to introduce them. The one with the umbrella is Herr Milosh Pavisish, the medical student from Agram in person. The other is His Excellency the Baron."

It occurred to Franzi that her practical joke had shed a very questionable light on all her previous stories, and that Georg might be inclined to doubt the existence of the two men whose ludicrous effigies he now saw seated on the sofa. She hastened to rectify her blunder.

"The gentleman from Agram really did have the cheek to turn up today," she said. "Just imagine, the doorbell rang at half-past six. I didn't budge – I knew it couldn't be you because it was far too early, and besides, you'd have knocked, not rung – so I sat there and let him ring, two or three times. In the end he went away – he's probably down in the street at this very moment, cursing in Serbo-Croat. You didn't see him, I suppose?"

"I may have," Vittorin said. "There was a scrawny little fellow with a red moustache pacing up and down outside the door."

This description was far removed from Franzi's mental picture of the young man from Agram. She shook her head.

"No, it couldn't have been him. Short, skinny, red moustache? That sounds more like the Baron."

"Really?" said Vittorin. "Does the Baron know your parents are away too?"

"Oh no, he doesn't have a clue," Franzi said quickly. "Unless, of course, Herr Milosh told him. It's a possibility."

Vittorin raised his eyebrows. "You mean they know each other?"

The situation was getting out of hand.

"No," Franzi said, "– I mean, of course they do, but only slightly. They're both members of the High Life Club – that's the extent of their acquaintanceship. But believe me, if I'd known it was the Baron I'd have given him a piece of my mind. You should see the letters he writes me, the cheeky devil! Let him stand down there and freeze, it serves him right. I'm going to make some tea now, Georg. Coming to the kitchen with me, or will you wait in here? I'll only be a couple of minutes."

She hurried out. Vittorin remained standing beside the stove, his head in a whirl, his face convulsed with shame and anger. One half of him called the other a contemptible coward.

It was an insult he wouldn't have tolerated from anyone else, but he repeated it, masochistically hurling it at himself again and again as he stared glumly into the fire. Yes, he was a contemptible coward – he didn't retract a syllable of it. Where had his courage fled to while she was in the room with him? He hadn't got a word out, and time was going by – inexorably ticking away. He had only a few minutes left. He must tell her, he couldn't put it off any longer. The opening words would be terribly hard to say, but once they were said the worst would be over. He *had* to come out with it. Ten-thirty at the station, and she still knew nothing . . .

All at once he heard a delighted laugh from the hall: Franzi had spotted his knapsack. She flung the door open with an air of triumph.

"I almost tripped over it," she exclaimed. "Your knapsack! Of course, I never thought of that! You had to pretend you were going away, or your family would have been suspicious. Where *are* you supposed to be off to, Georg? Tell me."

"Russia," he replied, but his courage failed him, and he uttered the fateful word so quietly that she didn't hear. She put her arms around his neck.

"Did they believe you?" she asked. "I'll tell you something, Georg: I don't care if they know you're with me or not, I really don't. What's the point of playing hide-and-seek? Whatever I do, I'm prepared to take the consequences. I've never been a coward."

She looked up at him with her girlish mouth set in a determined line and a radiant smile in her eyes, ready to forget the whole world in his arms, but he was blind, deliberately blind, to her expression.

She picked up his knapsack and put it on the table.

"My goodness, it's heavy. Let's see what you've got in there."

She undid the draw-string, and the first thing that came to light was the red notebook containing Vittorin's Russian vocabulary lists. She peered at the unfamiliar script.

"What's that," she asked, "Greek?"

"No," he said curtly, harshly, "it's Russian."

"You mean you've brought some homework with you? What odd ideas you have, George. I doubt if you'll get much Russian learnt tonight or tomorrow!"

A photograph fell out of the notebook as she deposited it on the table. It showed a tall, stern-faced young woman stiffly posed in front of a painted backcloth – a tulip bed. Her narrow-waisted gown had puffed sleeves.

"Who's this?" Franzi asked.

"It's a photo of my mother as a young woman," said Vittorin. "You never knew her. I'm supposed to look like her. I always take it with me when I . . ."

The moment had come. He'd reached the point of no return.

". . . when I go away for any length of time," he went on. "Women used to wear puffed sleeves in those days, around 1900. It wasn't the prettiest of fashions, but that's the only picture of her I've got. I had it with me all the time, in the trenches and later in the prison camp."

Franzi stared at him in sudden alarm.

"You don't mean you're really going away, Georg? Answer me! *Are* you, seriously? You are, and you only tell me now? Where are you off to?"

Vittorin took his mother's picture from her and replaced it in the red notebook.

"Russia," he said. "Don't look so upset. I'll be back in a week or two."

"You once mentioned wanting to go back to Russia some time. So you really meant it," Franzi said in a low, dejected voice. "What do you plan to do there?"

"I can't tell you – it's not the kind of thing one discusses with a woman. There's something I've volunteered to do – unfinished business, if you like. Don't ask me any more. You needn't worry, I'm not going alone – there are two of us – and I'll be back in a few weeks' time. I've got a new job to come back to, too – personal assistant to a business tycoon. At least, I may have second thoughts. He's a rather shady character –

in fact, to be quite honest, I suspect he's a bit of crook, but who isn't these days? He pays well, that's the main thing, and he's going to keep the job open till January 1st – I fixed it with him."

"When are you leaving?" asked Franzi, thoroughly subdued by this torrent of words.

"My train goes at half-past eleven," he said swiftly, trying to sound off-hand, "but I'll have to be at the station by half-past ten. You'd better get ready quickly if you want to see me off. I can't stay much longer."

She gazed at him in silence, her eyes filling with tears. Stung by the sight because he knew he was in the wrong and wanted to forestall her reproaches, he adopted a harsh, hostile tone.

"If you want to make a scene go ahead, but it's pointless, I can tell you that right now. I don't have the time. I'm not going to miss that train on your account."

She made no reply, just went to fetch her hat and coat.

The last tram had gone, so they had to walk. Franzi didn't utter a word the whole way to the station.

Once in the booking hall they were accosted by Kohout, who was carrying a wooden army suitcase and sweating with excitement. All he spared Franzi, when introduced, was a cursory, uninterested glance, a clumsy little bow, and a swift, rather moist handshake.

He deposited his suitcase on the ground beside him.

"You might have turned up a bit sooner," he told Vittorin, peering nervously in all directions. "I was here on the dot. It really wasn't necessary to invite Emperger to see you off. I don't like that man – never did. You haven't told him I'm going too, have you?"

"Of course not," Vittorin assured him, "since you didn't want me to."

"I hope you haven't told anyone else," Kohout pursued with a wary glance at Franzi, who was standing a few feet away. "What about your girl-friend?"

"She only met you two minutes ago and she probably didn't

even catch your name," Vittorin said soothingly. "I can't understand why you're so jumpy. What are you scared of? You're your own boss, after all. You're answerable to no one but yourself."

Kohout broke out in another sweat. He screwed up his eyes and wrung his hands.

"Another few minutes and the train'll be in," he said. "Do me a favour and go and claim the seats, will you? I'll leave my suitcase with you."

"Why," asked Vittorin, "are you off somewhere?"

"Of course. I was only waiting for you. You don't think I want to bump into Emperger, do you? I'll leave that pleasure to you. Me, I'm boarding the train at half-past eleven, not a minute before. Don't worry, I'll make it – and keep an eye on my case."

He waved his crumpled hat and strode briskly off.

Emperger was late. He appeared on the platform only minutes before the train pulled out, waving and smiling as he came. Agreeably surprised to find Vittorin in the company of a young woman, he kissed Franzi's fingertips with exaggerated gallantry.

The three of them stood outside the compartment in which Vittorin had successfully battled for his seats.

"It was a real struggle to get here in time," Emperger reported. "I'm much too much in demand, I'm afraid. At half-past ten I had to collect a young lady from the opera and escort her home – not my type at all, incidentally, but one can't shirk one's obligations. She lives in the suburbs, to make matters worse, but luckily I borrowed a car. Some friends are expecting me at twelve. I simply couldn't cry off – one doesn't like to hurt people's feelings. And so it goes on, night after night. It's a mystery to me how I ever manage to get any sleep."

In token that he really wasn't exaggerating, Emperger loosened his silk scarf to reveal the dinner-jacket under his opera cloak.

Vittorin drew him aside.

"Will you inform the others that I've gone to Moscow?" he asked.

"Of course, tomorrow without fail," Emperger assured him. "That's to say, I'm rather out of contact with the Professor. Incredible how quickly one loses touch with people – it's simply that they all have interests of their own. So you're really serious, eh? You're off to Russia to carry on the war single-handed, *pour ainsi dire*. My respects, Vittorin, I envy your determination and strength of character. As to the practical value of your mission, everyone's entitled to his own opinion . . ."

A menacing scowl appeared on Vittorin's face.

"But speaking for myself," Emperger said hastily, "I'm behind you all the way. A man's word is his bond, and when I think what that swine Selyukov . . . What a delightful girl-friend you have, Vittorin – a pleasure to behold. A recent acquisition? I congratulate you on your good taste, anyway. From the way you spoke, I always assumed you were a recluse."

Vittorin had ceased to listen. In his mind's eye, he had just brushed past Grisha, Selyukov's orderly, and marched into the staff captain's office to demand satisfaction. He could picture the uniform, the St George's Cross, the cigarette between the slender, faintly tanned fingers, the smoke rings, the fire on the hearth, the books on the desk. All these he could visualize quite clearly, but Selyukov's face remained vague and insubstantial. He searched his memory in vain: he had forgotten the face of his mortal foe. Just as this agonizing realization dawned on him, the locomotive emitted a shrill whistle. He jumped on to the step and the train got under way. Franzi clung to his hand for a moment longer.

"Will you write to me?" she asked, sounding as if she had just emerged from the depths of a dream.

"I'll write you from Moscow," he called. He felt a sudden, burning desire to say something loving and affectionate, but the distance between them was already infinite.

He lingered on the step. It struck him as odd that the other

86

two, who had only met a few minutes ago, should be standing side by side and waving to him as if they belonged together, but he didn't dwell on the thought. He turned away, content beyond measure to be leaving a city in which his life had become no more than a shadowy limbo.

He made his way to the compartment. Kohout was already there and had put his army suitcase, which was adorned with painted tulips and roses, on the luggage rack.

"Well, that's that," said Kohout. He drew a deep breath and mopped his perspiring brow. "All's well. We'll be over the border in another few hours."

Emperger insisted on driving Franzi home. It would give him the greatest pleasure, he assured her. He had time enough, and besides, he wasn't in the habit of letting young women walk home unescorted at this late hour.

Franzi remained thoroughly monosyllabic, so the task of making conversation devolved on him alone. He shone a torch in her face, pointed to her eyes, and quoted Shakespeare:

> Here did she fall a tear. Here in this place
> I'll set a bank of rue, sour herb of grace . . .

Seeing that she knew no English, he changed the subject. He was on the threshold of a brilliant career in banking, he announced. He might even have a car of his own in a few months' time – quite something, eh? – but hadn't yet decided on any particular make. He had a nice little bachelor apartment, not that he was entirely satisfied with it, of course – he needed more room for his books, and besides, one liked to spread oneself – but it wasn't easy to find anything suitable in these dreary, Bolshevik-ridden days. He was no bourgeois – far from it: he found the right-wing politicos a trifle stupid, and he certainly wasn't "behind the times" – he used the English phrase – but he could not raise any enthusiasm for the left-wing extremists either.

Franzi was then informed that he had until recently been

involved with an actress – a very well-known one, what was more. Relationships of that kind had their drawbacks, of course. Celebrated artistes tended to be capricious and one didn't always find it easy to indulge their more outrageous whims, so he'd broken it off with her. But although he was in the thick of society life – never a day without some invitation or other – he often felt extremely lonely.

When they pulled up outside Franzi's apartment, Emperger told her that he didn't really feel like going on to his party after all. To put it crudely, the people who were expecting him could lump it. He thought it would be far more amusing to go to a bar – in congenial company, of course, because drinking alone was no fun. Although his manner cooled perceptibly when Franzi ignored this hint, he prefaced his farewells by asking permission to look her up from time to time in his friend Vittorin's absence, inquired where she worked during the day, and made a note of her telephone number.

Once upstairs in the living-room Franzi slumped into a chair, buried her face in her hands, and wept with noisy abandon. Racked with sobs, she gave free rein to her bitter disappointment. At length, feeling better, she wiped away her tears and went over to the mirror, where she inspected her red and swollen eyes with a kind of wry satisfaction.

A defiant, despairing exuberance overcame her. She yearned for a wild orgy, a frenzied, self-destructive bacchanalia. Her eyes still brimming with tears, she hurried to the kitchen and made a bowl of punch. When it was standing ready on the table, she played the gramophone with a total disregard for the neighbours, who were, she told herself, welcome to hear what a good time she was having. And while the gramophone churned out operetta hits, jazz, and the overture from *Die Meistersinger*, she chain-smoked and drank punch – glass after glass of it – even though it turned out that she'd forgotten to add any sugar.

What with all the punch she'd drunk and all the crying she'd done, Franzi became drowsy. Around two in the morning she fell asleep on the sofa, fully dressed, between the Baron and the young man from Agram, whose umbrella had slid to the floor.

The train pulled into the frontier station three hours late. Vittorin awoke from a restless sleep, aching in every limb, to find that Kohout had climbed on the seat and was getting his case down.

"Where are we?" he asked, still half dreaming. "What time is it?"

"Five a.m.," Kohout replied hoarsely. "Neither night nor day. I've got a headache – do I look as if I hadn't slept a wink? Hurry up, we have to get out here. Passport control, customs inspection."

Carrying their luggage, they trudged across the track and joined a long line of waiting figures. The queue progressed slowly, step by step. The man at the door admitted only a handful of passengers at a time.

"Got any cigarettes with you?" Kohout whispered. "Here, stick a few of mine in your pocket. Twenty's the limit, and I don't want any trouble."

They had to wait half an hour before their turn came. The immigration officer was sitting in a kind of booth just inside the door. Kohout handed him his passport and stood there hunched up against the cold.

The official took the passport and studied the particulars. He glanced at Kohout's face for a moment and exchanged a few words with a uniformed figure beside him, then pointed to a bench in the background.

"Go over there and wait," he said.

Kohout turned as white as the wall.

"But my suitcase," he stammered. "I have to get it checked by customs. What's the matter?"

"You'll find out in due course," the official said calmly. "Go over there and wait for me."

"What's wrong?" Vittorin demanded anxiously. "Aren't our passports in order? We're together."

The man looked up.

"Together, eh? In that case, wait over there too. I won't be long."

He nodded to his colleague, who shut the outside door. Then he examined the other passengers' passports.

Vittorin deposited his knapsack on the bench beside Kohout's wooden suitcase.

"What have you been up to?" he hissed. "Is there something wrong with my passport? If so, I'd sooner you told me right away."

Kohout leaned his head against the wall and said nothing.

Meanwhile, the official had finished checking the other passports. He stood up and beckoned to them.

"You two, come with me."

"Where to?" asked Vittorin.

"You'll see. Don't make a fuss, just come along."

Vittorin was told to wait outside an office while Kohout and the official went in. The sign on the door read: "Inspector, Frontier Security Service."

Their passports were forgeries – that was the only explanation. Vittorin gritted his teeth and longed for it to be over: the waiting, the interminable waiting, the questioning, the return journey. The return journey? No! He was determined not to go back. If they confiscated his passport he would have to sneak across the frontier on foot.

The door opened and Kohout emerged. Behind him came a man carrying his wooden suitcase.

"It's all a misunderstanding," Kohout said in a hoarse voice. He blinked nervously. "It'll be sorted out in no time. You go on ahead, I'll catch you up."

"Go in," the man with the suitcase told Vittorin, "the inspector's waiting. You can talk afterwards."

The inspector, a fair-haired, middle-aged man with a neatly trimmed moustache, gestured to Vittorin to sit down. The immigration officer was standing beside his superior's desk in an attitude of attention.

"Georg Vittorin, commercial employee," the inspector

began. He handed Vittorin's passport to his subordinate. "Read me out the particulars."

He then proceeded to ask Vittorin a number of questions concerning his destination, his connection with Kohout, the amount of money in his possession and how he had come by it. His answers were taken down in writing.

"Isn't my passport in order?" Vittorin asked.

"Your passport is quite in order," the inspector told him. "There's nothing to prevent you from continuing your journey. As soon as you've signed this, you may go."

Vittorin breathed a sigh of relief.

"I'd like to wait for my friend," he said. "We're travelling together."

The inspector stroked his blond moustache.

"Your friend is under arrest and will be brought before the relevant district court," he announced. "He admits to having embezzled the following sums from his employer, Dr Sigismund Eichkatz of No. 11 Grosse Mohrengasse, Vienna II: 270 lire, 118 reichsmarks, 420 lei, and 1860 kronen. The money was found in his possession."

"I had nothing to do with it," Vittorin exclaimed in horror, "– absolutely nothing, I swear. I give you my word of honour!"

The inspector raised his hand.

"Had you been in any way compromised by circumstantial evidence or your friend's statements," he said, "I should have ordered your arrest. Please sign this declaration. If you hurry, you can still catch the train."

Kohout wasn't on the platform. It was only when the train pulled out that Vittorin caught a final glimpse of his friend.

He was standing near the boiler-house, flanked by two policemen and staring at the ground. Vittorin waved goodbye as he passed, but Kohout didn't notice. He was engaged in an animated soliloquy, from the look of him, because he was shifting from foot to foot and wringing his hands.

NO-MAN'S-LAND

Novokhlovinsk, a town some twelve miles south of Berdichev, consisted of three or four mean little streets and a
marketplace. The handful of fishermen's huts near the river
were grandly referred to by the local inhabitants as "the
suburbs". When the Austrians withdrew, the inn in the marketplace, the "Hotel Moskva", had been requisitioned by the
staff of the 3rd Ukrainian Volunteers as officers' quarters and
orderly rooms. The staff telegraph office was installed in the
schoolhouse, which had served as a quartermaster's store during the war. The station lay outside town, and anyone trying
to reach it on foot in winter had to wade there through knee-
deep snow.

This was the limit of Vittorin's progress to date, it having
proved impossible to go any farther. The Ukrainian Volunteers were holding a line between Novokhlovinsk and
Berdichev, and facing them was the Red Army's 2nd Lettish
Rifle Regiment.

Vittorin had rented lodgings in a cobbler's house and seldom
ventured out. His room, which was dark, shabby and ill-
furnished, did duty as a bedroom, living-room and kitchen
combined. The cobbler himself had taken his tools and retired
to a sort of lumber-room.

On the fourth night after his arrival he was roused by someone hammering loudly on the front door. He pulled on his
coat and made his way down the creaking stairs. The cobbler
opened the door. The tall, gaunt, bushy-eyed man standing
outside wore neither overcoat nor fur jacket in spite of the cold.

Huddled in the snow beside him and muttering incessantly was a figure swathed in a brown leather trenchcoat.

Raising his lantern, the cobbler saw at a glance that the tall man was a Russian officer. He was about to slam the door and bolt it when Vittorin intervened.

"Who are you?" he asked. "What do you want?"

The stranger raised a hand to his astrakhan cap in salute.

"Captain Stackelberg of the Nizhgorod Dragoons," he said in a hoarse voice. "I'm looking for lodgings for myself and my brother officer."

"Lodgings? There are rooms for Russian officers at the Hotel Moskva."

The captain shook his head.

"Not for us – we don't belong to the volunteer army. My comrade is sick. Unless I find him a warm room and some dry clothes soon, he'll die on me here in the snow. I can't carry him any further."

"What's the matter with him?"

"I don't know – a fever of some kind. You see? He's delirious. He's just completed a very taxing journey. He needs rest, a warm room, and a bed."

There was only one bed in the house, but Vittorin didn't hesitate.

"He can have mine," he said. "There'll still be room for the two of us – we'll manage somehow. Come inside."

The captain saluted again.

"Thank you," he said, and turned to his friend. "Mitya, on your feet! Do you hear me, Mitya? That's wonderful – now you want to spend the night in the snow! Get up, there's a fire burning inside."

He patted the snow off his friend's leather coat and re-addressed himself to Vittorin.

"My comrade's name is Dimitri Alexeevich Gagarin. Those people over there" – he gestured toward the east – "they shot his father, Count Gagarin. You aren't Russian, but the name may be familiar to you."

★

93

They lodged together in the cobbler's room for three whole weeks. Stackelberg slept on the floor, Vittorin on a makeshift bed consisting of two chairs and a fur jacket. The nursing and housework they shared between them. In the morning Vittorin set off for "the suburbs" in quest of bread, flour, eggs, sheeps' cheese, or fish. Meanwhile, Stackelberg swept the room and lit the stove. The local physician, an elderly man who had once been the medical officer of a Volhynian regiment, looked in on his patient every evening. When they were alone again, Gagarin, his sunken cheeks still flushed with fever, would sit up in bed and listen in silence while Vittorin and Stackelberg engaged in endless conversations about Europe, Russia, and their personal experiences.

"Why should I keep anything from you, after all you've done for us?" Stackelberg said one evening. "You'd guess the truth anyway, sooner or later. This was Mitya's third trip through the lines from Moscow, carrying certain papers and documents. I take delivery of them on behalf of the legitimate government. Sometimes I act as a courier myself."

"Is it that simple?" Vittorin asked eagerly. "I mean, is it as easy as all that, sneaking through the front line? Your friend is little more than a boy – he can't be eighteen yet – and it must take some nerve . . ." He broke off, reduced to silence by a hoarse bark of laughter.

"Nerve?" said Stackelberg. "He's so brave it's positively sinful, but the front line, as you call it, is a myth."

"Seryosha," the sick man called feebly, "when do I get my tea?"

"It won't be long, Mitya, just be patient," Stackelberg told him, and a gentle note crept into his gruff voice. "In Moscow they make tea out of turnips, but this is the real thing. You don't believe me? Ah, Mitya, you don't believe a thing unless it's staring you in the face, that's the kind of fellow you are."

He sliced some bread before turning back to Vittorin.

"Yes, the front line is a myth. There aren't any trenches. The Reds occupy the occasional farmhouse, post a lookout on the roof and a machine-gun in a window embrasure, and

94

there's their front line for you. As for the Ukrainian Volunteers, they make speeches, wrangle over whether their officers
should wear epaulettes, hold meeting after meeting, elect a
regimental commander one day and dismiss him the next.
They put up posters: 'The Volunteer Army is fighting for
democracy. Join our ranks, help defend Russia!' Fine words,
my friend, but they don't wash with me. That's not the Russia
I'm ready to die for."

A vigorous shake of the head betokened that the subject was
closed. He took the patient some tea and a boiled egg.

"There, look," he said, indicating the egg with a tobacco-
stained fingertip, "I've brought you a little barrel with two
kinds of beer in it. Now eat and drink up, Mitya, and be
thankful you've kept body and soul together."

Whenever Vittorin headed for "the suburbs" in the morning,
his route took him past a snowed-up timber yard. The plank
fence enclosing it was covered with posters printed by the
counter-revolutionary government. Sheets of blue, green and
white paper bearing proclamations addressed to the Ukrainian
people rubbed shoulders with caricatures of Lenin, Yoffe,
Dzerzhinsky, the Cheka boss, and Sverdlov, the Tsar's
murderer. Also to be seen were gory, garishly coloured
illustrations of Bolshevik atrocities. One of these, which
depicted a raid on a village, showed Red Guards with repul-
sively brutish faces mowing down peasants as they fled from
their blazing cottages, seizing their womenfolk and driving
off their livestock. Standing in the foreground in red-braided
breeches and glossy riding boots, the sleeves of his leather
jacket adorned with the Soviet star, was a Red Army officer
whom the artist had endowed with a resemblance to General
Voroshilov. He was leaning on his sabre and looking down,
with an air of diabolical triumph, at the bloodstained corpse
of the village priest. Beneath, in flamboyant red letters, was
the caption: "This is how they liberate our Russian brothers."

Vittorin lingered in front of this poster whenever he passed
the fence. The Red officer's arrogant smile held him in thrall,

filled him with impotent rage. *The way he stands there in his patent leather boots and riding breeches – well-groomed to his fingertips, the perfumed murderer. At home he washes his hands in eau de cologne and reads French novels, and the women are for ever chasing him. And I – I'm still stuck here in this godforsaken hole, getting nowhere fast . . .*

It was an immense effort to tear himself away from the poster. When he got home, he raised the subject of Selyukov with Captain Stackelberg.

"Mikhail Mikhailovich Selyukov?" said Stackelberg. "No, the name means nothing to me. You'll have to consult the War Commissariat's personnel records, though God knows what kind of a mess they're in. Mikhail Mikhailovich Selyukov . . . So he's gone over to the revolutionaries – betrayed the Tsar and sworn allegiance to the Soviets? In that case he'll be serving on a front like this one here. He won't be a staff captain any longer – a battalion commander, more like. He was in the Semyonov Regiment, you say? Perhaps, but everything's gone haywire – you don't know where you are any more. Our Nizhgorod Dragoons have been renamed 'Lassalle's Own Red Cavalry Regiment' – that's the kind of thing that's happening these days. If he's as much of a low-down, bloodthirsty sadist as you say, you'd better look for him in the Lubyanka. That's where the worst of the scum are based."

"The Lubyanka?" said Vittorin. "What's that?"

"You've never heard of the Lubyanka? Why, God preserve you, the Lubyanka is the great revolutionary slaughterhouse, the headquarters of death. It's the nerve centre of the Moscow Cheka."

Count Gagarin, who was sitting beside the stove wrapped in blankets, looked up.

"You don't know the Lubyanka? Well, I do, God knows. I went there and was issued with a pass stamped 'CR', meaning 'Counter-Revolutionary'. Why CR, I wondered – my father had never dabbled in politics. Anyway, I was admitted to the office by a fellow posted outside the door, a sailor with a red arm-band. The commissar sitting at the desk wore glasses and

96

had a shawl tied round his head – maybe he had toothache. He's a Christian soul, I told myself, so why shouldn't he take pity on me? I handed him my pass. 'What can I do for you, citizen?' he asked. 'Comrade,' I said, 'I only arrived from Petersburg this morning. My father was brought here on Tuesday. I've come to inquire the reason for his arrest.' The commissar consulted his list. 'No, he's not here.' – 'Please, comrade,' I said, 'have another look.' That annoyed him. 'He's not on my list, I tell you. Try again tomorrow, you can see I'm busy. Next!' – 'But I was sent here,' I said. 'You *must* have his file.' He banged the desk with his fist. 'Get out, you're wasting my time! Next!' He ignored me and started writing."

Stackelberg had risen and was pacing restlessly up and down. He took a glass of red wine from the table and went over to his friend.

"Have some of this, Mitya," he told him in his gruff voice. "Drink up, it'll make you feel better, you'll see."

"There were people waiting outside, women with tear-stained faces, but I didn't budge. He's lying cold and hungry on some damp cellar floor downstairs I told myself. The commissar looked up. 'What, still here? Go to the devil! Push off!' At that moment someone came in with a newspaper. The commissar took it and began to read. All at once he turned polite. He beckoned me over with a grin, and his voice went smooth as syrup. 'What a fortunate coincidence! I couldn't be more delighted. I'm in the pleasant position of being able to pass on some information. There, read it for yourself.' I took the paper – it was the *Izvestia* – and there it was, on page one: 'Shot last night on the Khotynski Field: General S. I. Nelidov' – then someone else, a professor whose name I didn't know, and then . . . I clung to the edge of the desk. A white mist gathered before my eyes and I fell to the ground – I didn't even have time to cross myself."

Stackelberg had rolled himself a cigarette. He sighed as he lit it with his lighter.

"Yes," he said, "God's world is a sad place. Great, holy Mother Russia is ruled by an army of executioners. Be patient,

Mitya: we'll crush them like eggshells. There'll come a day when their blood will be washed from our Russian soil with holy water."

Stackelberg had been out all day. It was nine in the evening when he finally returned, chilled to the marrow and wet through. He tossed his astrakhan cap on to the table and brushed the hair out of his eyes. Then he stooped to poke the fire in the stove.

"It's just as I said," he announced without straightening up. "The Volunteers have received reinforcements and ammunition. There's fighting ahead. The front is coming to life."

This was bad news, Vittorin knew. It might rule out any possibility of getting through the lines. Dismayed, he turned to Count Gagarin and tried to read his expression. Minutes went by. Outside, the blizzard continued to rage. Gagarin cocked his head and thought awhile.

"Well," he said at last, "so it's tonight, God help us."

Vittorin stood up. If the front came to life their venture would assume the nature of a reckless gamble, and yet . . . Count Gagarin was determined to keep his word. Vittorin went over to him. He tried to thank him, but he was still groping for the right words when the young Russian officer shook his head with an embarrassed smile.

"Why thank me? Anyway, what's all the fuss about? It's a mere stroll, twelve versts."

"Twelve versts by the Devil's reckoning," growled Stackelberg. "It's nearer twenty, Mitya, and don't forget the snowstorm."

"All right, call it twenty – we still won't freeze to death. What are you trying to do, Seryosha, get me to break my word and blush for shame? Back home on the Don our Cossacks have a saying: 'Toss your heart over a ditch and your horse'll jump after it.'"

The captain shrugged his shoulders and made no reply.

Very little more was said. Count Gagarin completed his preparations: binoculars, map, compass, a small flask of brandy, food for two days. Then he carefully checked his Smith & Wesson revolver and stowed it away in the pocket of his grey peasant smock.

They left the house an hour before midnight. Stackelberg bade them farewell on the outskirts of the fishing village.

"Go now, Mitya, and may God preserve you."

He kissed his friend on both cheeks in the Russian manner, then shook Vittorin's hand.

"I owe you thanks for bread and salt, roof and hearth. I won't forget. Goodbye and good luck."

They set off along a track defined by straw-wrapped posts jutting from the snow. On their right lay the gleaming ribbon of the frozen river. The blizzard had temporarily abated, and a menacing, malevolent moon sailed overhead. The wind drove tousled clouds along and shook snow from the bare branches of hazel and whitethorn bushes. The fishermen's huts receded into the gloom, and the wintry solitude lay heavy on Vittorin's soul.

It was about three in the morning. The moon emerged from between the wind-blown clouds racing across the sky. By its light, Count Gagarin made out the dark shape of a farmhouse to the right of the track. He halted.

Snow was still falling heavily, but it was a little less cold. Vittorin was close to collapse. He staggered along like a drunken man, slipped twice and fell, scrambled to his feet again, toiled through the snow with his eyes shut. The breath rasped in his throat. His feet were numb with cold and his cheeks chapped and burning. At last he reached Gagarin's side.

"Do we have much farther to go?" he groaned.

"We've only covered eight versts at the most." Gagarin pointed to the farmhouse. "We can rest there and get a little sleep. It'll do you good."

"Isn't it occupied?"

Gagarin shook his head. "There aren't any people in this part of the world – we're between the lines. They're a sad sight, these abandoned houses. Peasants lived here once – lived as their forefathers did, slept and got drunk and beat their wives, prayed to God and tilled the soil. The earth is black – grain thrives here. Now they're all gone, where to, no one knows."

He released his safety catch – it was possible that some patrol had bivouacked in the farmhouse – and they made their way inside. Moonlight filtering through gaps in the roof disclosed that the place was deserted.

"There's some straw over there – yes, and a horse blanket!" Gagarin exclaimed. "This isn't a peasant hut, it's a palace fit for a tsar. You'll sleep as snug here as an angel curled up beside God's stove."

Vittorin was so exhausted he flopped down where he stood. Gagarin draped the blanket over him and thrust a bundle of straw beneath his head. He himself perched on the table and lit a cigarette.

"Aren't you going to get some sleep?" Vittorin asked.

"Somebody has to keep watch. I've got the brandy here, but we'd better save it for tomorrow."

"Everything's gone all right so far, hasn't it?"

Vittorin found it an effort to speak. His chapped and blistered lips were smarting.

Gagarin didn't reply.

"You'll be going back the way we've come," Vittorin went on. "Will the captain be waiting for you at Novokhlovinsk?"

"No. He's under orders to head for Tiraspol through Polish territory. Scattered Russian units have formed themselves into a new army down there on the Dniester."

"And you? What will you do?"

Silence fell. Gagarin seemed to be pondering the question. All Vittorin could see of him in the gloom was the glowing tip of his cigarette.

"I'll play hare or hound, depending on how the hunt goes," he said eventually. "Who can tell what the next hour will bring? I may wear my regiment's blue cherkesska again, or I may die like a rat in some Cheka cellar. It doesn't pay to speculate on such things. My soul will reach its appointed destination come what may."

"And you really believe that the old Russia, the Russia you love, will be reborn?"

"Perhaps," said Gagarin, sounding weary and despondent all of a sudden. "Perhaps. Russia is undergoing an ordeal by fire. We aren't privileged to know what the outcome will be."

He took a final pull at his cigarette and got off the table.

"It's cold in here," he said in an altogether different voice. "Will it disturb you if I dance a *lezginka* to warm myself up?"

The farmhouse was still in darkness when Vittorin awoke. He felt as if he'd been asleep for no more than a few minutes. A dull, distant rumble could be heard. He raised his head and listened.

"Shall we wait till the storm blows over?" he asked drowsily.

"Rub your face with snow, that'll soon wake you up." Count Gagarin's voice came from somewhere near the door. "That's hell speaking, not heaven. The Volunteers' artillery opened up half an hour ago – they're getting ready to attack. You didn't hear a thing, though, just went on sleeping like a baby. Ready to go? We'll have to take a different route. There's no time to waste."

Snow stung their faces as they emerged from the farm house. Gagarin pointed in a south-easterly direction.

"See? There's the forest, dark as damnation. Stay close behind me, this is a bad stretch: a powdering of snow on a thin layer of ice and marshy ground beneath."

They trudged through the darkness of night and the grey light of dawn for two long hours, sheltering among clumps of willow whenever the blizzard became too fierce. Once, when the beam of a searchlight came gliding across the snow-mantled hills and fields, Gagarin flung himself to the ground. By daybreak they had reached a sparse belt of birch trees straggling up the side of a hill. At the top they called a halt. Bluish-grey clouds were scudding across a cold, translucent sky. Visible through the trees was a distant horizon veiled in mist.

"Now would be the time to make some tea," said Gagarin, "but we can't. Look down there."

He pointed at the valley. A detachment of Red cavalrymen had paused to water their horses on the banks of a frozen mere. Three of them had dismounted and were punching a hole in the ice with the butts of their carbines. The patrol commander, who was sitting his horse a few feet away, seemed intent on the distant bombardment.

Gagarin led off again. They descended the hill and made their way along a deep ravine forming the bed of a frozen stream. For a long time their route took them across level ground thickly overgrown with bushes. At one point Gagarin seemed to lose his way. He consulted the map and compass, made a sharp left turn, and they were back on course again.

Toward nine in the morning he paused, pointing to some telegraph poles and a bullet-riddled signalman's cabin.

"We've crossed the railway line," he said. "Another quarter of an hour and we'll be safe."

Now that the mist had lifted they could see their destination, Berdichev Forest.

"Only another quarter of an hour," Gagarin went on, "but I'll feel happier when we've got this last stretch behind us. The wind has blown the mist away, which isn't good. If there's a patrol on the edge of that forest they'll be invisible to us but quite capable of spotting us at a thousand yards." He shrugged. "Well, we've got to get across somehow. We can't fly like birds, so we'll have to run like hares. First, though, I'll take a bit of a look around."

He stowed the binoculars in his pocket and scaled a pine tree that was leaning over at a slight angle. The artillery fire in the north had slackened, but the rattle of a machine-gun could be heard nearer at hand. The branches swayed and groaned, snow trickled down from above, and a crow, cawing harshly, circled the tree.

Suddenly a shot rang out from the forest. Vittorin looked

up in alarm, but Gagarin hadn't moved. He remained perched in the pine tree with the binoculars to his eyes in the attitude of one watching and listening. A minute went by. Then he started down again, slowly and carefully transferring his grip from branch to branch. Once on the ground he stood leaning against the tree trunk.

"Time to say goodbye," he said. "You'll have to fend for yourself from now on. Take the compass and the map. If you run into a sentry on the other side, produce your papers and knock him out while he's examining them. If there are more than one –"

"Aren't you coming with me?" Vittorin broke in.

"No, what's the point? I'll be honest with you: I'm scared. It's shameful, I know, but there it is."

Vittorin stared at him in silence.

"You may not believe me," Gagarin pursued in a low voice, "but it's God's own truth. Why shouldn't I be afraid, when I love life so much? You have a duty to perform – a great mission, you told me so yourself. You've got to get across. Hurry, don't waste time or it'll be too late."

"And you'll stay here?"

"No, I must go back. It would be lovely to lie here in the fresh air, close my eyes and dream the dream of the earth."

He slid to the snowy ground. His cap had fallen off, and the moist hair was clinging to his forehead.

"You're wounded!"

Gagarin shook his head.

"Yes you are, you're wounded," Vittorin exclaimed. "Let me take a look."

"All right, so I'm wounded," Gagarin replied with an impatient gesture. "For heaven's sake get going. When you reach the outskirts of Berdichev, send a peasant with a sledge – he can fetch me tonight. It was a Lettish sniper. He was over to the left there, on the edge of the forest. I spotted him just too late – he got me in the leg. And now hurry. Keep to the right or you'll bump into the patrol. Get a move on, I'd hate to have brought you all this way for nothing."

103

"I'll find a sledge and fetch you myself," Vittorin said. "What if the patrol finds you first, though?"

"Stop asking questions, you're wasting time. Don't worry about me, I know what to say to those fellows. I'll spin them a yarn – tell them I've deserted from the Volunteers to fight for Red Russia. They'll relieve me of my pound of tea and bars of soap. Then they'll cart me off to a field hospital, end of story. No long goodbyes, comrade. Take your courage in both hands and run for your life."

He ran for his life, but he didn't get far. Halfway to safety he ran into the Red patrol.

One bullet whistled over his head, another grazed his ear. He threw himself down in the snow, panting, and lay there with the blood pounding and roaring in his temples.

"Don't shoot!" he yelled as soon as he had caught his breath. "Deserter! Don't shoot!"

Four Red Guards emerged from behind a snow-drift and advanced on him, rifles at the ready. Their leader, who wore a sackcloth coat and a red cockade in his cap, looked down at Vittorin with a mocking expression.

"A deserter, eh? Trying to sneak through the lines in a peasant smock? Well, we'll soon see what kind of deserter you are. Where's your friend?"

Vittorin had sat up.

"What friend?"

"Don't lie, you bastard!" the patrol commander bellowed. "The man in the tree – where did you leave him?"

Vittorin wiped the sweat from his brow.

"Over near the signalman's cabin," he said, "but he may have turned back."

"Well, he won't have got far. You go first, and don't try to run for it or you'll take a bullet with you."

They found Count Gagarin beside the signalman's cabin. He had removed his boot and bandaged his shattered knee with a strip of cloth. When he saw the Reds coming he took a couple of long pulls at his cigarette and fumbled in his pocket. With no sign of haste, he produced a ribbon in the colours of Imperial Russia and carefully wound it around his sleeve. Then he reached for his revolver, which was lying beside him in the snow, put it to his temple – the barrel glinted briefly in the winter sunlight – and pulled the trigger.

The patrol commander hurried to his side. He picked up the dead man's hand and examined it.

"I thought as much," he said. "A landowner's son – an officer in the White Guards. Well, he saved us the trouble. Very thorough, he was." He turned to the others. "Go through his pockets."

No one took any notice of Vittorin. He could have fled, but he stood there stunned, gazing in horror at the young Russian officer sprawled in the snow with bloodless cheeks and eyes closed, dreaming the dream of the earth.

"He was only a youngster," said one of the soldiers. "You can almost smell the mother's milk, but he had a sweetheart already. Look, he kept her picture next his heart."

He tossed the photograph into the snow.

"What shall we do with this one, comrade?" the soldier went on, jerking his thumb at Vittorin. "Another spy – the officer's orderly, maybe. Shall we send him to join His Excellency?"

The patrol commander strode up to Vittorin.

"We'll let the CO decide," he said. "Take him to the rear for questioning."

Vittorin, shut up in a barn immediately behind the front line, waited in vain to be summoned for interrogation. Everyone seemed to have forgotten about him. The Red sentry detailed to guard him left his queries unanswered, as did the man who relieved him at noon. An hour later Vittorin was marched off to Berdichev.

Brooding silence reigned in the streets of the town. It was growing dark by the time Vittorin and his escorts got there, but no lights were visible anywhere. In the local flea market, people were trying to sell such personal possessions as they could spare. A timid-looking girl was offering a dealer some kitchen utensils and a yellow silk curtain. Elsewhere, a bent old man was shuffling around with a Chinese vase in one hand and a pair of patched canvas shoes in the other. Dealers and sellers scattered in panic as the escorting soldiers neared the marketplace, all except the old man with the Chinese vase, who tried to hide behind a stall.

The raised boardwalks had been broken up for fuel that autumn. A woman in a tattered black silk dress was sitting on the steps outside the church. Without raising her head, she held out both hands when she heard the soldiers pass by. A sentry emerged from the shadows and shone a flashlight on Vittorin and his guards. Townsfolk conscripted for work on the front-line fortifications were silently, dejectedly mustering in a courtyard. Doors, walls and fences were plastered with notices from the local soviet requesting every inhabitant to contribute three sets of undergarments for the Red Army's use.

At Grigorov Prison, Vittorin's name was entered in the register. He gathered from what his escorts said that he was suspected of spying for the counter-revolution, but the words made little impression on him.

It was not until the cell door closed behind him that the pressure under which he had laboured all day began to ease. He saw by the meagre light of an oil lamp suspended from the ceiling that the cell housed a dozen men or more, some lying on plank beds or on the bare floor, others huddled up on bales of straw, and one seated on a broken crate. The sight was somehow reassuring; alone no longer, he was one of many companions in misfortune.

His fatigue was compounded with an urge to sit down and ponder his predicament in peace – to put what had happened in its proper perspective. Slowly and cautiously, he slid down the wall into a sitting position. Just as he did so, someone close beside him emitted a wild, shrill cry that ended in a hiss like the snarl of an enraged cat – a cry fraught with anger, fear and despair.

"Don't touch me! Be careful, don't touch me! Can't you see I'm dead?"

Startled, Vittorin made out an unnaturally contorted figure lying stiff and motionless on a plank bed facing the wall.

"It's outrageous, quite outrageous," the figure moaned softly. "Holy and Almighty God, they won't let me sleep."

An old man rose from his place beside the window and came over to Vittorin, picking his way carefully between the prisoners on the floor.

"Take no notice of him," he said. "Those folk upstairs have driven him out of his mind. He ought to be taken to a hospital, but the sick have no claim to preferential treatment here. Come with me. I'm in charge of this cell – I'll show you a place."

There was more room near the window. The prisoners had crowded together in the middle of the cell to avoid the snow-laden wind that whistled through the broken windowpanes. The old man sat down beside Vittorin.

"You don't come from this town, do you?" he said. "What are you accused of? Me, I'm a profiteer. My wife and I had a little flour and sugar left. She baked some cakes and I sold them in tea-rooms and on street corners. That's my crime – that's why I'm here. They arrested me when the hunt for Artemyev began. Artemyev – don't you know the name? Artemyev, a veteran Social Revolutionary, a terrorist, a subversive of the Tsarist era. He's reputed to be on his way to Moscow to get even with Zinoviev, Lenin, Kamenev – all of his former friends – on instructions from the Mensheviks' executive committee in Paris. Our new rulers fear Artemyev more than all the White Guard generals put together. He knows how to fight, you see. He doesn't issue proclamations, he uses dynamite and infernal machines . . ."

Vittorin clenched his teeth to stifle a groan of rage and despair. He, too, had a score to settle, but he was detained here by an absurd mischance. Fate had treacherously sided with his enemy.

"I haven't been questioned yet," he whispered angrily. "When will I be summoned for interrogation?"

"If you're lucky, not for a long time," the old man told him. "They may even forget about you."

"But I *want* to be interrogated, don't you understand?" Vittorin exclaimed. "I want my rights, that's all – my human rights."

The old man raised his hand in a weary, disconsolate gesture.

"Human rights?" he said. "Don't talk nonsense. Anyone sent here has forfeited his human rights. As for being interrogated, you'd be wise not to expect too much. Your interrogation will last two minutes, they won't listen to a word you say, and if the examining magistrate takes a dislike to your face he'll have you shot out of hand. That's all interrogation means."

Vittorin stared silently at the barred window.

"Human rights?" the old man went on. "Look at poor Bobronikov there, the self-styled corpse who startled you just now. Before the Revolution he had his own jewellery store. They brought him here – maybe he'd done a little black-marketeering – but he wasn't downhearted. 'Many's the time I've entertained the commissars at my home,' he said. 'My wife, Iraida Petrovna, will take the necessary steps.' For the first few days he amused himself by making raffia shoes and weaving little baskets out of wicker brought him by the Red Cross nurse. Then the prison governor had a bright idea. 'Citizen,' Bobronikov was told one day, 'come with us for questioning.' He was marched off to a cellar containing the bodies of two men shot a few hours before. 'Well, Citizen Bobronikov,' said the governor, 'now it's your turn. You've had it too good for too long, stuffing yourself with our bread and fish soup.' He made him kneel down, came up behind him with his revolver, and fired two shots past his ear. Then he said – it was his idea of a joke – 'All right, that'll do for today.' Bobronikov just lay there groaning. He wouldn't budge, so they had to carry him back here. Since then he's been in the world hereafter. He doesn't worry about his human rights; he keeps calling for a priest and a choir and begging to be buried."

There was silence in the cell for a while.

"Now he's asleep," the old man resumed. "He's probably dreaming that he's in the next world, weaving little baskets and raffia slippers in the presence of God. By the way, there's a pitcher of water in the corner. You won't get any bread tonight."

He blew out the oil lamp and groped his way back to the window. While settling down for the night he pointed at the ceiling.

"Hear that?" he whispered. "It's the governor. He paces up and down his room all night. He can't sleep -- the dead give him no peace."

Toward seven in the morning the door was flung open. A warder came in and shone his acetylene lamp on the face of the man lying nearest him.

"Citizen Bobronikov," he shouted, "get your things ready. You're off to the station."

Bobronikov, the "Corpse", leapt to his feet with a shrill cry and fled into a corner, where he threw himself down and lashed out with his fists and feet. The old man tried to pacify him but was bitten on the finger for his pains. Hysterical screams and cries for help issued from the cell next door, which was crowded with women prisoners. Two soldiers, alerted by the commotion, hurried in and put an end to it. They pounced on the demented man and dragged him outside.

No one even contemplated going back to sleep. A bleak, cheerless day was dawning. Vittorin found the remains of some bread and cheese and two cigarettes in his pocket. He had just begun to eat when a tall man came over, gave a courteous little bow, and stated his name and profession. He was Leonid Vassilich Avdokhin, an attorney who owed his imprisonment to denunciation and intrigue on the part of his domestic servants. According to custom, he informed Vittorin in a soft, melodious voice, it was the latest arrival's job to swab the cell floor. With a covetous glance at Vittorin's cigarettes, he added that he hadn't smoked for a week and would gladly relieve him of that chore.

Having pocketed the cigarettes, Avdokhin politely but firmly insisted on keeping his part of the bargain. A little exercise would do him good, he said. While he was kneeling on the floor and wielding a damp swab, a bald-headed little man planted himself in front of Vittorin and addressed the cell at large.

"Just look at our new boy! See what a prince he is, getting someone else to do his work for him? It's disgraceful – I wonder he isn't ashamed!"

The bald man, a former employee of the local soviet, had been jailed for persistent embezzlement and bribe-taking. He was permanently at odds with all the inmates who could not lay claim to a proletarian background. The attorney came to Vittorin's aid.

"You should stay in your corner and keep quiet, Ivan Sergeevich – very quiet. Everyone knows what kind of a worker *you* were. Don't expect me to kneel in awe before the likes of *you*! You took your fellow citizens' roubles with one hand and pocketed them with the other – that was *your* idea of an honest job!"

The former Soviet clerk went white with rage and showered Avdokhin with abuse, calling him a dirty profiteer, a mangy rat, a louse to be crushed underfoot. Then he castigated a young man with carefully parted hair, an actor from Kiev, for having given the lawyer an approving nod.

Hostilities became general. Semyon Andreevich, a teacher from the municipal girls' school, turned on his immediate neighbour, an elderly tramp.

"Stop crowding me!" he bellowed, digging him in the ribs. "Keep your distance, you filthy old scarecrow, or I'll break every bone in your body. The way you spread yourself, any-one would think you had two backsides. Clear off, get lost! I never want to see you again."

The cell senior turned to Vittorin and shrugged.

"It's like this all the time. They've forgotten how to coexist like human beings. They yap at each other like dogs."

The altercation was cut short by the arrival of the Red Cross nurse, who was bombarded with questions from all sides. To the inmates of the cell she represented their sole link with the outside world and a happier previous existence, but she was forbidden to engage them in conversation. Silently, she handed out the day's bread ration and administered some drops from her medicine chest to Storoshev, a former landowner who lay on his bunk, racked with fever and wrapped in a blanket. The tramp, who had retreated into the darkest corner of the cell to avoid his neighbour's attentions, complained of lumbago and asked for some cranberries to rub into his back. Cranberry juice, he assured the nurse, was a sovereign remedy for consumption and bee stings as well as backache. He had been prescribed it by a monk in the Yakovlev Monastery named Amfilogi, or Beloved of God.

The actor sidled up to the attorney. Stroking the reddish beard he'd grown while in prison, he glanced at the nurse's departing figure and addressed Avdokhin in an undertone.

"Did you notice the way she looked at me, Leonid Vassilevich? She's in love with me, I've known it for days now. She only comes here for my sake."

Meanwhile, the old tramp had waxed garrulous.

"This Amfilogi, this Beloved of God," he said, " – he lived at the Yakovlev Monastery, which has many saintly relics. People come to see them holding lighted candles. In the old days I used to be given a consecrated loaf, some tea, sugar and dried oatmeal, and forty kopeks. When I turned up there this autumn I found that the monks had nothing themselves – they were going around the villages begging. There's another monastery nearby containing the relics of some other great and holy martyrs. They don't give you much there, but everyone gets twenty kopeks. However, I said to myself, it's an age since you visited the monastery at Berdichev, so I trudged all the way here, and what did I find? The pious monk had been driven out to make room for some commissars, as they're called, but commissars are no good. They don't do pilgrims any favours."

"They arrested you, the Reds – the Communists," said the actor. "They did you that much of a favour."

"I'm not sure if it was the Reds or the Communists, Your Excellency," the old beggar replied. "How would I know a thing like that? God alone can tell them apart. Other people have customs you can recognize them by. For instance, I've been in the land of the Germans and the Tatars, who are also called Kalmucks. The Germans put tobacoo in their homemade brandy, that's how you can tell them. The Tatars shave their heads and live on fish. Tatar habits, those are."

He went on to describe the hospitality and gifts he'd received at various monasteries, but he was talking to himself alone. His voice sank to a drowsy, monotonous murmur. Only isolated words could be picked out – "stockfish", ' groats and honey", "dumplings", "cheese pancakes", "eighty versts", "Father Porphyri, God bless him!", "the Deacon Aristarch" – so everyone soon stopped listening to him.

That evening the former Soviet clerk was summoned to the governor's office "with his things". He turned pale when he heard his name called, but rose without a word and bundled up his belongings. The little palliasse he'd brought with him to the prison he bequeathed to his neigbour, a fishmonger from Shmerinka. Then he said goodbye to his cell-mates, even to the attorney and the actor with whom he'd been on such bad terms.

The fishmonger sat down on the palliasse at Vittorin's side. "He says it's because he quarrelled with his boss," he whispered, "but he took bribes. He won't be back, you mark my words. The same goes for the others in here – they'll be lucky to survive. Me, I've been promised my release by the governor if I denounce six counter-revolutionaries." He subjected Vittorin to a speculative stare. Then he said softly, "I've already got four."

Two more prisoners arrived the following day, a Red army deserter and a civil engineer from the Berdichev machine-tool factory, which had been shut down for lack of fuel and raw materials. The engineer, a clean-shaven, bright-eyed young man, promptly introduced himself to the other inmates and gave them a grimly humorous account of the reason for his arrest.

"I subverted the authority of the Soviet regime, comrades – that's the kind of devil I am. I told my works manager there was only one can of kerosene left in Russia, and that belonged to Lenin."

He went on to report that the Cheka hadn't yet managed to capture their mortal enemy, the veteran terrorist Artemyev. House searches were in progress day and night in Berdichev, Zhitomir, Ovruch and Kiev.

"They questioned Comrade Vera Zhedoeva, his partner in the attempt on General Prince Urussov's life seven years ago. She admitted going to Kiev to meet Artemyev, but he never turned up – he must have seen they were watching her. He is in Kiev, though, that's for sure. Someone spotted him in a suburban lodging house two days ago, but he'd gone by the time they came to arrest him. Well, they'll get their hands on him sooner or later."

"Why should they?" said the schoolmaster. "He doesn't go around with his identity written all over him."

"Yes he does," the engineer retorted. "It's easy enough to pick out a hawk in a flock of jackdaws. I saw Artemyev in Moscow before the war, at the trial of the 'Seventeen'. I'd recognize him anywhere. One look at his face and you know at once who he is."

Conversation proceeded until the attorney, who was standing beside the window, gave a low cry.

"God Almighty!" he exclaimed. "What have they done with Bobronikov? They must have shot the poor fellow."

Pale as death, he pointed to a young man sauntering across the prison yard with a riding crop in his hand, spurs jingling.

"That's the governor's deputy, and he's wearing Bobronikov's fur coat and cap . . ."

When evening came, the cell's population was swollen by eight peasants taken as hostages from villages in the neighbourhood, one of them an old man of eighty-two. It was no longer possible to lie full length, so the prisoners sat crowded together.

"It's only for tonight, citizens," were the warder's parting words. "The governor says he'll attend to your comfort tomorrow."

The landowner, who had been ejected from his prison bed, sat swathed in a blanket near the door. No one had heard him utter a word in the previous days. He had awaited his end in silence, but now he began to speak in a sepulchral voice.

"The Starets, the great saint who lies buried at Tsarskoe Selo, has put a curse on us. There's no more sun in Russia now, no more light or life. Poison failed to lay him low and bullets failed to kill him, so they strangled him with their bare hands. In God's kingdom, where the righteous take their ease, he raised his voice in accusation against the land of Russia, and the Almighty hearkened unto him."

"Enough of your saint!" the schoolmaster snapped. "Rasputin was a fraud, everyone knows that – he led a disgraceful life. Besides, there isn't a God, there are only devils, and Russia's swarming with them."

The old tramp shook his head.

"You've studied books, Your Excellency, and you must be one of the wisest and best-educated men alive, but it can't be true that there isn't a God. There's a God all right, as sure as Christ is lord of us all, and I can prove it. Judge for yourself, Excellency. I'm walking along the highroad with eighty kopeks earned from a farmer for working in his fields. Then I see an inn. 'It's hot,' I say to myself. 'Go in and quench your thirst, but with tea, not strong drink.' However, the landlord brings out some homemade vodka and I leave the inn without a kopek to my name. 'Perdition take all inns and taverns,' I tell myself. 'Old Satan has bewitched me yet again, may I be thrashed for yielding to temptation!' And now, Your Excellency, listen to what happens next. I'm almost on the outskirts of town when two fellows come my way. They pick a quarrel with me and beat me with their sticks like a post-horse. Well, I got the thrashing I asked for, so who if not God heard me ask for it? There is a God, Your Excellency, you can see that yourself."

"You've got the intelligence of a turnip, that's all I can see," said the schoolmaster. "I'm delighted you got your thrashing, and . . ."

He broke off. Rifle fire and confused cries could be heard coming from the streets outside the prison.

At six the next morning the nurse entered the cell followed by an officer with his arm in a white sling.

"The Reds have been overthrown," the nurse announced. "The Volunteers have occupied the town. Any prisoner with friends or relations prepared to vouch for him is free to leave."

Not a word, not a movement. Someone in the corner started sobbing quietly. All at once the tramp rose. He thrust the actor aside and went up to the officer.

"I see you're with the 3rd Ukrainian Volunteers, Lieutenant," he said. "Be good enough to send for your commanding officer. I'm Artemyev. I'll vouch for everyone here."

People hurried out into the street from their homes and offices, from tea-houses, cellars and places of refuge. They exchanged congratulatory hugs and clustered together in vociferous groups. The same exultant and delighted cries rang out on all sides:

"They've gone – the Bolsheviks have gone! They cleared out during the night!" – "I told you so: I said they couldn't hold out for more than three weeks!" – "The chairman of the executive committee has been arrested!" – "I woke up in the night, heard those shots, and . . ."

The main thoroughfare had transformed itself into a promenade. There was a sudden reappearance of long-forgotten Tsarist uniforms, ladies' silk hats, jewellery, choice furs. It was as if the town's inhabitants wanted to prove to each other that the Bolshevik reign of terror had failed to change their ways.

The commander of the Volunteers was standing in conqueror's pose on the corner of Mikhailov Street, nodding and saluting in all directions. The silver braid on his blue military tunic glittered in the winter sunlight. Saffyanikov, an ex-member of the Duma who had spent two months hiding from the Bolsheviks in the back room of a cabbies' tavern, smilingly acknowledged his friends' congratulations. Elegant sleighs and officers' horses stood waiting in front of the Passage Hotel, where the regimental band of the Volunteer Cavalry was giving a concert. The Jews of the town had gone to ground. Posters outside the municipal theatre advertised a gala performance. Cossacks were bivouacking in the marketplace.

While light and life were flooding through the streets, fighting continued on the outskirts of town. Three Communists barricaded themselves inside a warehouse near the freight depot and defended it against a half-company with revolvers and hand-grenades. When two of them were wounded, the third surrendered. A Red Army instructress arrested in the act of dressing up as a man killed herself with a bullet from her revolver. A Red sentry guarding the ration store in Uman Street refused to quit his post. Out of ammunition, he fought off the mob with his rifle butt, a tight-lipped giant of a man with blood streaming from a head-wound. He was offered quarter but paid no heed. A Volunteer officer, who happened to be riding past, dispatched him with his service revolver. The mob poured into the ration store over his dead body. All they found was a basket of onions and a few pounds of black flour adulterated with chopped straw.

Toward noon a violent snowstorm set in and the streets emptied. Vittorin suddenly found himself alone on the deserted boulevard. Now that all those beaming, excited faces had disappeared and the cries of joy had died away, it occurred to him that he had no share in the happiness of the liberated town. Although he had escaped a futile death and was no longer in custody, he was back where he had been four days ago: outside Soviet Russia and far from his goal. All his trials and tribulations had been in vain. He had a momentary vision of the young officer who had lost his life on Selyukov's account. Cheeks pale and eyes closed, he lay in the snow while a Red Army soldier bent over him and rifled his pockets.

Vittorin gave an involuntary groan. Gagarin had died so

young, but his death hadn't taken him, Vittorin, a step further. He doubted if he would ever get to Moscow unaided. Meanwhile, Selyukov was striding arrogantly through the streets of that white stone city, strolling quirt in hand along Petrovka and Tverskaia, or sitting in his office and pouring scorn on humble petitioners. "Ah, so it's you. What a fortunate coincidence – I couldn't be more delighted to see you, believe me. Your father? He was shot last night. And now get out, you can see I'm busy. *Pashol!*"

Or perhaps he was riding into villages at the head of a requisitioning detachment, herding peasants together and mowing them down . . .

It was while these thoughts were running through Vittorin's mind that he suddenly recalled Selyukov's face, the loathsome countenance he'd forgotten: eyes like those of a bird of prey, thin lips set in a cruel, mocking smile, features inhuman. A Satanic mask, that was how Selyukov's face appeared to him now.

The snow swirled about him unceasingly as he came to a halt and debated what to do. First he must find somewhere to sleep for an hour or two. He was hungry, too, not having eaten all day. Such money as he still had left was sewn into his cap. He walked on, intending to remove it from the lining in the shelter of the next doorway, but his path was barred by a young man in working clothes.

"Excuse me, comrade, would you be good enough to come with me? Someone wants a word with you."

"Who is this someone?" Vittorin demanded.

"Don't worry, he's a friend. I'll take you to him."

Vittorin was shown into a room on the first floor of an elegant town house. It had probably served as the office of a Bolshevik commissar, because pictures of Lenin, Trotsky and Liebknecht shared the walls with a motley assortment of Communist proclamations and posters: "Long Live the Fraternal World of the Working Class!" – "Universal Education for the Proletariat!" – "We Forge Your Guns, You Grow Our Bread!" The room reeked of stale tobacco smoke. Seated at a circular table strewn with newspapers and pamphlets were three men so intent on their conversation that they seemed oblivious of what was going on elsewhere in the room. A girl in a dark school uniform was furiously battering away at a typewriter. Cartridge cases and empty cans littered the floor.

"Comrade Artemyev," said Vittorin's companion, "here's the man you wanted to see."

It was only then that Vittorin recognized his former cellmate. The veteran revolutionary was standing at a window some distance from the rest. He had shaved off his beard and now looked thoroughly West European despite the tattered peasant smock he still wore. He took no notice of Vittorin. His entire attention was focused on the cringing, terrified figure of the schoolmaster, who stood before him with his arms outstretched in a bizarre attitude of supplication.

"Comrade Poshar," Artemyev called to one of the three men sitting at the table, "take this down. The following items were found in the prisoner's bundle: twelve thousand Romanov roubles, eighty thousand Duma roubles, a canvas pouch containing picric acid, and a small-bore Colt revolver. I identify them all as my property. There can be no doubt, therefore, that he robbed me while in prison."

"It's a mistake, I swear it," the schoolmaster cried piteously. "I'm innocent. I've no idea how those things found their way into my possession. It's a complete mystery to me."

"Be quiet, Semyon Andreevich, you can't expect me to believe that!" Artemyev's expression was half indignant, half sorrowful. "Whatever the reason – greed, spite, or ingrained habit – you robbed me. Now turn out your pockets. Ah! So you took my Soviet roubles too, did you? They aren't worth much, but you didn't sneeze at them either. All right, tell me: what am I to do with you?"

The schoolmaster wiped some beads of sweat from his brow.

"I don't understand," he moaned, "I must have done it in my sleep. For Christ's sake have mercy and let me go. I've been an honest man all my life. It's only now, in these accursed days . . ."

Artemyev raised one hand and let it fall again.

"As far as I'm concerned you can go to hell," he said scathingly. "Wait, not so fast – don't forget your bundle. And no more experiments of this kind, or you really will end up against a wall."

Vittorin's companion suddenly threw his cap on the ground and roared with laughter. The three men at the table joined in while the youthful typist spluttered into her handkerchief. The schoolmaster paused in the doorway. He glared at the girl, spat, and disappeared in a flash.

"He caught on at last," the girl said, still laughing.

Artemyev shook his head. "No, he didn't. He's as thick as a doorstep, that man." He turned to Vittorin. "Ah, there you are, comrade. Would you mind seeing if your own belongings are in order?"

Vittorin undid the drawstring of his knapsack. The red notebook was still lying on top, but tucked between the clothes beneath it, to his amazement, he saw a brown leather pouch that didn't belong to him.

"All right, hand it over," said Artemyev. "There aren't any roubles inside, but no matter, I'll take that too. All good things come from God."

The blood surged into Vittorin's cheeks.

"Are you suggesting I stole it?" he demanded angrily.

Artemyev fended off the imputation with both hands.

"No, no, why should I make a joke at your expense? I wanted to thank you for doing me a little favour and retrieve my property, that's all. Remember what a fix I was in and you'll understand. Lydia! Lydochka! Comrade! Give that machine a rest, I can't hear myself speak."

The clatter of the typewriter ceased. Artemyev took the leather pouch from Vittorin and put it on the table.

"You see," he went on, "they arrested me just as I was on the point of leaving town. I had all kinds of things on me, but the militiamen didn't search me. Why should it have occurred to them that a tramp's pockets were stuffed with explosives and detonators? So there I sat in the cell. For someone in my disguise, the prison was a safe place to be. Everybody was too busy looking for Artemyev in town to bother about an old tramp in custody. But then, comrade, I learned the governor's name. Sixteen years ago, when I was preaching rebellion at the artillery barracks in Karkov, he was with the secret police. Later on he joined us and became a revolutionary – we fought side by side on the Moscow barricades. Since then we've gone our separate ways. Today he's a Bolshevik, whereas I'm an anonymous subversive again. He wouldn't have recognized me if he'd visited our cell, but he's an experienced type. 'Hey, you with the shifty eyes,' he might have said. 'Come here. Let's see what you've got in your pockets.' In a predicament like that, I had no choice: I divided up my things and palmed them off on other people."

Vittorin turned pale. "You mean that pouch contains an explosive of some kind?"

"Mercury fulminate," Artemyev replied, "but don't be alarmed. It got damp, so there was little risk of an explosion."

"What if they'd found it on me – what if they'd shot me?" Vittorin said bitterly. "Would you have been entitled to go on living?"

"I'm up against a whole regime, an entire political system," said Artemyev. "You don't appreciate what revolution entails. When Stromfeld tried to blow up the Moscow Government building in 1902, forty innocent people lost their lives."

"Stromfeld's operation was ill-conceived and ill-prepared," said one of the men at the table. "It was bound to fail."

"That's beside the point," Artemyev told him, turning back to Vittorin. "Now, comrade, if you'd be so kind, take another look among your things. A small white cardboard box – yes, here it is. Now look in your left-hand coat pocket: a batch of identity cards bearing the Military Commissariat's official seal. Aren't they there? Damnation, I'd forgotten: you don't have them. I got rid of them on that engineer who accused Lenin of hoarding kerosene. After him, Alyoshka! No, wait, there's no hurry, I can always find him at his factory. Well, comrade, that's that. May I offer you a cigarette? You're from Germany, aren't you? A prisoner of war? Where are you bound for?"

"Moscow," said Vittorin.

Artemyev started whistling, and for the first time Vittorin heard the tune that was being sung the length and breadth of Russia.

"Where are you rolling, little apple?" Artemyev quoted. "You will ne'er come back again . . ." He grinned. "To Moscow, eh? Why venture back into the forest when you've just escaped the wolves?"

"Because I've a bone to pick with one of the pack," Vittorin replied.

Artemyev studied his face intently, then gave an almost imperceptible nod.

"I thought as much. So I wasn't mistaken: 'there's fanaticism in those eyes' – that's what I said to myself when they brought you to the cell. However, I'm still not quite clear about you. What party do you belong to?"

An expectant hush descended on the room. Vittorin realized that they were all waiting for him to reply – that everything depended on the next few moments.

"I don't belong to any party," he said, determined not to stray from the truth because he knew that he could never deceive a man like Artemyev. "I'm operating on my own, for purely personal reasons." After a pause he added, "Is it possible to get to Moscow? That's all that interests me."

"Where there's a will there's a way," Artemyev replied with a chuckle. "Very well, let the apple roll. Comrade Dolgushin is leaving here tonight. He'll take you with him as far as the railway station at Pecherka-Slava. From there . . ."

A black-bearded man in the background leapt out of his chair.

"Excuse me, Comrade Artemyev, but what are you thinking of? We know nothing about this German, and – "

Artemyev cut him short with a gesture.

"Our friend distrusts intellectuals," he told Vittorin. "He's almost a Bolshevik in that respect. Comrade Dolgushin," he continued, addressing the bearded man, "when Lieutenant Gromov approached us in 1911, it was you that told him, 'We know nothing about you. Show us what you're made of.' So he went off to Rostov the next day and gunned down the chief of police in broad daylight. I remember what you said at the time. You said –"

"At the time, acts of terrorism based on personal initiative were useful to us," Dolgushin broke in angrily. "Today they only harm the Party. They lend our operations a disorganized appearance and alienate the Europeans."

"Alienate the Europeans?" Artemyev laughed uproariously. "So you still hope for assistance from *them*? From whom, exactly? Surely not from the newspapermen who ride around Russia in Trotsky's private train and gorge themselves on caviare? Enough!"

He turned to Vittorin.

"There's a carter named Yankel Hornstein in Sukharov Street. Dolgushin will meet you outside his place at nine tonight. Now it's my turn to say, 'Show us what you're made of.' How much time do you need? When shall I hear from you?"

Vittorin drew himself up. He confronted Artemyev like Lieutenant Gromov, the police chief's assassin, who had long since vanished into a Siberian salt mine. Now that he was sure of getting to Moscow, the remainder of his mission seemed child's play.

"I'll be in touch a week from now," he said, and picked up his knapsack.

LA FURIOSA

Moscow, arsenal and armed camp of world revolution, was undergoing a Messidor 1793 of its own.

A bloody fog brooded over the soil of Russia. Fierce fighting was in progress everywhere, and the white armies, those "hirelings of foreign stockholders and their lackeys", were gaining ground on every front. Orenburg and Ufa had fallen to Kolchak's Cossack regiments, Kazan was under threat from the Czechoslovaks advancing on the Volga. Soviet government forces were faring no better in the south. General Denikin, who enjoyed French support, had proclaimed his intention of hanging Budenny, "the renegade sergeant", and Trotsky, whom he called "the Jew Leiba". Repulsed at Nikopol and beaten at Kremenchug, Red troops had given up the Donets Basin, evacuated Poltava, and abandoned Kharkov to the enemy. The "black bands" led by the peasant anarchist Makhno, hitherto allied with the Soviets, deserted to the counter-revolution. At Tula the 4th Red Infantry Regiment murdered its commanding officer and joined forces with the rebel peasants of Vyenev. In the north, General Yudenich's army was preparing to attack Leningrad with the support of the British Navy.

Faced with this predicament, the men in the Kremlin resorted to heroic measures. Under a decree proclaiming the Soviet Republic to be in extreme danger, all able-bodied workers were drafted into the Red Army. Factory yards became parade grounds. The woodworkers, textile workers and paper-mill workers raised a regiment apiece, and wildly cheering crowds applauded these units as they left for the front after a mere six days' training. Anaemic and undernourished Russian clerks who had never before handled a gun were mobilized and hurled into battle. A call for help went out to the Baltic destroyer fleet, which succeeded in doing what everyone had thought impossible: it steamed up the Neva, negotiated the Mariinsk canals, entered the Volga, and subjected the Czechoslovak lines to a murderous and wholly unforeseen bombardment.

Trotsky and his staff of former Tsarist officers sped between the battlefronts by express train. There were eleven fronts in all, and Vatsetis, Trotsky's Lettish military adviser, was rumoured to have forecast that they would soon be augmented by a twelfth, to wit, starvation. Although food and fuel were in short supply, the munitions factories continued to function. "If our coal runs out," Kamenev told a gathering of foundrymen, "we'll stoke our furnaces with the pianos of the bourgeoisie." Muscovites undertook two-day journeys by rail to obtain a sack of potatoes. The itinerant traders who used to peddle garlic, dried fish and cranberries in the streets of Moscow had disappeared overnight. All that could now be bought were buttons, shoe polish and notebooks.

One government decree ordained the surrender of all privately-owned bicycles, binoculars and torches; another mobilized the bourgeoisie and set them to cleaning streets and military installations. The Communist Party threw open its ranks to all who wished to join. In Moscow alone, twenty thousand people registered within three days. The streets were filled with long lines of workers queueing up at counters for hours, not for food, but to hand in donations toward the equipping of the Red Army. The work force at a match factory formally resolved to "overthrow the class enemy by boosting output". At Kazan Station, a man was regularly seen distributing fur coats, shoes, pocket watches, meerschaum cigarette holders and petrol lighters to troops bound for the front. When arrested, he admitted having robbed passers-by, night after night, "in order to regale our valiant Red Army men with riches wrested from the bourgeoisie".

Lorries laden with soldiers, machine-guns and ammunition boxes roared through the city in an unending stream. Two batteries of heavy guns on their way to Yaroslav Station bore the inscription: "They'll hear us in Paris!" One of the battery commanders mounted the roof of his truck and addressed the crowd that had escorted him to the station. "The real front is here," he declared, "here with you in Moscow. We out there are only covering your rear."

His point was taken. The counter-revolution had yet to be finally crushed in Moscow. It was said that the headquarters of the Moscow garrison had been mined by White conspirators, that the general staff of all the White Guard organizations was secretly based in a building on Smolensky Boulevard, and that a coup d'état had been planned to coincide with a forthcoming religious festival. These rumours were continually refuelled by the mass arrests and executions that took place every day.

Being unable to lay hands on every conspirator, the masses vented their revolutionary spleen on the stone emblems of the *ancien régime*. Tsarist monuments were torn from their plinths. When the statue of Alexander II in Sokolniki Gardens was smashed to pieces, the park attendants and two *petites bourgeoises* raised their voices in protest, not on behalf of the emancipator of the serfs, but because a pair of thrushes had nested in his metal crown.

Statues and busts of the great revolutionaries of the past sprouted everywhere, though many of them vanished as quickly as they had appeared. A bust of Bakunin by a Futurist sculptor disdainful of "the bourgeoisie's reactionary methods of representation" – he had fashioned it out of bottle sleeves, matchboxes, electric light bulbs, box lids, telegraph wire and raffia shoes – was hurled into the gutter by a brief resurgence of counter-revolutionary sentiment. Not far from the Iberian Madonna in Red Square, on the other hand, it was possible to see a revolutionary monument which, though crude, was nonetheless effective: an outsize axe embedded in a massive block of white stone bearing the inscription, in big red letters:

"The White Guard". One morning, old Prince Kochubey was found on the steps of this monument with a bullet in his head. His three sons had all lost their lives in the civil war, one as a Red Army soldier, the other two as officers in Denikin's forces. The old man had kept the wolf from the door during his last few days on earth by working as billposter.

Such was Moscow in March 1919: a city gone mad, a city through whose streets a sick, tired and hungry Vittorin, his clothes in rags, trudged in search of Selyukov.

He looked for Selyukov in the streets traversing the centre of the city, in government eating-houss, in the dance halls where sailors and Chekists disported themselves, in the hutted encampments on the outskirts. He lingered outside the War Commissariat building and scrutinized the faces of the people streaming past him. His money had run out even before he reached Moscow, so he lived as an "illegal", spending the night under bridges or in empty barns and shacks outside town. When hunger became too much for him he suspended his investigations for long enough to earn a few roubles by devising propaganda posters for a Soviet printing works to which he was directed by the labour exchange. For two whole days he drew potbellied bourgeois smuggling their money-bags across the frontier and White generals fleeing from Red bayonets. On the third day he skipped work to look for Selyukov at the Party's club for revolutionary officers. He was reprimanded on his return and given to understand that concentration camps had been established for the disposal of slackers, shirkers and saboteurs.

In search of a job that would leave him more spare time, he worked as a day labourer loading timber for half a pound of bread and a bowl of soup. In the afternoons he mingled with the crowds that thronged Kuznetsky Bridge, Sukharov Square or Strastny Boulevard, ever on the look out for Selyukov.

Vittorin's series of conjectures, which he held to be logically irrefutable conclusions, had persuaded him that Selyukov must be in Moscow. Although he persisted in that belief, even after three long weeks of fruitless research, he changed his investigative technique. Having learned that all officers in the old army were obliged to register in accordance with a Soviet decree promulgated some months before, he abandoned his post on Kuznetsky Bridge and spent hours in various government information bureaux. There he waited his turn with the serene self-assurance of a man on the brink of success. The official would listen with an air of suspicion, impatience, or stolid indifference, demand to see his identity card and trade union membership booklet, ask him a number of questions, and eventually tell him to return the next day or direct him to another department.

At last he found the right place. He was instructed to enter the name and personal particulars of the officer in question on a preprinted buff card. A surly-looking clerk tossed the completed card on to a plate overflowing with crusts of bread and cigarette ends and told Vittorin that he could either wait or come back in an hour's time. Then he turned on two old ladies who were scrubbing the floor.

"Get a move on!" he snapped. "Hurry it up – and stop jabbering in French all the time!"

An hour later the card was back in Vittorin's possession. There it was in black and white: Mikhail Mikhailovich Selyukov, formerly a staff captain in the Semyonov Regiment, resided on the third floor of No. 15, Tagansky Square. The accuracy of this information was attested by the registrar's signature and the imprint of a greasy thumb.

That night Vittorin spent two hours standing outside No. 15, Tagansky Square. The faint glow issuing from the third-floor windows suggested that Selyukov was still awake. With bloodshot eyes and murderous thoughts revolving in his brain, the enemy of mankind must be restlessly pacing his apartment, robbed of sleep by the dead. Or did he sense the danger that threatened him? No, Selyukov had no cause for concern, now that he had sided with the Revolution. "We have no finer associates than the officers of the old imperial army," a Bolshevik orator had recently told a rally in Arbat Square. "Last year they helped us to put down the Social Revolutionaries. After all, what have we deprived them of? Just their gold epaulettes, nothing more." No, Selyukov would no longer be wearing his gold epaulettes and Order of Vladimir. Instead, he would be bowling through the streets of Moscow in a car driven by a tipsy sailor, tossing his coat to a Red Army orderly, issuing orders, signing death warrants, herding defenceless bourgeois into camps, ordering careworn petitioners out of his office, sending drunken soldiers into villages to carry off the peasants' horses or womenfolk at gunpoint. Such was the Selyukov who now paced the third floor of No. 15, riding crop in hand.

Vittorin realized that it would be folly to barge in on Selyukov alone and unarmed, with no means of enforcing his will. If he did, his enemy would find it only too easy to humiliate him yet again. *Pashol?* No, not this time. He must adopt a different approach and lay his plans with care. He already had a scheme in mind, and he proceeded to put it into effect the very next morning.

He paid another visit to the labour exchange. There were vacancies for engineers, unskilled workers, persons who could read and write, and persons with special linguistic and commercial skills. Vittorin declined a post as accountant at a timber yard and requested a personal interview with the director of the labour exchange. Thereafter, armed with a recommendation from the latter, he betook himself to the metallurgical section of the Public Health Commissariat, which was looking for an "expert in West European languages".

The head of this section was a handsome old man whose finely chiselled features and bohemian shock of hair suggested a cross between a scholar and an artist. He examined Vittorin's papers, found them in order, and engaged him in a conversation that ranged from food shortages in the Balkan States to Swedish pig-iron exports and, after touching on numerous other subjects, culminated in a discussion of Taine's ideas on the philosophy of history. He then expressed satisfaction that Vittorin was a German and, thus, not the kind of person to

128

idle as soon as he secured a job. He knew the Germans, he added; he had spent three years working in the Hamburg docks.

Vittorin's task was to synopsize the financial sections of the leading English, American and German newspapers. He signed on at eight every morning and remained at his desk until late at night.

His work found favour. After a week he was given a bigger food ration, a certificate stating that he was a government employee, a voucher for two shirts and sundry other garments, twelve hundred Soviet roubles in crumpled notes, and, since he had no legal abode, a permit entitling him to requisition a room in a bourgeois apartment.

That had been his objective all along, and that was why he had toiled at his desk until all hours, day after day. It was possible, nay, certain, that Selyukov enjoyed exemption from billeting orders, but no matter; Vittorin was uninterested in acquiring a room or "legal abode". The permit, that wondrous little piece of paper, would empower and authorize him to enter Selyukov's apartment. "Do my eyes deceive me, or is it you, Mikhail Mikhailovich? What a fortunate coincidence! We still have some unfinished business to discuss . . ."

The hour had struck; his dream, his recurrent dream, was about to come true. Escorted by a brace of Red Guards with Mauser pistols in their holsters and hand-grenades in their belts, he set off for Selyukov's apartment.

He drew a deep breath as he stood outside the door on the third floor of No. 15 and saw Selyukov's name on the brass plate: "M. M. Selyukov" – Mikhail Mikhailovich. His heart was pounding. He didn't ring the bell yet, he took his time and waited for the turmoil in his chest to subside. Then he heard the strains of a violin! Who the devil could be playing a Bach gavotte in Selyukov's apartment? Stupidly, his heart continued to thump. It had all been so simple: an inquiry at the records office, No. 15, Tagansky Square, and now, three floors up, "M. M. Selyukov". So simple – almost too simple.

He rang the bell at last. Selyukov was beyond that door.

Selyukov beyond that door? All at once it struck Vittorin as strange and well nigh incredible that Selyukov should be inside. It had all been too easy. No last-minute snags or hitches. Up three flights of stairs and there it was, a door like any other. Was it really possible that his great moment should seem so mundane? There it was on the brass plate: "M. M. Selyukov". Selyukov, staff captain, Semyonov Regiment. There could only be one such, but still the violin played on.

Vittorin rang the bell once more – calmly and imperturbably this time. His hand had ceased to tremble.

And then, as the strains of the violin died away and shuffling footsteps approached, he knew, without being able to account for his absolute certainty, that the door wouldn't open on Selyukov after all.

The tall, gaunt man in the doorway looked somewhat ridiculous in his cherry-red dressing-gown and embroidered slippers. He started back in alarm when he made out the two uniformed figures on the gloomy landing. For a moment he stood there transfixed, but he regained his composure almost at once. He ran a hand over his sunken cheeks as if merely put out that visitors should have found him unshaven.

"Can I help you?" he said in a tone of polite inquiry.

"I've been instructed to requisition a room in your apartment," Vittorin told him, rather at a loss. "Here's my permit."

The man took the piece of paper and held it in his hand without even glancing at it. His haggard face broke into a courteous smile.

"You're welcome to a room here. Please come in."

"Your name is Selyukov?" Vittorin asked.

"Selyukov? Yes, that's right. Mikhail Mikhailovich Selyukov."

"How many bedrooms are there in this place?" one of the soldiers demanded sternly.

"Three. Two large and one small – it's more of a dressing-room, really."

"Do you do any kind of work that entitles you to an apartment with a dressing-room?" the soldier pursued.

"No, I don't work, I just live from hand to mouth," the man in the dressing-gown replied. After a pause he added, "There used to be three of us, but now I'm on my own."

The other soldier, who had been standing in silence at the head of the stairs, said abruptly, "Vanka, let's have that light." He took the torch from his companion and shone it on the face of the owner of the apartment. Then, with a hoarse, unpleasant laugh, he said, "My respects, Excellency."

The light went out.

"So it's you, Kolya," said the man in the cherry-red dressing-gown, his voice devoid of surprise or alarm. "Sober for once, I note. Well, you've certainly come to the right place this time."

"Your most humble and obedient servant, Excellency," the soldier said, still chuckling. "I recognized Your Excellency at once."

"You're a trifle late, Kolya," the man in the dressing-gown rejoined. "Natalya Alexeevna and little Lussya are beyond your reach, but I'm still here, so off you go at the double. They'll pay you in full for me, I'm sure – every last kopeck."

The soldier turned to Vittorin and clicked his heels.

"If your requirements in respect of a room have been met, comrade, we'll be going. Come on, Vanka. My respects, Excellency!"

"You just witnessed a bizarre reunion," the man in the dressing-gown told Vittorin when they were alone together. "Kolya used to be a manservant of mine, but I threw him out of the house for persistent pilfering. He doesn't remember me kindly, so he'll take his revenge. Well, let him. I'm not Selyukov, as you've gathered; I'm Baron Pistolkors, formerly a gentleman-in-waiting to the Tsar. The Bolsheviks have done me the honour of putting a price on my head – rightly so, since I was a member of the Committee for the Preservation of the Fatherland and caused them a certain amount of trouble.

You're a foreigner. Have you come to observe our revolution in progress – to find a Russian Danton or Robespierre? Believe me, our Dantons and Robespierres are an unedifying sight at close quarters. This apartment? I bought it from an officer in the Semyonov Regiment, together with his papers. That's right, his name was Selyukov. In Petersburg everyone knew me, but here I could hope to lose myself in the crowd, that's why I bought his papers. Natalya Alexeevna was still alive then."

His face became even greyer and more sunken. He stared silently into space for a moment.

"Diphtheria, so the doctors said," he went on, "and she took our little Lussya with her. Perhaps it was better that way – I'm a spiritual pauper compared to my wife. The real Selyukov? He's not in Moscow any longer – he left for the front with his regiment. On the other hand, perhaps he didn't. Who can tell where an apple rolls to these days?"

He asked Vittorin to be content with the smaller of the two bedrooms for a couple of days. After that he would have the whole apartment to himself.

"I'll be arrested," he said. "Kolya always was a rat. He'll go to the Cheka and denounce me, it's a foregone conclusion."

"You mean you're going to let them arrest you?" Vittorin protested. "Why give up without a struggle? You must leave at once, this minute – you can't stay here. Don't you have a friend who would put you up for the night? Tomorrow you can leave the city and go into hiding somewhere else."

The former courtier listened with polite attention. All that conveyed his low opinion of this advice was a dismissive little gesture.

"Thank you, friend," he said, "but why should I cling to my empty husk of a life? Ever since the morning when I laid little Lussya's body on a sledge – well, I've been a trifle lonely, a godforsaken burden to myself. Do you smoke? Here, please help yourself, they're old stock. I'll have one too, if you don't mind."

He lit a cigarette, then changed the subject.

The Revolution? He regarded it as a successful slave revolt, nothing more, and spoke with detestation of the Bolshevik leaders, whom he called "expropriators of human dignity". Lenin he loathed above all others. He went to the open window and pointed to the domes of the Kremlin, which were bathed in gold and purple by the setting sun.

"There sits Vladimir Ilyich, whetting his iron sickle," he said. "There used to be an old peasant prophecy: 'A priest and a gipsy will sit on the Tsar's golden throne.' Well, Vladimir Ilyich is no gipsy. He's more of a priest with no chasuble but plenty of incense. He has beguiled Russia with fine words and contaminated our young people with the poison of the age: 'Liberty, justice, the creative energy of the proletariat, the emergence of the anonymous masses from centuries of darkness into the sunlight of the new era . . .' What if it's all an idiotic lie – what then?"

The man whose fate had been sealed by Vittorin's great mission finished his cigarette in silence.

"Do you know the poems of Baratinsky?" he asked at length. "Yevgeny Baratinsky? You don't know his elegies?"

> Proud city, erstwhile mistress of the world,
> pilgrims now pause with melancholy mien
> to marvel at the ruins of your splendour.
> Did victory's brave guardians forsake you?
> You linger, mute and silent, down the years,
> a sepulchre of nations long extinct.

"Baratinsky entitled that poem 'Rome', but today it should be renamed 'Petersburg'. I possess the original in his own handwriting."

Pistolkors opened a desk drawer and took out an ebony casket. It contained what he termed "flotsam of the centuries collected in the course of my travels – curios and treasures from every land and age". These he spread out on the desk with loving care. They were objects of disparate value: coloured copperplate engravings from England, Japanese woodcuts, Persian miniatures, a Dürer print, a Rembrandt drawing, a self-portrait of E. T. A. Hoffmann dating from his time at Bamberg; two letters, one from Talleyrand to the King of Naples, the other from Balzac to a Polish noblewoman; two army orders from General Skobelev; a hotel bill from which it emerged that Stendhal had paid two thalers and eight silver groschen for a night's lodging, a cup of chocolate, and the ordering of a coach; a handwritten sheet of music from a youthful composition by Moussorgsky, no longer extant; and, finally, a hotch-potch of letters, petitions, diary sheets and verses by Russian poets, complete with a list of names.

When the owner of this miscellany noticed that Vittorin paid little heed to his remarks and kept trying to reopen the subject of Selyukov, he replaced his "curios and treasures" in the casket and the latter in the desk. Then he retired to his room.

Such was Vittorin's only conversation with Baron Pistolkors, a stubborn upholder of the *ancien régime* who had advised the Tsar – disastrously, as it turned out – to refuse the liberal members of the Duma an audience in January 1917 . . .

Pistolkors spent the ensuing days closeted in his room, playing the violin – Bach, for the most part, and the melancholy, impassioned melodies of the early Italians. Vittorin never again set eyes on him, perhaps because the baron regretted that lack of human companionship had prompted him to confide so fully in a stranger, or perhaps because he had no wish to disclose that the cherry-red dressing-gown was the only garment he possessed.

He played the violin from morning till late at night. He was in the middle of Tartini's "La Furiosa" sonata when the men from the Cheka came to fetch him.

A priest who had been discharged from Lubyanka Prison the previous day brought Vittorin a note from Baron Pistolkors. It was dated and headed: "From life's back yard". The former gentleman-in-waiting asked for his violin, a few books, and the brown woollen rug he had used as a curtain. The world of men, he wrote, was a crass and cruel place. Malice, vindictiveness and petty-mindedness were the Holy Trinity of the age. He also asked for some cigarettes to help him establish "a tolerable relationship" with his fellow prisoners.

Vittorin could not find the woollen rug among the Baron's belongings and decided to give him his own fur coat instead. When he presented himself at Lubyanka Prison with his bundle the following morning, however, he learned that the man for whom its contents were intended had been shot in the yard of the Alexander School two hours before.

He sold the violin in the flea market. Instead of going back to his office he roamed the streets every day on the lookout for soldiers returning from the front. Vittorin was quite at home in Moscow by now. He knew the days on which underclothes and shoes were for sale at the market stalls in Sukharev Square. He could distinguish Soviet and Kerensky roubles from the bank-notes of the Don Government and the Lettish and Georgian Republics. He wore a Russian smock. He knew where to go to get food and when it was distributed. He also knew how to converse with front-line soldiers in their own idiom and could induce even the most taciturn among them to talk to him.

Where Selyukov was concerned, however, he made no progress at all. The conflicting reports he received were irreconcilable. The Semyonov Regiment had covered itself with glory during the capture of Orsk, he was informed one day, only to be assured the next that it had months ago been disbanded on account of anti-revolutionary sentiment. It turned up in two different places within hours, once victoriously advancing through Siberia, once riddled with scurvy and completely *hors de combat* on the northern front. Selyukov himself had been appointed a divisional commander at Kharkov, had been killed at Kupyansk while serving as an artillery spotter, had embezzled the regimental funds and deserted to the enemy at Yuryev – and all this within the space of a single week. Vittorin's informants were unanimous on one point only: that they had encountered Selyukov at the front. They recognized him instantly from Vittorin's description.

Despite these setbacks, and for want of any other expedient, he persevered with his inquiries. He haunted the vicinity of railway stations and accosted soldiers in search of a bed for the night, offered to put them up at the apartment, plied them with tea and cigarettes, bought cartridge-case lighters from them. When they departed after hours of talk and little sleep, they left behind a smell of makhorka tobacco and wet sheep-skin, leather jackets and horse dung, anise oil and onions, cabbage soup and rain-sodden grass.

It was a routine that persisted until the evening Vittorin came across someone who hailed from a different kind of battlefront.

When Vittorin approached the man near the freight station, he had just eaten a snack standing up and was stowing away the remains – a hunk of black bread and a pickled gherkin – in his knapsack. All that distinguished him from the front-line soldiers around him was the pair of glasses he wore. The button on his old gunner's cap was dyed with red ink. On the strength of the glasses, Vittorin guessed him to be an orderly-room clerk with a battalion headquarters in transit from one front to another.

It turned out that the man had nowhere to sleep. Tired out after a long train journey, or so it seemed, he responded monosyllabically to Vittorin's questions on the way to Tagan-sky Square. Once in the lobby of the apartment he removed his tattered grey overcoat, an unproletarian proceeding which Vittorin had observed in none of his previous visitors.

As soon as they entered the Baron's study, the soldier's manner underwent a strange and startling change. Every sign of diffidence and fatigue vanished. While Vittorin was making tea he toured the room and examined the desk and bookcase with particular interest. Then, more like the master of the house than a guest, he walked through the dressing-room to the bedroom, whistling softly as he went. Having inspected the whole apartment, he went to the window and peered down into the street.

"What time is it, comrade?" he asked without looking round.

"Seven o'clock."

"Seven, eh?" he murmured. "They haven't changed, the mangy dogs! The old Russia has gone, swept away by time and tide, but those priests' sons are still there, still the same as ever. The only difference is, these days they hunt me in the name of Bolshevism. Once upon a time, when I was manning the barricades, they sang 'God save the Tsar'. Cowards, that's all they are – scared of their own shadows."

Vittorin, busy with the samovar, had only caught the last few words. "Who's scared?" he asked.

"Scared and stupid – yes, stupid as well. They're a bone-headed bunch."

"Who are you talking about, comrade?"

"The Cheka police, of course. At this very moment, those pumpkin-eaters are searching the apartment I left this morning."

"You have an apartment?" Vittorin exclaimed. "You mean you haven't just come from the front?"

The stranger slowly turned to face him.

"Why pretend, comrade? I've been watching you for the past week, surely you spotted me? If you didn't, what kind of an 'illegal' are you?"

Vittorin reached for his revolver, but it had disappeared.

"Stay where you are," he blurted out. "Keep away from me. What do you want?"

"Forget about Comrade Mauser," the stranger said. "I want to know what organization you belong to and who sent you here, that's all. I've admired your work – your efforts to establish contact with military personnel. You're obviously operating in accordance with some definite plan. You've entertained men from seven different regiments in the last few days, here in this room."

Vittorin was dismayed. "Seven or seventy," he retorted, "what business is it of yours?"

The stranger shrugged.

"Artemyev may be right in thinking that you belong to some right-wing officers' association," he said. "There's a so-called 'Rebirth League' in Moscow, but we haven't managed to get in touch with it."

Now that he had heard a familiar name, Vittorin felt less at sea.

"So you're one of Artemyev's men," he said. "You should have said so in the first place. I know Artemyev – I've had dealings with him. Where is he? Is he in Moscow?"

"He's here all right. Did you read about that raid on the armoured car full of cash from the Leather Distribution Centre? That was Artemyev. You're looking slightly reassured, I see. I'm sure we'll come to some agreement in the end. You might even offer me a cup of tea."

"What is there to agree on, comrade?" asked Vittorin, his suspicions rekindled.

The stranger waved him into a chair and sat down opposite.

"Seen as a whole," he began, "the situation is as follows: the anti-Bolshevik forces are fragmented. They lack definite guidelines and a unified chain of command. Take your organization, for example. It operates within the army, making random attempts to establish contact. We, too, are interested in forming Party cells inside the Red regiments. In other words, we're using two stones to kill the same bird. Why? Because instead of working in harness with us, your organization –"

"I don't belong to any organization," Vittorin interjected.

"Your friends, then, if you prefer to put it that way –"

"I have no friends in Moscow."

"Let's not quibble over words. Your superiors –"

"I have no superiors in this matter," Vittorin said flatly.

"You mean there's no driving force behind your operations – no political party or movement?"

Vittorin had a fleeting vision of the fat, flushed, ever-perspiring face of his old comrade Feuerstein.

"I'm operating alone," he said, downcast all of a sudden. "I don't have anyone to help me. There used to be an organization, but it collapsed."

"I can't expect you to trust me right away," the stranger

said after a pause. "You're bound to be wary of everyone including me, I realize that."

"It's the truth," Vittorin insisted. "My best man was arrested and the last person to help me shot himself: Count Gagarin – know the name?"

"No, it doesn't ring a bell. You may be telling the truth, comrade, but if your organization has collapsed, where does that leave you? What's the point of working in isolation? You'll soon be faced with a choice between joining us and discontinuing your activities. No, don't shake your head, you know I'm right. You can't operate indefinitely in Moscow without –"

"I'm not staying in Moscow," Vittorin broke in. "There's nothing more I can do here. I'm going to the front."

"You're leaving?" said the stranger, and a look of surprise flitted across his face. "Is that definite? I regret your decision, comrade. We might have put some important work your way. When are you thinking of going?"

"I can't say for certain. I want to go to the front, but to one particular regiment. That's the snag."

"What snag, comrade?"

"I doubt if the district commission takes account of personal preferences."

"What strange ideas you have, comrade," said the man in glasses. "What do you need the district commission for? We have the rubber stamps of every regiment, every regimental headquarters and regimental committee, every divisional staff and military academy – even of the War Commissariat itself. We have travel permits, letters of appointment, blank forms of all kinds. We even have the official seal of the executive committee of the Moscow Soviet. We'll provide you with a nice little piece of paper, never fear." He broke off. "Doesn't this apartment have a second exit? Pity . . ."

Artemyev was spending the night at a hostel in the Presnya district. Two hours later he received the following report pencilled in the margin of a sheet of newsprint:

"Where premises are concerned, the apartment of the

139

German whom I was instructed to watch would lend itself admirably to the manufacture and storage of bombs. Furthermore, its windows overlook Tagansky Square, where the headquarters of the Wool Trading Agency and the Sickness Benefit Office are situated. This could be of relevance to our organization's financial position, given that it would enable us to keep watch and pick the most favourable moment for a raid. The chairman of the house committee is known to me. He takes bribes and should present no problem. I had a conversation with the German. Although he was evasive, I managed to ascertain that he belongs to a right-wing group dedicated to the formation of a bourgeois government. What points to this is that one of the rooms contains photographs of ex-Premier Goremykin, General Efimovich, and other representatives of the imperial régime. Active cooperation with this group cannot, however, be recommended. It is in the throes of disintegration, and its leading lights are in prison. The German has decided to abandon his conspiratorial activities and leave Moscow. In my opinion, he could at most be employed as an observer."

Vittorin met Artemyev at an eating-house installed in the basement of a house opposite Spassky Gate formerly owned by Prince Kudashev. The place served fish soup, boiled turnips, and, quite often, little earthenware bowls of thin, unsweetened coffee. In the afternoons it was almost always crowded with employees from the nearby government offices who wolfed their food and were swiftly replaced by other customers waiting on the spiral wooden staircase. At midday, however, Artemyev and Vittorin had the place to themselves.

The veteran revolutionary sat astride a bench with his cap tilted back and a cigarette dangling from the corner of his mouth, one eye on Vittorin and the other on the entrance to the cellar. He seemed to be known here, because a nod from him sufficed to banish the pockmarked waiter to the cubbyhole that served as a kitchen.

"Moscow's a big place, but I tracked you down for all that,"

Artemyev began. "I'm glad you're still in the land of the living. You've worked really hard, collecting all that information about the Red troops and their headquarters. A useful form of activity, comrade, but what of our conversation at Berdichev? Weren't you planning to take some form of positive action against a certain individual?"

Vittorin stared at the table.

"I still have that end in view," he said. "I've never abandoned it."

"Remember Dolgushin?" Artemyev went on. "You know, the man who accompanied you to the station? 'Comrade,' Dolgushin said to me when he got back, 'I know a terrorist when I see one. That German will never kill Lenin or Rakovsky. He'll go to Moscow and try all kinds of things, and they won't amount to a row of beans.' Dolgushin's a lathe operator by trade. He's had thirty years in the organization – specializes in blowing up bridges. He dislikes and mistrusts intellectuals. Russia was deep in snow when he said that about you. Now the peasants are cutting hay."

"I know," Vittorin said despondently. "I've wasted a lot of time. All my efforts have gone for nothing."

"So what are your future plans, comrade?"

Vittorin, still staring at the table, shrugged his shoulders. His face took on a weary, apathetic expression.

"I'm no stranger to bitterness myself," Artemyev said. "There are days when I feel as if I'm bound hand and foot – entangled in a sort of shroud. It's hopeless, I tell myself; luck has deserted me in favour of the other side. I'll be killed and there's no one to take my place. What will remain of me when I've been shovelled into the ground? Will the great Russian people – the people of the steppe villages and factories, the people I love – will *they* appreciate what I've lived and fought for? There's a terrible void inside me at such times. Then a new day dawns and my spirits revive. I'm still alive and kicking, I tell myself. The priest isn't handing out candles yet – he hasn't anointed my head with oil or sprinkled my chest with earth."

"You're right." Vittorin looked up. "I'll leave Moscow and start all over again."

"So you're leaving. Would you be prepared to go out into the villages and further our cause among the peasants?"

Vittorin shook his head. "I want to go to the front."

"Why there, of all places?" Artemyev protested. "You think they'll welcome you with wine and roses? Village work is important. The peasants' guilds have always been our major source of strength."

"I must leave for the front," Vittorin said firmly.

"Must you really? I used to say 'I must, I must', but now, when I ask myself why I had to do certain things, I can't find one good reason. You want to go to the front? Very well, I won't try to stop you. The front it is, then. I've got as many forms and rubber stamps as any commissar. First, you'll need a movement order. 'The War Commissariat confirms that . . .' What are you full names?"

"Vittorin, Georg Karl."

"Georg Karlovich Vittorin. 'The War Commissariat confirms that Comrade G. K. Vittorin . . .' Year of birth?"

"1889.

" '. . . born in 1889 of proletarian parents, has been transferred to . . .' Which regiment?"

"The Semyonov Regiment."

"That unit has been renamed 'Karl Liebknecht's Own' and forms part of the Second Moscow Rifle Division, currently holding the Kharkov-Belgorod Line. In what capacity do you wish to join the regiment, comrade? Shall I assign you to the transport section? Can you drive a car or ride a horse?"

"I can't do either," Vittorin replied apologetically.

"Well," said Artemyev, "no one can be good at everything. If wolves could fly, God wouldn't have created the eagle. All right, how about a hand-grenade instructor? Would that suit you?"

"I don't have the technical knowledge."

"Oh, come now, surely you can throw a hand-grenade? Anyway, what's all this talk about technical knowledge? Take

142

the medical corps: any fool who used to sweep the floor of a chemist's shop can call himself a doctor nowadays. Here's your movement order, here's your travel warrant, and here's your permit from Moscow Military District. The latter entitles you to draw a three-day ration of bread and sugar from the stores at garrison headquarters. One more thing, comrade: don't go back to your apartment."

"It was officially allocated to me," Vittorin protested. "I've every right to . . ."

He broke off. Artemyev glanced at the waiter, who had just emerged from his cubby-hole.

"Your apartment has been under surveillance since last night," he said in a low voice. "I owe it to you to point out that three Cheka policemen have been posted in Tagansky Square. They plan to arrest you."

"Why should anyone arrest me, comrade?"

"An odd question. The Cheka have become aware of your activities, that's why. You weren't very discreet."

"But all my things are there – my clothes and so on."

"Are they worth risking your neck for? We'll provide you with all you need. You'd better leave today, and whatever you do, don't go anywhere near that apartment. You promise? Very well, take your papers."

Vittorin pocketed them and, in so doing, became a Red Army soldier.

He had all he needed to get him to the front – equipment, papers, food for the journey, and, concealed on his person, the revolver essential to his grand confrontation with Selyukov – but still he hesitated to take the ultimate step. It seemed so final and irrevocable that he was reluctant to be over-hasty. Twice he set off for Kursk Station, and twice he turned back, deterred each time by the same misgivings. Could he be certain that Selyukov was still serving with the regiment in whose ranks he had originally entered the civil war? Mightn't the former staff captain have quit the service? Mightn't he have been assigned to rear echelon duties, given command of one of the newly raised regiments, or transferred to some divisional headquarters? Vittorin was anxious to reassure himself on that score before leaving Moscow for good.

He spent two days looking for men from "Karl Liebknecht's Own", whether wounded or on leave, but none of the soldiers he encountered wore shoulder-straps bearing the initials "K. L." Instead of returning to the apartment, he slept at a lodging house on the Leningrad road. On the morning of the third day he joined a procession of suburban factory workers singing revolutionary songs as they marched to the Kremlin to attend a rally there.

Moscow's factories were at a standstill that day. Vittorin learned that the workers of Milan had seized power, and that street fighting had broken out in Elberfeld. Because the simultaneous nature of these developments suggested that world revolution was imminent, the embattled proletarians of Western Europe were to be honoured with rallies, revolutionary demonstrations, processions, public entertainments, and a Red Army parade.

Most government offices were shut, but staff at the headquarters of the various departments remained on duty till noon. Vittorin left the procession in Red Square, formerly Imperial Theatre Square, and had no difficulty in gaining admittance to the War Commissariat.

Only two people were in the Personnel Records Office at this hour: an oldish man with a sparse goatee and a bald head – clearly the head of the department, because he was reading *Pravda* – and a weary-looking girl engaged in numbering documents of some kind. Vittorin addressed himself to the girl.

"I need some information, comrade. I should like to know the names of the battalion, platoon and section commanders of a certain front-line regiment."

"I'm sorry, comrade," the girl replied in a soft, melodious voice. "I'm not allowed to disclose information of that sort."

Vittorin was determined not to be put off. For a moment he considered producing his papers as evidence that he was bound for the front and anxious to know the names of his future superiors, but he abandoned the idea in case the documents were recognized as forgeries. He tried another tack – one that seemed less risky.

"In this instance, comrade," he pleaded, "perhaps your orders will allow you to make an exception. It's a genuinely deserving case. I've requisitioned a room in a family's apartment. The wife is sick, there are three children, and the husband's at the front. She hasn't heard from him for two months. Put yourself in her position, comrade."

Vittorin could tell that his story had made an impression. The girl seemed to be wavering, reconsidering. She glanced inquiringly at her boss, who was still engrossed in his newspaper.

"The woman has her husband's parents to look after as well," Vittorin went on. "Two months without a word, imagine! She asked me to make inquiries. The last time she heard, he was commanding a battalion of the Liebknecht Regiment. His name is –"

"No," the girl broke in, "it's pointless going on, we can't give you any such information."

Just then the head of department put his paper down.

"One moment," he said, and turned to Vittorin. "The battalion commander you mentioned – which regiment was he serving with?"

"The Liebknecht, formerly the Semyonov Regiment."

"Be patient, comrade, and you'll have the particulars you're after. Wait here while I make the necessary inquiries."

He left the room. The girl glanced nervously at the door to satisfy herself that it was almost shut.

"For heaven's sake go!" she whispered. "Go, or an innocent family will suffer. Along the corridor on the right, down two flights of stairs, and you'll be out on the street. Go quickly! Oh God, it's too late . . ."

The head of department returned, accompanied by a burly, thickset man with a broad face, prominent cheekbones, and the lustreless eyes of a dead fish. He wore a flat green cap and a uniform adorned with red piping and the Soviet star in gold.

The girl's expression had gone quite blank. She bent over her desk and went on numbering documents in the margin. Her boss beckoned to Vittorin.

"What was the name of that battalion commander?"

"Mikhail Mikhailovich Selyukov."

"Address?"

"No. 15, Tagansky Square. He's at the front, though."

"I know," said the head of department. He turned to the man in the red-braided uniform.

"Take three of your men and escort this comrade to the said address. Arrest any persons you find there and march them off to the Special Tribunal for questioning. The head of the family is a traitor." With a glance at Vittorin, who was looking utterly dismayed, he added, "The Semyonov Regiment, as it used to be known, deserted to the enemy four days ago, officers and all."

Outside the door bearing the brass plate inscribed with Selyukov's name, Vittorin made one last attempt to avert the consequences of his initiative.

"I tell you, comrades, you're wasting your time. You won't find anyone there. It's all a misunderstanding."

The three Red Guards leaned on their rifles, waiting for an order of some kind. Their peasant faces, broad and bearded, were quite impassive. One of them had removed his cap and was mopping his brow. The Cheka officer fixed Vittorin with his dull, fishlike gaze.

"We'll see," he said brusquely. "Give me the key. You don't have it? If the place is really empty you'll be paying the Lubyanka a visit yourself. Then you'll tell us where to find those people."

He tugged at the bell-pull.

The bell's harsh, jangling note terminated in a plaintive tinkle, then silence. Vittorin had heard it only once before, and that was when he had stood outside, heart pounding, with a requisition order in his pocket. Baron Pistolkors had been playing a Bach gavotte. Where were those sounds now? Gone for ever. The rooms were deserted, devoid of all human presence. The violin reposed on some stall in the flea market, and buried somewhere in a prison yard were the remains of the old courtier who had bidden farewell to the world, farewell to his memories, with the melancholy, fervent strains of "La Furiosa".

Vittorin gave a sudden start. Footsteps could be heard inside the deserted apartment. As they approached the door, a crazy notion flitted through his head: Pistolkors had returned from the dead to fetch his violin – no, it was cold below ground and he wanted the brown woollen rug – no, nonsense, it was Selyukov! Selyukov was back in Moscow, back in his apartment, home from the front . . .

"Who is it?"

An unfamiliar voice. Vittorin had never heard it before.

The Cheka officer hammered on the door with the butt of his Mauser.

"Open up! House search!"

The door remained shut. The only response was an oath and an alarm signal: two short, shrill, piercing whistles.

"All right," the Cheka officer yelled, "Break it down!"

Rifle butts reduced the door to matchwood. A shot rang out. The bullet, which was meant for Vittorin, grazed his shoulder. The soldiers burst into the lobby and hurled themselves at the man who had fired it. He resisted fiercely, but they pinned him to the ground. The Cheka officer hurried past them into the living-room, gun in hand.

He found it deserted. The first thing he saw was a hand press with a pile of leaflets beside it, the ink still wet. Some yellowish powder had been spread out on the desk to dry, and the chairs were littered with tin boxes, metal cylinders, pieces of lead, glass tubes.

The Chekist went over to the desk, took a pinch of powder, and sniffed it. A sound made him look up. Artemyev was standing in the doorway leading to the dressing-room.

The man from the Cheka didn't recognize him. All he saw

was someone who had fallen into his clutches and was at his mercy. He blew the powder off his fingertips.

"Are you the owner of this apartment? A hand press, leaflets . . . So you've set up a clandestine printing works, have you? Come here!"

Artemyev scrutinized the Chekist's face.

"Are you a Russian?" he asked. "You look more like a Kalmuck or a Buryat to me."

"I'll ask the questions and you answer them!" the Chekist snapped. "What's this powder here?"

"Groats," said Artemyev. "I live on them."

"You seem to be in a humorous mood. Well, you'll soon get over it. You're under arrest."

"Under arrest, eh? That's an empty phrase. It takes more than words, even to catch a chicken. You'll have to do better than that. I'm Fyodor Artemyev."

The Cheka officer turned pale. The hand holding the Mauser trembled and his forehead became beaded with sweat. He stared at the object in Artemyev's hand, conscious that he would never leave the room alive.

"Give yourself up, the building's surrounded," he pleaded hoarsely. "Your position is hopeless, even you must realize that. The Soviet authorities want no bloodshed – they may consider imposing a more lenient sentence if you volunteer to work for the proletarian masses. I know Dzerzhinsky and Steklov – I'm acquainted with them both. I'll speak to them, I'll use my influence on your behalf. Stay where you are, keep that hand still! I don't want to have to shoot you, but –"

"If only you'd shut up," Artemyev broke in with a sigh, "but you can't stop blathering."

The soldiers had entered the room with their rifles at the ready. Artemyev was suddenly overcome by a wild desire to escape his enemies once more, lose himself in the crowd, start work all over again. For a second or two, his alert brain juggled with a series of ingenious, audacious, futile plans.

He discarded them all.

"Welcome," he told the Red Guards. "You've turned up at a bad moment, comrades."

He took a step forward. Nestling in his hand was a cylinder of shiny, reddish metal. He tossed it into the middle of the room.

Vittorin had already left the building by the time the bomb exploded. He collided with a street lamp, recovered himself, heard a woman scream, saw her throw up her arms and make for the shelter of a doorway, saw a cabby in the middle of Tagansky Square whip up his horses like a madman, heard a tinkle of broken glass.

He ran off without a backward glance. Getting as far away as possible – that was his only thought as he plunged into a maze of unfamiliar streets. He hurried past people with his face averted, convinced that they were Chekists, informers, or militiamen in disguise.

Not that he knew how he had got there, he found himself outside a church. Too exhausted to go any farther, he went in. There was an effigy of St Nicholas the miracle-worker in one of the side aisles. He subsided into a niche beneath it and shut his eyes.

It was four in the afternoon when he left the church. He felt calmer now, and the risk of being recognized and arrested seemed less immediate. He went up to a young woman selling matches on a street corner – they cost sixty roubles a box – and asked her the way to the station.

By now, the public festivities had reached their climax. A cortège was wending its way through the Sadovaya to the strains of a bizarrre funeral march: the parliamentary system was being borne to its grave. Behind its coffin, jeered and hooted by the crowds, walked actors got up as generals and priests, distillery owners and financiers. America, symbolized by an enormous money-bag, was being hauled along Smolensky Boulevard. A proletarian poet stationed on the steps of St Paul's recited revolutionary tirades against the bad old days, the bourgeoisie, the late Tsar's armies. In Arbat Square, where a makeshift circus was performing, European monarchs and politicians were portrayed as hyenas, wolves, alligators, feline predators and gesticulating monkeys. Wilson, Vandervelde and Lloyd George played the role of clowns.

Vittorin's ears were last assailed by the voice of Red Moscow outside Kursk Station, where men armed with megaphones invited all present to participate in the crowd scenes of a revolutionary play, *The Storming of the Winter Palace*, and broadcast the latest news: the city of Perm had been captured by Soviet troops; Red partisan detachments had derailed an ammunition train behind the Kolchak army's lines; last but not least, the counter-revolutionary Artemyev, that mortal enemy of the Soviets and hireling of foreign capital, had been killed while attempting to evade arrest and due punishment.

Vittorin stopped in his tracks when tidings of the great rebel's death rang out across street and square. He had no notion of the circumstances, no inkling that he himself had delivered Artemyev into his enemies' hands. All that struck him as odd was that providence should have granted Artemyev just time enough to facilitate his, Vittorin's, departure for the front. It was almost as if that had been the underlying purpose of Artemyev's colourful career.

But there was no time to dwell on this now. Vittorin extracted the movement order and travel warrant from the leg of his boot. Then, with the papers in his hand, he made his way into the station.

CHARGE!

The Penza Division's 3rd Red Rifle Regiment had originated under enemy fire in the front line itself. Formed at the end of June 1919, it had taken part in six engagements and the defence of Kharkov during the summer campaign, borne the brunt of the enemy's assault at Valki, and had received two honourable mentions in communiqués issued by the pan-Russian bureau of the War Commissars. By early November, when the rain had become incessant, the severely depleted regiment was in position facing a White brigade south-east of Miropol.

The regimental commander was a veteran captain who had lost his right arm in Carpathia and signed his orders left-handed. The first battalion was commanded by Seaman Stassik, the second by Comrade Storoshev, a stove fitter by trade. Both had completed a command course in Moscow, and both had been awarded the Order of the Red Banner. The third battalion existed on paper only.

Also under regimental command were a light field gun battery and a reconnaissance detachment made up of specially trained men. In command of this detachment was a Moscow University student who had volunteered for combat duty. His name was Berezin, and he had a girl-friend and an old mother in Moscow.

One dank November morning, Berezin returned from a patrol to the quarters he shared with the second-in-command of No. 1 Section. These consisted of a barn made semi-habitable with the aid of a worm-eaten table and a few chairs. Part of the interior was illuminated by the flickering light of a candle stuck in the neck of a broken bottle. A private soldier named Yefimov was crouching in front of the little cast-iron stove, feeding it with the damp remains of a broken crate.

Berezin hung up his crumpled, muddy greatcoat to dry. Then he went to the stove and warmed his hands at it.

"Where's the German?" he asked. "Is he out?"

"No, asleep. He's over there." Yefimov jerked a thumb at the shadows behind him.

"Still feverish?"

Yefimov shrugged. "Maybe it's fever, maybe something else. He feels cold – he shivers all the time. The medical orderly came and tried to give him some drops, but he sent him away."

Berezin proceeded to pull off his boots. Yefimov put some water on the stove to heat and continued his report.

"About the rations, comrade. They haven't issued any bread today, only cans of bully beef. One between two, that's all they had. This one's for you, though. The German won't eat a thing. He's only thirsty – kept asking for water all night long." Yefimov paused. "Well, comrade, how are the Whites faring? They sent over some shrapnel yesterday. I heard some rifle fire, too. Have the wolves' teeth grown again?"

"They're in clover, the swine," said Berezin. "It's groats and milk for them. You can hear them praying and singing after evening muster. They have regimental priests, the way they had in the days of the Tsar. They even have psalm singers."

The figure in the corner stirred. Vittorin rubbed his inflamed eyes, threw off his coat and blanket and sat up.

"Is that you, Berezin? Why shut the door? It's unbearable, this heat – for God's sake let some air in. Well, did you see him?"

Berezin, who had produced a cup with a broken handle from his knapsack, knelt down beside the stove. He carefully wiped the cup on the hem of his jacket and filled it with tea.

"Aren't you going to open the door and let some fresh air in?" Vittorin exclaimed.

"You think it's still summer outside, but that's because you're feverish," Berezin told him. "It isn't hot in here, with all the wind blowing through the cracks."

"I'm all right – there's nothing the matter with me. So you didn't see him?"

"Who?"

"The White officer – the one your men call 'the Whistler'."

"No, I didn't come across him. A patrol passed within twenty paces of us in those willow thickets beyond the embankment. Later on, at dawn, I met another – nearly bumped into it, the mist was so dense."

Vittorin shut his eyes. When had he first heard of the White officer who whistled as he led his men ino the attack, riding crop in hand? Who lined up Red prisoners, told their officers to step forward, and, still whistling, gunned them down? Brooding hatred had impelled Vittorin to seek him everywhere and question every White deserter, but it was only now, as he lay there in the barn, stricken with fever and consumed by his endless obsession, that he had become convinced that "the Whistler" and Selyukov were identical: Selyukov the well-groomed, perfumed murderer who strolled through life with a quirt in his bloodstained hand . . .

"Berezin," he said faintly, "tell me what happened when you got his horse."

"I already did," Berezin replied. "Ten days ago, it was. We'd shot the man's charger from under him, hoping to capture him alive, but he just stood there with an arrogant look on his face, smoking a cigarette and emptying his revolver at us. Marushin was killed right beside me."

Looking arrogant, smoking as he blazed away . . . Who had ever seen Selyukov without a cigarette?

"Well, go on. What happened then?"

"Nothing – I told you. We came under enfilading fire and had to withdraw."

Vittorin sank back on the straw with a groan. His eyes were smarting – the barn seemed full of red mist. We had to withdraw . . . Selyukov wouldn't have escaped if *he'd* been there. *He* wouldn't have withdrawn, enfilading fire or no. He would have taken cover and fought on . . .

A shiver ran down his spine. Too restless to lie still, he rose, draped the coat around his shoulders and began to pace the barn like a caged beast.

I'm sick, I can feel it. My fever's worse – I ached in every joint last night. Sooner or later they'll send me to hospital, and where will the regiment be when I get back? It's going to be withdrawn and sent into action on another front, the CO said so. The lorries are ready and waiting at Miropol. Where will the apple roll to next? The Revolution switches its troops from front to front, Storoshev says. The Revolution wins its battles with blood and gasoline. And over there, beyond the shell-torn sugar factory, is Selyukov. By tomorrow I may be in hospital. I must act – I must force the issue . . .

"Berezin?"

Berezin didn't hear. He was stretched out with the candle beside him, reading *The Red Front-Line Soldier*.

"Berezin, are you going out again today?"

"Yes, this afternoon, with a four-man patrol. They want to know what our friends across the way are up to. No patrols tonight, only listening posts." Berezin returned to his newspaper. "Honestly, these know-it-all journalists! Listen to this: 'The army perceives itself to be the product of the economic, social and political forces that govern us.' He may have learnt to write that way at Party rallies, but he won't earn many plaudits at the front. Comrade Yefimov, keep the fire going – that's an order! I don't talk about economic forces to my men. 'You're heroes,' I tell them, 'you're invincible. And now, follow me.'"

"I'll take that patrol off your hands, Berezin. I'll go out today instead of you. You're tired – you haven't slept."

"And you're ill, comrade," Berezin said. "I couldn't take the responsibility."

"I'm not ill!" Vittorin cried, shaking with fever. "All I need is wind, rain, fresh air, exercise. I'm rotting away in this place.

The lice are eating me alive, that's what's wrong with me. Let me go in your place, comrade."

"All right, damn you," said Berezin, "go."

He yawned, took a final look at the stove through half-closed eyes, and settled down for a sleep.

Vittorin did not return from patrol until darkness had fallen. He sent his men straight to their quarters and walked on down the path, skirting a fence and a clump of alders on his way into the dip beyond.

Fat beads of moisture dripped from overhanging branches, and the air reeked of sodden earth and stagnant water. The whitewashed farmhouse that served as regimental headquarters was a pale blur in the gloom. The sentry delivered his challenge in a low, lilting voice.

"*Stoy! Kto takoy!*"

Vittorin came to a halt.

"*Svoy*. One of yours."

"Password?"

"Comintern."

Outside the CO's office Vittorin encountered the regimental commissar, an athletic young man with a mass of curly brown hair.

"I've a report to make, comrade," Vittorin said, his fingers stiffly aligned with the peak of his cap. "The Whites are entertaining some important visitors tonight."

The commissar, a veteran of two campaigns and the great street battle at Kiev, studied Vittorin's face intently.

"What exactly did you see, comrade?"

"I spotted some officers in French uniform and horses with English harness. I also observed a cavalry signals section laying a telephone line outside the schoolhouse."

"What time was this?"

"Five p.m."

"And you noticed nothing out of the ordinary apart from that?"

"No – that's to say, yes: a lot of activity in and around the schoolhouse. Runners coming and going, that sort of thing."

"You observed no troop movements?"

"No."

Was that a malicious, mocking glint in the commissar's eye? The farmhouse floor lurched beneath Vittorin's feet and the rafters seemed to be closing in on him, but he clenched his teeth and kept a grip on himself. He held the commissar's gaze without a tremor, subduing his fever by sheer willpower.

"Those officers you saw," the commissar said after a brief pause, " – they may have been inspecting the White lines on behalf of some higher command. Where were you when you saw them?"

"On the roof of the farmhouse we shelled last week."

"So you managed to infiltrate the enemy outposts?"

"I did."

"Casualties?"

"None. I left my men behind and went on alone."

The commissar preserved an interminable silence. Another question? Another trap? Vittorin's temples throbbed. He clenched his teeth still harder to prevent them from chattering. Like every other joint in his body, his knees ached with dull insistence. He wouldn't be able to stand there for much longer, he could tell. Another few seconds, and –

"Very well," said the commissar. "I'll pass your report on."

It was eleven o'clock at night. A paraffin lamp was burning in the CO's office, and above it floated a dense grey cloud of tobacco smoke. Hanging on the wall were greatcoats, caps, a cartridge belt, and a carbine. A map lay spread out on the table, and running across it were two lines of flags, one red, one blue. On the far side of the blue flags, in the territory occupied by counter-revolutionary troops, lay a penknife and the CO's silver repeater.

Three men were sitting around the table, studying the map.

The regimental commander stood near the window, his right sleeve hanging limp at his side. The stove, which was almost out, crackled softly to itself. Seaman Stassik, commander of the first battalion, levelled his dead cigarette at the field telephone and vented his wrath on the staff officers at divisional headquarters.

"They're still arguing," he said with a scornful laugh. "First they've got to discuss the strategic and operational status of the entire front. One of them may even have made a suggestion, but the others will have pounced on him and cited half a dozen textbooks to prove that his plan is worthless. It's a straightforward military problem, but they peer at it through their glasses and see difficulties everywhere: it's the wrong time of year, the ground's flooded, the regiment can only muster eleven hundred rifles, the troops are inadequately equipped –"

"What's more," the regimental commander cut in, "the Whites have got barbed wire entanglements and machine-guns and their artillery is superior to ours. Add that and you'll have listed all the objections I put to the divisional chief of staff an hour ago."

Storoshev, the taciturn commander of the second battalion, nodded to signify that he shared the CO's misgivings. He disliked reckless gambles and favoured the delivery of well-prepared blows that were guaranteed to destroy the enemy. There was nothing impetuous about his brand of courage. Seaman Stassik was made of different stuff. Whether in action or at cards, with women or in argument, he always strove to clinch matters quickly. He laid his broad, red hand flat on the table and leant forward.

"Perhaps, comrade commander," he bellowed, "perhaps you also reported that our fraternal discipline was poor, and that our Red riflemen have refused to advance?"

"Our discipline is good," the CO said calmly, "but it takes more than fraternal discipline to render enemy positions ripe for assault."

Stassik eyed Storoshev across the table. "It almost sounds as if he wants Their White Excellencies to give us the slip," he muttered.

The one-armed captain had overheard. He flushed and took

two steps in Stassik's direction, but the regimental commissar forestalled him.

"Comrade," he told Stassik sternly, "the regimental commander must be treated with respect. I am jointly responsible for all his decisions. Unless you withdraw your imputation at once, I shall report this incident through official channels."

Seaman Stassik, who had captured two enemy guns at Valki in the thick of a fusillade, looked as sheepish as a scolded schoolboy. He started to say something, but the CO brushed his apology aside with a negligent gesture and resumed his post at the window. Just then the telephone rang. He picked it up.

"3rd Red Rifle Regiment, Penza Division. Commanding officer speaking."

He stood motionless with the receiver to his ear, staring at the coats and caps on the wall as if they were the source of the voice addressing him. A minute went by. Then he squared his shoulders and repeated the orders he had just been given:

"At 0600, fresh troops advancing from the direction of Yamnoye-Sobolevsk will mount a flank attack on the White Markov Brigade deployed between Zirky and Ivanovka. The 3rd Red Rifle Regiment will distract the enemy's attention by launching a diversionary attack at 0545."

The CO replaced the receiver. Turning to the regimental commissar and his two subordinates, he said, "You heard that. We must now make the necessary preparations. Your battalion, Comrade Stassik . . ."

The three men bent over the map without a word.

Trees and bushes detached themselves from the nocturnal gloom. Gradually, the sky above the paling hills became tinged with the light of dawn. Red Guards in sodden greatcoats crouched in their shallow, hurriedly dug foxholes, which were knee-deep in turbid yellow rainwater. The rifle bullets whistling over their heads made a sound like a whiplash whenever they struck stones or embedded themselves in tree-trunks. Artillery fire probed the terrain. First came a distant rumble like thunder, then a banshee wail that prompted everyone to hug the ground, and somewhere among the ploughed fields a brown geyser of earth would spurt into the air.

Vittorin peered over the low breastwork with his mud-caked entrenching tool held protectively above his head. An artillery duel was raging in the west. The enemy's heavy guns set up a continuous roar. Puffs of black and sulphurous yellow smoke appeared above the ridge. They belched forth fire and steel, but still the line of riflemen advanced. There was little to be seen but an endless succession of cotton wool cloudlets dispersed by the wind. Sometimes, too, tiny figures could be discerned. They raced down the slope, flung themselves to the ground and disappeared from view.

The issue would be decided over there, Vittorin knew. He shut his eyes, and his thoughts were instantly pervaded by dreamlike confusion. The scurrying figures were all in league with him. They had made his cause their own, so he could lie here and rest. A telegram bearing the Kremlin seal had arrived from Moscow at noon. "Message to all fronts: The following man is to be detained . . ."

Forward! There he stands in his riding breeches and patent leather boots, quirt in hand. He stands there all alone, but his face is invisible. No one can tell it's Selyukov because his shoulders are enveloped in a huge, sulphurous yellow cloud. "To be detained . . ." There they are already, the Red Guards, sprouting from the earth like mushrooms! They recognize him at last, converge from all directions and hem him in. He stands fast, though – he doesn't retreat. His breath is like fire, and the cloud around his shoulders emits a thunderous roar:

"Pashol!"

The thread of Vittorin's daydream snapped. He jumped as a piece of shrapnel whistled over his head: the shell had landed only ten yards short of his foxhole. A fierce fusillade was lashing the breastwork. When the rifle fire slackened for a moment or two, a figure materialized among some juniper bushes not far away. It sprinted, flung itself down, vanished into a furrow, reappeared. The man's face could now be seen.

It was Berezin. He sprinted another few yards, vaulted over the breastwork, and stretched out beside Vittorin, panting hard.

Berezin had been reconnoitring the approaches and knew the terrain. He got his breath back and proceeded to outline the situation.

"It doesn't look too good," he shouted above the din of battle. "We've pulled back on the right – the Whites are counterattacking. See those flares? Our people are calling for artillery support."

Berezin produced a notebook from his pocket and jotted down a message. He drew a rough sketch-map and marked the position of two enemy machine-guns he'd spotted, then tore out the sheet and handed it to Vittorin. His men were waiting for him in a nearby shell crater. Cautiously, he climbed out of the foxhole and crawled across the bullet-lashed ground until he vanished among the juniper bushes as suddenly as he had appeared.

The platoon commander had dug in behind the point at which the firing line formed an obtuse angle. He was a flaxen-haired youngster with a soft and girlish complexion that had earned him the nickname "Sonyechka" in the regiment, but he had spent seven months at the front and risen from the rank of bugler to that of platoon officer.

Vittorin handed him Berezin's message. Sonyechka read it and refolded the slip of paper. Then he scanned the enemy lines through his binoculars.

"We must silence those machine-guns," Vittorin urged him in a hoarse voice.

Sonyechka deposited the binoculars on the ground beside him and shook his head.

"That's a job for the artillery," he said. "You look like Satan on Christmas Eve, comrade. Are you sick?"

"Fever, but the MO and I have jointly decided to ignore it," Vittorin replied. He made a feeble attempt to smile, but the next moment his features resumed their tense, fanatical expression. His feverish brain had become obsessed with the idea that his platoon must occupy the village and cut off Selyukov's line of retreat. "We can't just go on lying here," he went on. "Our offensive has been checked. Why don't we take the initiative and attack?"

"I've received no such order," Sonyechka replied. "The lie of the land isn't good: three hundred yards of rising ground and no cover. We'll stay put till the rain washes us away, you mark my words. Hey, comrade!" He beckoned to a man in the firing line. "Take this and run like hell. Deliver it to battalion headquarters."

He rose and handed the man the slip of paper.

Vittorin had also risen. "So you won't advance?" he hissed between his clenched teeth. "You're scared. No wonder they gave you a girl's nickname!"

But Sonyechka didn't hear. A ricochet had severed the great artery in his thigh. His face went limp and he collapsed, scrabbling at the ground.

"Battalion headquarters," he repeated in a whisper. "I'm done for, comrade, take command. Don't waste ammunition, return fire only when attacked. Our present line . . ."

The breath began to rattle in his throat. He tried to tear open his coat with both hands. Then his head fell back and he lay still.

"Stretcher-bearer!" Vittorin shouted, but the medical orderly and his assistant were nowhere to be seen.

The soldier bent over Sonyechka and unbuttoned his great-coat and tunic. "No need for a stretcher, comrade," he said. "He'll never dance at another wedding. His troubles are over."

And he proceeded to pull off the dead man's boots. The bullet that had hit Sonyechka decided the fate of the entire platoon. Vittorin sprang to his feet.

"Comrades," he cried, "I'm in command now. We're going to advance – we're going to annihilate those traitors over there. The proletarian Fatherland demands it. The proletarian Fatherland is in danger. Comrades, save Russia!"

There was no answering voice. The Red Army veterans surveyed the open country ahead of them with an experienced eye. Any movement, however small, would be spotted by the enemy, yet they obeyed. Silently, they prepared to advance.

"Fix bayonets!" Vittorin commanded.

A faint rattle ran down the line. Silence fell, broken only by the whine of bullets. And then, quite suddenly, a song went up from the doomed men's ranks. One of them softly hummed it and the others joined in. Their voices gained strength, rising heavenward like a chorale, until they were all singing in unison:

> Where are you rolling, little apple?
> You will ne'er come back again.
> There'll be listed dead tomorrow
> a hundred more Red Army men.

"Forward!" yelled Vittorin, and their voices were drowned by the roar of exploding shells.

Very few of the attackers managed to penetrate the enemy's withering fire. Half-way to the village, the insane assault collapsed. Hemmed in on both sides, the Reds held out for a while behind the hedges and trees of a small orchard. When their cartridges were gone they withdrew to a shell-shattered farmhouse with the carcass of a big, shaggy dog sprawled outside the door. Here they fought off the enemy one last time with hand-grenades and rifle butts. A few minutes later, when the roof caught fire, they decided to surrender.

One of the prisoners who staggered out of the building, half stupefied by the smoke from the smouldering debris, was Vittorin.

He was now lying in the yard of the devastated sugar factory whose smoke-blackened walls, when they loomed out of the mist that morning, had seemed so mysterious and unattainably remote, as if they marked the boundary of another world. So there he lay, and huddled against the wall with weary, despairing or apathetic faces lay the other survivors of the charge. Two sentries in the uniform of the Kuban Cossacks stood leaning on their carbines in the middle of the yard while a third sat perched on the shaft of a farm cart, playing his accordion.

Vittorin's adventure was at an end. He had planned to confront Selyukov as a free man with his head held high, but no, fate had forbidden it and flung him back into Chernavyensk Camp. The wheel had come full circle: he was a prisoner and Selyukov his master once more. It was inevitable, preordained. A sick, prostrate, defenceless prisoner – that was what fate wanted him to be on the day of reckoning.

But no, he wasn't as defenceless as he'd been at Chernavyensk. There his thoughts had centred on his home and family and a grand reunion, but that was all behind him and had come to nothing. Now that he had sampled all the terrors of the age, life meant nothing to him any more. If Selyukov came now, he was ready for him.

He pictured his confrontation with Selyukov. There he was with the Order of Vladimir and St George's Cross on his chest. Do you remember me, Mikhail Mikhailovich? Yes, Selyukov remembered him. He knew what awaited him and turned pale. Vittorin drove his fist into Selyukov's arrogant face, imprinted as it was with all the vices in the world and all the evils of an atrocious age. Another blow, and another. Selyukov staggered back and drew his sabre, but he, Vittorin, was no longer there. Chernavyensk Camp had been abolished long ago, so where was he now? In a farmhouse with sunflowers and white roses painted on its wooden shutters. Before the door, denying access to all comers, lay a shaggy dog. "He's dead, and he guards the dead," said a voice that sounded strangely like an accordion. What was the source of this pain that kept boring into his head and chest? Bullets were zipping past. He knelt down behind a wood-pile and fired back, and suddenly Berezin was beside him, his face convulsed with anger. "Who gave the order to advance, you? Why did you do it?" – "Why? Because I had to. It was preordained, don't you see? All the vices in the world are imprinted on that face . . ."

Vittorin's leaden eyelids drooped. Dreams came and bore him off. They hauled him through icy torrents and across burning desert sands, swept him up into whirlwinds and down into murky depths. Then, wearying of him, they released their grip and he drifted up into the light of day.

An order rang out across the factory yard.

"On your feet! Fall in!"

Sleep and pain deserted Vittorin like leeches that have drunk their fill. The time had come. He stood up ramrod straight. The other prisoners formed a line on either side of him.

"Commissars, Red officers and enrolled Communists, forward march!" ordered the sergeant.

Vittorin and four others stepped forward. A sixth man followed after a moment's hesitation. The remaining prisoners closed up behind them.

"Halt!"

They halted. The man beside Vittorin muttered, "They're going to shoot us, all six of us, that's for sure. So be it. Let them plough me over if they must." He nudged Vittorin in the ribs. "There he is!"

"Who?" Vittorin whispered.

"The Whistler. Here he comes, the swine, don't you see him?"

"Twenty-seven prisoners, Your Excellency," they heard the sergeant say. "Six of them are enrolled Communists."

A curtain of red mist descended on Vittorin's eyes, and through it he saw the face of his devilish quarry. He uttered a cry and lurched forward.

"Mikhail Mikhailovich, do you remember me?"

The officer turned his head and saw one of the prisoners tottering toward him like a drunken man. He raised his revolver, then lowered it again.

"You?" he exclaimed. "For heaven's sake, how do you come to be with these people? Have you turned Bolshevik?"

"Turned Bolshevik," Vittorin repeated. He couldn't grasp where Selyukov had gone or why another man had taken his place – a man whose face he knew. It was Captain Stackelberg, who had shared his quarters at Novokhlovinsk. What did he want, and where was Selyukov?

"Tell me the truth, for God's sake!" Stackelberg cried. "Did they compel you to go to the front? Why are you fighting against Russia?"

"I volunteered," Vittorin said haltingly. He gazed past Stackelberg in search of Selyukov but failed to find him. Selyukov had vanished.

"Very well," Stackelberg said, "you may go. A Russian officer keeeps his word, even to the likes of you. You may go, I haven't forgotten. You're free, understand? You may go."

Vittorin understood. He took a step forward, but the strength that had sustained him until now was exhausted. He swayed and fell headlong, and darkness and silence descended on him.

The sergeant ripped open his greatcoat and tunic.

"I thought as much, Your Excellency," he said. "The Reds are sending us typhus now. He's already got the rash on his chest."

Stackelberg turned away with a look of disgust.

"Contaminated inside and out," he said. "Typhus and Bolshevism, it's all the same. Take him away."

But a moment later he recalled that the human wreck on the ground at his feet had once, in days gone by, been his friend.

"To the lime pit, Your Excellency?" inquired the sergeant.

"No," said Captain Stackelberg, "to the hospital at Lebedin."

And the harsh, angry note in his voice was that of someone ashamed of an involuntary remark, a secret thought, or an unbidden tear.

WHERE THE APPLE ROLLED

From his bed Vittorin could see the bare branches of an acacia and a little patch of sky thick with snow clouds. His recollections were hazy: muddled, terrifying dreams, thirst, Sonyechka's death, agonizing sensations of fear, a tune played on a piano accordion, a red mist, a buzzing in the ears, piping hot bath-water. His encounter with the cavalry captain from Novokhlovinsk had completely vanished from his memory.

The nurse told him that he had been in the isolation ward for three weeks, that two Kuban Cossacks had brought him in at four one morning, and that a sealed envelope had been left for him. The doctors had predicted the very day on which his fever quickly subsided, she said, and the brown blotches on his hands were nothing to worry about. She also assured him that his clothes and papers would be returned in due course.

That was as much as she could tell him, nor did the envelope provide any explanation of the events immediately preceding his admission to hospital. All it contained were two hundred French francs in small notes.

In the days that followed Vittorin had time to debate his future course of action. The hunt for Selyukov was still on. He realized that he had gone astray – followed a false trail. Now he must begin all over again. Far from being disheartened, he knew precisely what he had to do and could hardly wait for the day when he would be discharged. It came sooner than he expected.

Russia's fate was sealed at the end of December. Red troops had captured Novocherkask in the east and Balta and Tiraspol in the west. Although the White front continued to hold out between Poltava and Kharkov, plans for a withdrawal were in preparation at General Denikin's headquarters.

The hospital was evacuated early in January. While the White regiments streamed south toward the Crimea and the Caucasus, there to make one last stand on behalf of their doomed cause, Vittorin headed for the village of Staromyena, which lay south of the Donets in the Government of Kharkov.

"Grisha, Selyukov's orderly," he had written in his notebook. "Grigory Osipovich Kedrin (Kadrin?) from the village of Staromyena, Glavyask Railway Station, Government of Kharkov."

It was late in the afternoon when Vittorin reached his destination. The village of Staromyena straggled interminably along both sides of the highroad, which was as wide as a river. Rooks fluttered over snow-covered vegetable gardens, cawing harshly. Beyond the houses loomed the kiln and smokestack of the brick works where Selyukov's orderly had worked before the war. Vittorin questioned the village headman, a lanky, bearded peasant.

"Grigory Osipovich Kedrin? Yes, I know him, but he isn't here. He's serving as some officer's orderly. Last year, on the feast-day of the Ten Holy Martyrs of Crete, he came back from the Great Patriotic War and kicked up a rumpus because Asya Timofeevna had married the blacksmith. He beat her and set about the blacksmith as well. Drink, that was the main reason – he turned up here drunk, so I stuck him in the lockup till his mother came to collect him. The less said about liquor the better, though. They all drink like fish in this place."

He went on to inveigh bitterly against the inhabitants of Staromyena, who had secretly elected a village council and were only waiting for the Bolsheviks' arrival to kick him out.

"Today they cross themselves, but tomorrow they'll be spitting on their icons. God sowed the world with ten bushels of evil, and nine of them were harvested by the peasants of Staromyena. Grisha's a ne'er-do-well like all the rest. Yes, his mother still lives here. He sent her a letter – maybe she knows where he is. I'll take you to her, Excellency."

They found the old peasant woman standing at her cottage door, feeding the hens. It being Sunday, she was wearing a headscarf. Her face lit up when she heard that a gentleman from the city had come to see her son.

"Yes, Grisha's my boy," she told Vittorin. "I brought him up to the glory of God. Be gracious enough to come in, Your Excellency."

The interior of the cottage smelt of sour milk and damp firewood, pickled herring and boiled potatoes. A startled goose emerged from behind the table and flew at Vittorin, craning its neck and hissing angrily. Fast asleep on top of the stove lay a grizzled old peasant with a hare-skin cap pulled down over his ears. A little oil lamp of blue glass was burning in front of a faded picture of St Sergius.

'He wrote to me, but it was quite a while ago," the old woman said. "I saw the postman coming with his leather satchel. He called to me from a long way off. 'Agrafena Matveevna,' he shouted, 'there's a letter for you.' I went all weak at the knees as I took it. 'Where can he be?' I said to myself. 'He may not even have a corner to sleep and pray in.' Then I went and fetched Panteley, the sexton's son, who can read books and letters. He's the night watchman at the brick works."

She bent to pull up one of her red cotton stockings, which had slid down.

"My son Grigory Osipovich wrote in his letter that I was to sell the horse and the sleigh, but the officers had already taken the horse and the oats as well. They paid me in bad roubles. In the old days everything had its proper price, but today you have to take what you're given. 'Don't worry, I'll be back,' my son wrote, 'but not even I can tell when that will be. Look after the house, mother dear, and be careful with money.' He also wrote about the rain and the cold, and how there were Turks as well true believers in the city where he and his officer were living, and how the city was beside the sea, and he asked if I'd found his watch."

The old woman couldn't remember the name of the city. She opened the kitchen table drawer and proceeded to rummage in it for the letter. All that came to light were some slices of dried apple, a bunch of cockerel's feathers, a faded photograph of Grisha's father, a broken looking glass, a "Flight from Egypt" painted on wood, some copper coins, two clay pipes, a paper bag that emitted a cloud of plaster, a leather belt, and a battered frying pan.

"Holy Mother of God!" the old woman wailed. "It isn't here! Forgive me, Your Honour, I can't find it. I don't know where it can have got to."

The letter was eventually unearthed between the folds of a babushka at the bottom of a chest in which Grisha's mother kept tea, sugar and wax candles. One glance at the back of the envelope told Vittorin all he needed to know. Selyukov and his orderly were lodging with a merchant named Karabadian in the Kutaiskaya quarter of Batum.

"So that's where the Devil has taken him off to," said the village headman, wagging his head. "Batum? I've never heard of the place, Excellency, but you could ask the priest. He has a book that lists every city in the world."

Vittorin explained that he knew where Batum was and hoped to be there in three days' time. In his imagination he was already homeward bound. Russia lay behind him. Batum was just a minor detour, nothing more. Fate had smiled on him for once.

The old woman felt beneath the bolster on her bed and brought out a cheap copper-and-zinc watch.

"Your Excellency, gracious sir," she said, "if you see Grisha, give him this watch. It belongs to him. He left in a huff because he couldn't find it. I trust you to give it to him, Excellency. And tell him I can manage for hay and bread till March, but then I'll have to sell a sheep. The blacksmith's wife has run off, tell him, and tell him I sit here and pine for him.

I've bought a new sieve, but I don't have anyone to dig the garden for me. Tell him that too, will you?"

She accompanied Vittorin as far as the church, where his sleigh was waiting. The bell was tolling for evening service, and the women outside were crossing themselves. Vittorin climbed aboard and wrapped himself in a rug. It was twelve versts from Staromyena to the station. The village headman, who had been expecting a tip, scratched his neck and said nothing.

"His godfather, Gavrila Ivanich Shikulin, is dead. I don't have anyone to dig the garden for me. They took the blacksmith away for selling stolen horses. Tell Grisha I'm being careful with money . . ."

It was noon, and the heat was becoming unbearable. The cries of the street traders selling fruit, sherbets, baklava and pistachio cakes had lost a little of their shrill persistence. Vittorin, standing on the Sultan Validé Bridge that linked Galata with Stamboul, had at last spotted the *Aurora*, a steamer flying the Greek flag, a white St George's cross on a blue ground. The *Aurora* was sailing for Trieste at seven tomorrow morning and would be calling at Brindisi, so the shipping clerk had informed him. A berth in steerage without food cost sixty lire. Steerage passengers aboard Greek steamers were expected to feed themselves.

Vittorin had neither money nor passport. He'd lost all his money at cards last night – seventeen francs and half a Turkish pound wouldn't have been enough in any case – but today he would win, he felt sure. Sixty lire were all he needed. You could survive quite well for a week on bread and cigarettes. He knew; he'd done it.

What worried him far more was how to get hold of his travel documents by seven tomorrow. He had two passports and a Russian refugee pass issued by the Entente Commission at Batum, but Lucette had taken charge of all his papers and refused to hand them over. When he'd mentioned yesterday that he might have to go away – only for a day or two, and it wasn't absolutely definite – she'd made a terrible scene: tears, reproaches, it would be abominable of him to walk out on her now, he was the cruellest man alive, et cetera. Every waiter in the damned hotel had gathered in the corridor to listen.

Lucette was young and pretty and a dancer. She could have found a hundred lovers to take his place, but she disliked the Greeks with their "twelve-sous cologne" and detested "all these Levantines, who never wash". She would never willingly let him go, that much was certain.

Vittorin had searched their room this morning, while she was still asleep. He'd found the walnut casket in the wardrobe and stealthily, furtively slid the key from under her pillow, but all it contained was the business correspondence of the three "Toledo Girls"; letters from their Milan agent, letters from the owners of seedy nightclubs in Galati, Smyrna, Athens, Alexandria and Port Said; newspaper cuttings adorned with pictures of the trio; crumpled ribbons; withered flowers; and a whole bundle of letters signed "Pancrace". Pancrace . . . Ethel and Adèle, Lucette's fellow *danseuses*, had often mentioned a man of that name. Vittorin had no idea who he was or exactly what role he had played in Lucette's life; he only knew that the name was familiar.

His papers weren't there, however. Lucette had obviously hidden them elsewhere in the room. They must be wherever she kept her jewellery.

It was half-past twelve, and Lucette liked him to keep her company while she breakfasted. He would be late if he didn't hurry. The funicular would have got him to Pera in ten minutes, but he didn't have the twenty paras – last night had cleaned him out. Lucette rose at one. She smoked an Abra cigarette after breakfast, then took a bath. After that she played patience or amused herself with Ethel's pet parrot. Such was Lucette's day. If Lupescu called – the Rumanian owner of the Café Élysée, where the Toledo Girls were playing – she received him in a housecoat buttoned up to the neck. He didn't get to see much, poor man.

Vittorin had met Lucette in Batum. He'd earned just enough

that day, by working as a porter at the dock, to treat himself to a meal at a cheap café on Mariinsky Prospekt. A sudden downpour had prompted the three Toledo Girls to take refuge in the same scruffy establishment, and that was his first encounter with Lucette. Now he was doing all right. His lean days were over. He played the violin at the Café Élysée. Lucette contrived to get him a job in the band wherever she was appearing. When the Toledo Girls danced at night – whether as Spanish gipsies, exotic butterflies, priestesses of the God Shiva, or monocled dandies in dickies – he would look up from his score and follow Lucette's every movement. Even after so many weeks in her company, it still amazed him to reflect that such a woman belonged to him and no one else. When they were alone together and he held her lithe, supple body in a close embrace, he had to keep telling himself that she was Lucie d'Aubry, the dancer on whom a hundred pairs of lustful male eyes rested nightly at the Café Élysée. And when she lay in his arms with her eyelids drooping and her lips parted, silent and drained of energy, her voice and laughter seemed to ring in his ears.

He must go, for all that. It hadn't been an easy decision. He couldn't conceive of life without Lucette, but his self-imposed mission demanded a final sacrifice. When the Selyukov business was settled he would go back to her. Constantinople, Ruschuk, Smyrna – he would find Lucette wherever she was. He wouldn't leave her again.

He hadn't found Selyukov in Batum. Selyukov had left for Constantinople five months earlier, and Vittorin had followed him there. He'd inquired after him in every hotel in the city, in luxury restaurants and humble eating-houses, in bars, cafés and brasseries, in the seedy nightspots of Galata and the gambling hells of Pera. For three days now, he'd known that Selyukov was in Rome.

Rome, Via Nazionale, Hôtel Royal des Étrangers – that was where he would find the man. He no longer saw Selyukov as an arrogant Russian officer who had insulted him. Selyukov was the evil personification of a degenerate age. He was the medium through which Vittorin hated everything sordid that met his eye – all the crooks, currency speculators and human predators that had shared out the world between them. Constantinople under Allied occupation was swarming with these shady creatures, overflowing with men whose fingerprints were on file at police headquarters. Their vile, greedy, bloated faces were to be seen everywhere. They made money out of war, politics, espionage. While General Wrangel's army was putting up a last stand in the Crimea, they were profiting behind the scenes. They haggled, they cheated, they supplied both Whites and Reds with saddlery, horseshoe nails, revolver holsters, cleaning rag, axle grease, cans of tainted bully beef. They belonged to the highest bidder, and champagne flowed wherever they did business.

They were numerous, invulnerable and ubiquitous – in Paris, in Bucharest, in Vladivostock. Vittorin could avenge the humanity they were betraying, the world they had polluted, by exterminating just one of them, and his name was Selyukov.

The city streets were incandescent with heat. Vittorin had now reached the Grande Rue de Pera. Down in Galata, police duties were undertaken by carabinieri, but up here British bobbies held sway in blue and white armbands. On the terrace of the Hôtel de Londres, British and Greek officers rubbed shoulders with crooks, parasites and vultures of indeterminate nationality, not to mention their painted and bedizened womenfolk. The latter, too, were for sale if the price was right: to such men, pimping was a trade like any other.

The buildings flew the flags of the victorious Allies. Not a fez or tarboosh could be seen on the street. Strangers in their own capital city, the Turks remained indoors.

The members of the Café Élysée's floor show were housed on the first floor of a small hotel. In front of it, swinging his cane and puffing at a cigarette that dangled from the corner of his mouth, stood a young man with an effeminate face and flaxen hair slicked back on either side of a centre parting. He greeted Vittorin by raising two fingers briefly to the peak of his sports cap. Vittorin was reminded by this touch of familiarity that they had met at cards last night. Uneasily, he wondered what the man was doing outside his hotel. He might have lost all his money, but he didn't owe a centime, so what did Goldilocks want?

Goldilocks didn't appear to want anything. He turned and sauntered off down the street, swinging his cane.

Vittorin could hear Lucette's irate voice half-way up the stairs. He found on entering their room that Monsieur Lupescu had shoehorned his bulky frame into an armchair, in which defenceless position he was having to endure a torrent of insults and reproaches.

"I don't know how you have the gall to show your face here," Lucette snarled at him, quivering with indignation. "Some nerve, I must say, breezing in as if nothing had happened! You obviously make a habit of getting your friends in the press to vilify an artiste who takes her profession seriously. They're scum, those people, one and all!"

Monsieur Lupescu's face wore the look of a frightened rabbit. He was feeling guilty. Although the piece in the *Courrier de Pera* to which Lucette took exception had been inspired and paid for by him, he had unwisely neglected to check it before publication. Because he felt guilty, he strove to mollify the star of his floor show by half-agreeing with her.

"His write-up was a little on the skimpy side, I must admit."

But that only made matters worse.

"Skimpy?" Lucette said furiously. "*Skimpy*, did you say? No, monsieur, no one could have injected more venom into two short sentences. It's vile and infamous, and you choose to call it skimpy. What's more, to crown everything, you stick up for the swine. There, read it yourself, if you really enjoy seeing an artiste assassinated in print!"

She swooped hawklike on the newspaper, which was lying crumpled on the floor, smoothed it out with her fingertips, and held the review, which she already knew by heart, under Monsieur Lupescu's nose.

"Go on, read it and then have the effrontery to say another word in defence of that contemptible creature. Fine friends you have, monsieur! There: 'the programme also' – *also!* – 'featured the Toledo Girls. They gave of their best and were likewise –' *likewise!* – 'well received.' It's outrageous. In your place, I'd be ashamed!"

"The *Courrier de Pera* is an unimportant financial paper," said the owner of the Café Élysée, very apologetically. "Nobody reads it."

"Just because nobody reads what he writes, that man has absolutely no right to insult me in such a vile way. He must have been born and bred in the gutter, and you can tell him so from me if he ever has the nerve to show his face again. Was he by any chance a tall, thin streak of a fellow with a goatee beard and horn-rimmed glasses?"

She remembered seeing one of her fellow artistes, Ida Morrison, the Café Élysées's soubrette, in the company of a man with a goatee and horn-rims, but it hadn't dawned on her till now that he was a journalist.

"I've no idea who wrote the piece, I assure you," Monsieur Lupescu insisted.

"No idea, eh? You heard nothing, saw nothing, noticed nothing. You seriously expect me to believe that? Don't play the innocent! There's something behind this and you know it – you're no fool – but it amuses you to see me treated like dirt. Anyway, why are you sitting there like a monkey in a sideshow? Are you really so keen to waste my time? Go on, get out. I'm sick of the sight of you!"

She slammed the door on the hapless Monsieur Lupescu and turned to Vittorin with a beaming smile.

"He genuinely doesn't know who wrote the piece. He doesn't know a thing, but it's important to show him occasionally that I'm not to be trifled with. It was the Morrison girl, I've worked it out. She played this trick on Lupescu because he's not renewing her contract. Heaven knows what the fellow from the newspaper sees in her, the ugly bitch. He didn't do it for free, that's obvious."

"I don't find her particularly likeable," Vittorin broke in, "but you can't call her ugly."

Lucette threw him a pitying glance over her shoulder.

"I never knew your taste in women was so vulgar," she said. "*Mon pauvre garçon*, she's got arms like a coolie and a complexion like raspberry juice. If you fancy getting together with her, you need only say. Every man deserves the woman of his choice."

She went to the window and looked down into the street. Suddenly she gave a low cry.

"What's the matter?" asked Vittorin.

"Nothing," she said quickly. "A mosquito bit me, that's all. There's a storm brewing, the sky's gone all dark. We'd better close the shutters – no, don't bother, I'll do it myself."

Lucette had seen her former lover down below – seen and recognized him even though he hadn't looked in her direction. His build, his sports cap, his pearl-grey gloves and the way he swung his cane – all these were unmistakable. Her hands trembled as she closed the shutters. She'd known he was in the city, but she hadn't seen him till now. She still belonged to him in spirit, but common sense forbade her to live with a man who had treated her badly, robbed her, deceived her, and spent her money on other women. He was there, prowling around the hotel, watching and waiting for an opportunity to accost her. Feeling a trifle frightened – frightened of herself as well as him – she sought refuge with Vittorin. She stole up to him as softly as a cat, stroked his hair and rested her head on his shoulder.

"Do you still remember the little café in Batum?" she asked. "It was nice, wasn't it, our first meeting? For you it may be only a dim and distant memory, but I often think of it. I saw you, and I knew at once how things were with you, and that you didn't have two kopecks to rub together, but I didn't care. I thought you were a Russian officer. I don't know what appealed to me about you – perhaps it was the uniform, or perhaps . . . '*Comme tes yeux sont grands . . .*' Remember? You were humming the tune to yourself, and I knew it was the start of something. I was the one that spoke first, *mon petit*, in case you'd forgotten. I'm not sorry I did, are you? Well, are you?"

Without a word, he drew her close and put his arms around her. She shut her eyes.

"You really must lock the door when we . . ." she said softly. "You never remember, *mon petit*. I always have to remind you."

At one a.m., when the last customers had gone and the waiters were noisily stacking the tables and chairs, Vittorin had an interview with the owner of the Café Élysée. It took place in the dressing-room where Fred Musty, the resident comic, was removing his makeup with the aid of vaseline. After a long argument to which Musty contributed certain financial demands of his own, Vittorin obtained an advance of fifteen francs instead of the twenty he'd asked for.

With the money in his pocket he set off along Pera's main thoroughfare, then turned off down the small, unlit side street that led to the naval hospital. Outside a single-storeyed building he paused and rang the bell.

Although the Entente Commission had ordained that all places of public entertainment in Pera, Fondoukli, Top Hané and Galata should close at one a.m., there were one or two clandestine establishments where customers could while away the night behind locked doors. The bar-keeper who admitted Vittorin made his living out of a clientèle that turned up after one a.m.

There they were again around the table, the same peculiar types with whom Vittorin had played cards all last night. Jewel smugglers, perhaps, or cocaine dealers, or deserters from some ship – who could tell?

The little man with the wrinkled face and the massive watch chain was known as Coco. The broad-shouldered one who had just bellowed for a rum-and-kümmel went by the name of Buster. The bank was held by Weasel, a scrawny fellow with a sallow face and a squashed nose. The fair-haired man whom Vittorin had seen outside the hotel was also there. Goldilocks seemed to favour a more refined life-style than the roughnecks around him: he was drinking Greek champagne and smoking a Cercle du Bosphore. The cramped room reeked of liquor, violet pomade, musk, and "Maryland" tobacco. Little notice was taken of Vittorin's arrival. Play was already in progress.

Vittorin punted cautiously to begin with. A player with only fifteen francs in his pocket had to husband his resources. He only took the whole of the bank for the first few coups. If he lost, he passed next time. If the banker twice in a row drew the card known as *"le brutal"*, because it beat all the rest, Vittorin declined to stake on the principle that luck of that order was unassailable. By three a.m. he had doubled his capital. A quarter of an hour later he was down to his last three francs. At four he was within a whisker of the sum that would have enabled him to retire from the game. By four forty-five he had lost everything.

"God, it's hot in here," said the man nicknamed Buster. "Like an engine-room, it is. Let's make ourselves comfortable. If we open the window the landlord will have the police breathing down his neck."

He removed his jacket and played on in his shirtsleeves. Weasel, who followed suit, revealed that his right forearm was adorned with an elaborate tattoo comprising a crescent moon, a clenched fist, a creature resembling a hare, and a girl's head. Coco threw down his cards, pointed to the eight of hearts, and cried triumphantly, *"Oh là là!* Just in the nick of time, *monsieur le timide!"*

He had won the coup. Weasel pushed two crumpled notes across the table. "You wait," he muttered with grim determination.

The fair-haired man turned to Vittorin.

"Aren't you punting any more?"

Vittorin shook his head. "I'm out of cash," he said. He meant to sound off-hand, but his voice clearly betrayed how embarrassed he was and how eager to play on. "If the bank would advance me fifteen francs . . ."

"Very sorry," said Coco, who held the bank, "I don't accept coups on credit."

The fair-haired man lit another cigarette.

"Please allow me to help you out," he said. "Here are twenty francs."

Vittorin stared at him in surprise. "Thanks anyway," he said, "but I may lose. If I do, I'm not sure I'll be able to pay you back right away." The twenty-franc note was already in his hand.

"You won't lose," the fair-haired man said firmly. "Why not hock your jacket?"

"My jacket?" said Vittorin. "Is that meant to be a joke?"

"No, I'm quite serious. We all do it when we're going through a bad patch. It brings you luck, see? Sometimes there's a sort of jinx on me. I lose and go on losing for hours. Then I hock my jacket and my luck changes."

"What the hell!" Vittorin exclaimed. "All right, I'll try it. Here, take the thing."

Goldilocks smiled as he took Vittorin's jacket and put it on the chair beside him. Play continued.

They stopped playing at half-past five in the morning. Milk and vegetable carts could be heard in the street, and daylight was creeping through the chinks and knotholes in the shutters.

Vittorin had thirty francs – not enough for a steerage ticket, and nothing else mattered. He wanted to settle his debt, but the fair-haired man wasn't there. Vittorin had been too intent on the game to notice his disappearance an hour earlier.

He retrieved his jacket. Coco and Weasel were at the counter drinking black coffees paid for by Buster, who had won. The landlord opened the door. From the public gardens came a cool breeze laden with the scent of grass and acacia leaves.

They swiftly shook hands on the corner of Kabristan Street – "So long, see you tonight!" – and went their separate ways.

Vittorin was upstairs in the hotel corridor before he disco-

179

vered the loss of his room key. He rummaged in his pockets. Where could it have gone? Had it fallen out somewhere? Should he go back to the bar and look for it, or hunker down outside the door and wait for Lucette to wake and let him in? He was dog-tired. He wanted to sleep and lose himself in oblivion. He would have to wake Lucette – he hadn't any choice. He knocked, softly at first, then louder.

Not a sound came from inside, but the door of the adjoining room opened. Vittorin turned. It was Ethel, the English member of the Toledo Girls. Her face conveyed a mixture of surprise and indignation.

"So it's you, is it? What are you doing here? You're a nice one, you are – a real beauty and no mistake. What do you want?"

"What do I want? I want to go to bed, of course."

"You devil you, living on women! What did you get for that key? How much did he pay you for it?"

"Pay me? Who? What are you talking about?"

"You rotter! How much did that Monsewer Pancrace pay you to hand over the key?"

"Pancrace?" Vittorin looked appalled. "Would he be a fair-haired fellow with a face like a girl?"

"It was a low-down thing to do. You ought to be ashamed of yourself."

"He must have sneaked it out of my pocket."

"And you never noticed, eh? Don't give me that! Hey, what are you doing?"

Vittorin was furiously rattling the locked door. Ethel emitted a scornful little laugh.

"What's the idea? Fancy a threesome, do you? He's in there with her – turned up an hour ago. She screamed, called for help. Then they made it up. You'd better go."

Vittorin let go of the doorhandle and stared at the floor.

"If they've made it up," he said, "that cuts me out – there's no point in my staying. All right, I'll go, but what about my things?"

Ethel disappeared into her room. She returned with his

papers and the knapsack that had accompanied him to Russia and back.

"All the best," she said. "I'm not worried about you. With your looks and your talent, you'll always find some woman to live off."

He didn't answer. There was something tucked into his passport. Opening it, he found a hundred-franc note and a slip of paper inscribed *"Clear off!"*

Rage welled up inside him – rage mingled with a painful sense of loss and a burning desire to call the man out and drive his fist into that smooth-skinned, womanish face, but the thought of Selyukov outweighed all else. The *Aurora* was sailing an hour from now. If he hurried he would get there in time. He pocketed his passport, together with the money and farewell note.

"Give Lucette my regards," he told Ethel. "I didn't do it, but never mind."

He left with the feeling that he really had done it – and he had, now that he'd taken the hundred francs, but he didn't care. There were some things more important than Monsieur Pancrace.

An hour later the *Aurora* sailed slowly out of harbour with Vittorin on board. He stared wide-eyed at the city in which he'd been living. He surveyed its terraced gardens and minarets, its green-domed mosques and white marble palaces, its ancient, cypress-shaded cemeteries, its massive walls and gates; all this he saw – saw for the very first time – just as he was leaving it behind.

From Rome Selyukov's trail led to Milan, where it petered out. The ex-captain and his manservant had spent four days at a small *pensione* in the Via Cappelari, but Vittorin was unable to trace their movements thereafter.

Having run out of money, he was compelled to suspend his investigations and look for work. Life's squalls and tempests swept him along from place to place. In Genoa he worked as a waterfront coal-heaver, in Barcelona he addressed envelopes, in Narbonne he became an assistant house-painter. Time went by. Vittorin made all kinds of discoveries: that a man could live on cheese rinds and rotten fruit when work was scarce; that trains existed for travellers other than those with tickets; that in certain humble hostelries a piece of bread and a glass of wine could be purchased with cigarette-ends gleaned from the pavements by day. Sometimes, when your harvest of butts was plentiful, you could even get a morsel of salt meat, but those occasions were few and far between.

At Toulon his knapsack was stolen, at Marseilles he spent two weeks in jail. He became acquainted with the bread soup doled out by charity hostels and the stench of the sulphur fumes they used to disinfect the clothes of the homeless. Selyukov seemed infinitely remote. For all Vittorin knew, he might be in Algiers, Geneva, or Buenos Aires.

Then came the incident that changed Vittorin's fortunes and restored the freedom of movement denied him by his daily fight for survival: he was knocked down by a car on the Boulevard de la Corderie. The driver, an American, not only took him to a hospital but left enough money to cover his treatment and compensate him for his injuries. Several ribs had been fractured and both his arms were badly lacerated. When he left the hospital four weeks later, he was handed six hundred francs.

He set off for Paris the same day.

Wherever Selyukov was, one possible means of ascertaining his address did exist. In Paris, so Vittorin had learned from a fellow patient, newspapers were published by Russian émigrés of various political persuasions: ultra-conservatives, liberal monarchists, the Cadet Party, champions of armed intervention in Russia, advocates of reconciliation with the Soviets, Mensheviks, Social Revolutionaries – even a small group of Russian anarchists styling themselves "non-party". Every Russian refugee sought to keep in touch with his homeland and his scattered circle of friends by subscribing to at least one of these periodicals.

One bleak winter's morning Vittorin presented himself at the offices of *Pozledniye Nvosti*, a newspaper edited by Pavel Milyukov. It was his eleventh such attempt, but this time he was in luck. Mikhail Mikhailovich Selyukov's name appeared on the subscribers' list, and the paper had been mailed to him at the same address for the last eight months. The address in question: Apartment 16, 2nd Floor, 124 Währinger Gürtel, Vienna.

Vienna . . . He could have stayed put and waited – he could have walked down the street one day, turned a corner, and . . . He needn't have lifted a finger.

The clerk in the subscription department looked up in surprise when he heard Vittorin's hoarse, mirthless bark of laughter.

"I'm sorry," Vittorin said, gritting his teeth, "but it really is hilarious. Typhus, lice, starvation, war, imprisonment. Across Russia, half-way round Europe, through hell on earth in all its forms. I've slept on rotting straw and evaded arrest in Moscow. My comrades were shot in that accursed sugar factory. Marseille! Constantinople! I've rubbed shoulders with criminals from every corner of the earth, when all I really need have done, I see that now, was . . . Can you blame me for laughing?"

He fell silent and stared dully at the flickering gas jet.

"I don't understand," said the clerk. "If you wish to lodge a complaint, this isn't the place. You must apply to your legation – we can't help you. Was there something else?"

Fräulein Fifi had just been to the theatre. It was the third time this week: Châtelet the day before yesterday, the music hall at the Olympia on Tuesday, the Trianon today. They'd left after the second act. There had been a minor altercation in the foyer between Mario and his friends – these Italians were so temperamental – but only over where they should have supper afterwards, the Fantasio or the Chez moi. In the end they'd agreed on Adrienne's for the sake of the *coq en pâte*, its celebrated speciality. Mario knew all the best restaurants. Now they were sitting in the hotel bar, and it was boring. Mario and his friends were talking business, discussing stocks and shares such as Creusot, Hotchkiss, Gaz Torino, Randfontein. If Randfontein or Tanganyika went up in the next few days, Fräulein Fifi would get her platinum bracelet, she knew . . . There was dancing in the ballroom across the way – she could see the couples through the open door. The young Belgian had looked in just to say hello to her. He was sorry he couldn't stay, he said. An urgent appointment, but he'd be back in half an hour. An awfully handsome young man, he was. Polite, charming, good-mannered, well-educated – a real gentleman. Unpunctual, that was his only failing. When he said he'd be back in half an hour, he . . . Still, the half-hour wasn't up yet. He'd invited her to go to Brussels with him. An opera singer, a friend of his, would test her voice. "With a voice like yours, you can't fail to make your fortune, believe me, Fräulein Fifi. The makings are there. All you need is coaching." Brussels was a lovely city, so they said. Practise scales every day? Well, why not? Mind you, there wasn't a lovelier city in the world than Paris, but Mario only intended to stay another week. Poor Mario, he didn't know he'd be travelling back to Milan on his own, not yet, but he was the one who'd always said they would have to split up sooner or later . . .

Fifi had three alternatives: she could go to Brussels, London, or Menton. She had lots of friends. The architect whose name she could never remember wanted to take her to London with him, but London didn't appeal to her overmuch. London at this time of year? Ugh! The baron was the smartest of the lot. He lived in Paris, but he wasn't as rich as all that, according to Mario – his father kept him short. She wouldn't go to Milan, not for anything. Milan was a deadly place. It would be nice if the young Belgian showed up again . . .

Her glass was empty. A waiter appeared like magic and plucked the champagne bottle out of the ice bucket. Mario was still going on about East Rand and Crédit Mobilier. The waiter was supposed to be a genuine count – a Count Volkonsky –

whereas the Baron was just a baron. The Baron said *"tu"* to Mario. How did Mario come to know an aristocrat like him? Mario was a footwear manufacturer. He looked really comical in a dinner jacket, with his jet-black moutache and his fat red face.

Fifi drank a little champagne, just to pass the time, and all at once she felt sad. Tears sprang to her eyes, and she yearned to rest her head on Mario's shoulder. She knew precisely why she was feeling so tearful: because it had rained and snowed all day and the sun was nowhere to be seen; because she wouldn't be going to Milan with Mario; because she'd missed the third act; because the poor waiter was a genuine count and had to carry trays around. Life was so awful, so lovely and so sad, and time went by so fast.

But her fit of the blues soon passed. No more tears. She was suddenly in a good mood again – almost in high spirits. It was nice to sit here and watch people. She enjoyed trying to guess where they came from and what they did during the day. They were such a mixed bag: painters and other forms of genius, Parisian socialites, American tourists, bourgeois from the provinces. The pale, clean-shaven gentleman looked like an actor, probably a film actor. The plump man with the cigar came from Holland and was a wholesale butter merchant. Done any good business in Paris, Mynheer Vanderbeek? Really? Delighted to hear it. That fellow over there in the threadbare suit must be a student from the Latin Quarter. He was being reckless today and drinking a coffee here instead of in some cheap café. Why was he staring at her? Was he admiring her dress? It came from Madeleine's in rue Rougemont, my lad, if you're interested. What did he want? Why was he staring at her like that?

Fräulein Fifi's face took on a bewildered, helpless expression. She was just about to turn to Mario – "That man over there, what's he playing at?" – when the man in question raised his head and brushed the hair out of his eyes. Without knowing why, Fräulein Fifi got up and went over to his table.

"Georg! What are you doing here?"

"Is it really you, Franzi? I kept looking at you and wondering if it was you or not."

"Have I changed that much? What about you? Where have you sprung from? Tell me!"

They both spoke at once, asked a score of questions, talked at cross purposes. She glanced at Mario, but he was still deep in conversation and hadn't even noticed that she'd left the table.

"Hold on, I'll join you," she said. "And now, tell me all about yourself."

"You first. If you've come from Vienna, what news of my father and my sisters?"

"I don't know. They're fine, I think – I've been away for so long. It was just a holiday trip at first, but then I fell in love with the place."

"Have you got a job here?" Vittorin asked.

She tossed her head. "No, I do a lot of travelling. Menton, Brussels . . . I may study singing – the next few days will tell. One of my gentlemen friends –"

Vittorin scowled at her. "The baron, you mean?"

"You know?" she said, taken aback. "How come you know him?"

Then she remembered. A long-forgotten spectacle took shape in her mind's eye: two dummies ingeniously constructed of old clothes and seated on a sofa. She smiled.

"Yes, the Baron's here too – I see him sometimes – but my friend is that gentleman over there, the one with the black moustache. He's a big industrialist from Milan. I met him in Lugano."

Vittorin was still in the dark. He knew only that he had lost her, perhaps for ever. She belonged to someone else.

"Are you fond of him?" he asked. "Do you intend to marry him?"

"Yes – maybe, I mean, but what's the difference? He's a divorced Catholic."

Vittorin said nothing.

"Paris is wonderful, isn't it? Fantastically interesting. Do you like it here?"

186

Vittorin still said nothing.

"Don't keep staring at my hands," she went on, "I know they aren't my best feature. My, look at the fur that woman's wearing! Chinchilla!"

Vittorin had come to a decision. He looked her full in the face.

"What if I ask you this, Franzi? Will you come home with me – will you start a new life with me? Well, answer!"

The question took her by surprise. She was so bewildered she didn't know what to say.

"'What if?' – that's what you said, but you don't have any intention of asking me, not really."

"Yes I do! I want to know. In two day's time my mission will be over. Two days from now I'll be free. I'll work, I'll earn a living. That's the situation. And now, answer me."

Back to the dreary daily grind? Back to the typewriter? Up at seven every morning to brew the breakfast coffee on a gas ring? Living as a twosome in a back room overlooking an air well? Could she? It was unthinkable – he didn't have the first idea! However, she refrained from turning him down flat.

"Do I have to decide right away, Georg?"

"Yes, you do. I can't wait."

"It would be lovely," she said, "but it wouldn't work."

"Why not?"

"Why do you think! What would my friends say if I simply walked out on them? And besides –"

"So you won't?"

"No, Georg, it really wouldn't do. Don't be angry with me."

They were like two strangers all of a sudden. Neither of them spoke a word. Vittorin glanced at the clock – time was getting short. Franzi glanced over at Mario, uncertain how to say goodbye. There was nothing left *to* say.

There was the young Belgian at last! He paused in the doorway, smitten with indecision at the sight of her in the company of a man he didn't know – not her type at all.

187

"Please excuse me, Georg," Franzi said quickly, "I'm meeting someone. Will we see each other again?"

Vittorin had risen.

"I doubt it. My train leaves in forty minutes."

"Really?" She raised her eyebrows. "Forty minutes, eh? You're still the same as ever – always leaving on the next train out. Goodbye, Georg."

The young Belgian escorted her to the ballroom. She turned in the doorway and gave a little wave before settling herself in her partner's arms. Other couples glided past. Vittorin spotted the mauve-trimmed neckline of Franzi's dress and the gleam of her hair. Then she disappeared from view.

He continued to stand there, waiting for a final glimpse of her. Five minutes went by, then six. He would have to go. Numerous couples had passed the door, swaying to the music as they stared straight through him with an air of total indifference. Franzi might have been among them, he couldn't say for sure.

SELYUKOV

There were only three other people in the compartment from Innsbruck onwards. The old woman in the headscarf was bound for Bischofshofen to take up a post as cook at a Gasthaus there. The plump, bald, cheerful man, who travelled for a wholesale wine firm, had samples of numerous South Tyrolean wines in his case. As soon as they pulled out of Innsbruck he begged a slice of bread from the Gasthaus cook and cut it into four equal portions. Then he produced a tasting cup from his case and invited the others to sample his Terlaner, Traminer and St Magdalener. The young man in the sports jacket, a power station engineer, announced that he was off to South America in a couple of years' time. Brazil – that was the land of the future.

The wine salesman nodded. There was still money to be made in South America, he said. He used to have a relative in Lima, a maternal great-uncle to whom he would always be grateful for the remittances that had helped to finance his education. There were worse preparations for life than five years in high school. A certain standard of education was essential in his job. You had to be able to communicate with customers, find out what their interests were and what they liked to talk about; then the orders came by themselves. He'd been in the wine trade for five years. Before that he'd travelled for a type-writer manufacturer, but that was an absolute dog's life.

"Are you going to Vienna on business?" he asked, turning to Vittorin.

Vittorin, staring into space, didn't answer right away. He was picturing a room with red curtains, and standing in the room was Selyukov. The book on the desk was a French novel with a frontispiece depicting a naked woman. A shot! Selyukov had fired. The bullet ploughed into the door panel and splintered it. He had no time to fire again. It was Vittorin's turn now, but what if there was a woman in the room? Selyukov had a woman on the premises, that was absolutely certain; he'd got her hidden behind the screen. She would scream – she would call for help. Well, let her. Let her scream – let her telephone the police, it didn't matter what happened afterwards. Selyukov collapsed and lay quite still. He'd pulled the screen over on top of him as he fell . . .

"No," said Vittorin, "I'm going to Vienna for purely personal reasons."

The train made a longish stop at Salzburg. A little man with a remarkably pallid complexion was pacing the platform, his shoulders hunched up against the cold. His smart patent-leather shoes contrasted oddly with an unfashionable hat, an ill-cut overcoat, and a pair of excessively baggy trousers displaying only vestiges of a crease. He was muttering to himself as he went. Vittorin accosted him. The pale-faced man glanced at him, raised his hat, and walked on. Vittorin caught him up.

"It's Herr Bamberger, isn't it? Don't you remember me?"

The man came to a halt.

"Yes, I think so. That's to say, my memory's not of the best. Can you give me a little help?"

"My name is Georg Vittorin."

"Georg Vittorin – of course. Please forgive me for not recognizing you right away. What can I do for you, Herr Vittorin?"

"I had a conversation with you a couple of years ago, Herr Bamberger. I've often thought of you since. All I really wanted to ask you was: did you win your war?"

"My war?" Herr Bamberger looked mystified.

"Yes, you predicted the collapse of our currency, and you were right. You said there was going to be a war of each against all, and you were determined to win it."

"Forgive me, but I'm still not absolutely . . . what was your name again?"

"Georg Vittorin. You were renting a room in my father's apartment at the time."

Herr Bamberger smote his brow.

"I've placed you at last! My memory really does let me down sometimes. How are your sisters, Herr Vittorin?"

The power station engineer walked past. He respectfully raised his hat, but Herr Bamberger failed to notice.

"One of them got married," Vittorin improvised. "The elder of the two, but you probably knew that." He paused. "Or aren't you still in touch with my family?"

"I fear we've drifted apart," Herr Bamberger said politely.

"You grew tired of the room, I suppose?"

"Not at all. I simply found it more convenient to rent a small apartment near my office. What about you, Herr Vittorin?"

"I've been travelling for the past two years. France, Spain, Turkey, Russia."

"An educational tour?"

"Not really. I had some personal business to attend to abroad."

"And now? What are your future plans?"

"That's what I'd like to discuss with you, Herr Bamberger. I don't want to go back to the old routine – I've developed an aversion to the phrase 'a steady job'. I want to be free and independent. I want to work for myself, not help to line someone else's pockets."

Herr Bamberger stared silently, thoughtfully, into the middle distance.

"You want my opinion? Well, if I may offer you a word of advice –"

He broke off. A smartly dressed young man had just hurried up.

"Excuse me," the young man said with a little bow. "We're not leaving for eight minutes. Your call to Vienna will be through in another two. Would you like me to –"

"Thanks," Herr Bamberger cut in. "I'll take it myself."

He turned back to Vittorin.

"Do forgive me, I have to speak with Vienna urgently. Please remember me to your family. Ah yes, you asked my advice. I don't take too rosy a view of the immediate future – there's a cold wind blowing. If you want my opinion, obtain a modest but secure position in some well-established firm – that's your best hedge against the years to come. Delighted to have met you again, Herr Vittorin. My regards to your charming sisters."

And he set off for the stationmaster's office.

The engineer was waiting in the doorway of the compartment.

"Are you personally acquainted with President Bamberger?" he asked as Vittorin resumed his seat.

"Slightly acquainted, yes," said Vittorin. "Is he a president these days? What does the title signify?"

"He's the boss of C. L. F. Holdings, didn't you know? One of our biggest industrial tycoons."

"I see. What about the young man with him?"

"His private secretary, at a guess. An enviable job. Some folk have all the luck. He probably earns a minister's salary, goes on nice trips in a private railway carriage –"

"A private carriage?"

"Of course. That's why we're six minutes late, because we waited at Schwarzach for President Bamberger's private carriage. I doubt if we'll make up the time before we get to Linz."

Vittorin brushed a lock of hair out of his eyes and made no comment. He had only a fleeting recollection of the elegant young man who had inherited his share of life's *table d'hôte*.

"Bamberger's a dollar millionaire many times over," the engineer went on. "I read in the paper last week that he's acquired a majority holding in our company as well. I'm with Elektro-Union, by the way. How did you get to know him?"

"He once offered me a place in his private carriage," Vittorin said pensively, "but I turned it down. Our destinations were entirely different."

Suburban roofs and windows reflected the light of a bleak winter's morning. The puddles of melted snow had become coated with a thin film of ice overnight. Vittorin strode briskly

192

along, shivering in his thin overcoat but heedless of the wind that drove watery snowflakes into his face and the damp chill that penetrated his clothing. Oskar tried hard to keep in step. Every now and then he glanced sideways at his long-lost brother, alarmed by the strange, set expression on his face. This was his third attempt to engage Georg in conversation.

"I'm usually at the office by now," he said with an involuntary gesure in the direction of the Schottentor. "We start work at eight, but I've taken the day off. It's a wonderful invention, the pneumatic post. You scribble a couple of lines – 'flu or some other excuse – and you're off the hook. A schoolmate of mine died of 'flu six weeks ago. I'd been out drinking with him on the Saturday night and they buried him the following Thursday – it's as quick as that, and I never even knew. All I thought was, where's old Max, why haven't I seen him around? No, but what I meant to say was, you must write a job application complete with a *curriculum vitae* and leave the rest to me – I'm *persona gratissima* at the office. But don't say anything about not having had a job for years. Gloss over that, or it might make a bad impression. Is it really so difficult, finding a job abroad?"

"I never stayed long enough in any one place," Vittorin replied. "You know me, I've got itchy feet. I'm a born idler – Ebenseder says so, so it must be true."

"Never you mind what Ebenseder says," Oskar told him. "I don't like him any more than you do. I begged Lola not to marry the man, over and over, but when they retired Father early, that settled it. 'What else can I do?' she said. 'I've got Father and Vally's future to think of.' Well, Father's properly provided for now – whatever he makes on his little business deals he keeps as pocket money, and Vally's studying at the Conservatory. Ebenseder isn't a bad lot, he's just unlikeable. Lola may even have grown fond of him by now. You can never tell with women."

There was the apartment house, a building like any other. On the right of the entrance was a glazier's, on the left a florist's and a public lottery office. A small china plate announced that a physician specializing in internal diseases had his consulting room on the first floor. A small black dog was cavorting with some other dogs in the middle of the road, deaf to the pleas of its owner, an old woman laden with a shopping bag and sheltering under a patched cotton umbrella. Barrels were being unloaded from a dray.

Vittorin had come to a halt.

"Are you going write that application today?" Oskar asked.

"I don't know."

"If you gave it to me today, you might get an interview tomorrow."

"I don't think I'd better make any plans at present."

"You could start work on the first."

"It's hard to say where I'll be on the first."

"Will I be seeing you again today?"

"I can't tell you that either."

Oskar eyed his brother uneasily. "Won't you let me come with you?"

Vittorin shook his head. "No, it's something I've got to do on my own. No one can help me."

"I'll stay here, then," Oskar said. "I won't go home, I'll wait in the coffee-house across the street."

"All right, but if I'm not out in half an hour, don't bother to wait any longer."

"What do you mean?" Oskar protested. "I don't understand. What are you up to? I tell you this much: if you aren't out in half an hour I'm going upstairs to find out what's happened to you."

"If you insist," said Vittorin.

He had a vision of the street transformed. Heads were craning out of every window, onlookers crowding around the entrance. A lanky policeman had stationed himself in the doorway and was holding the throng at bay.

"Move along there!" – "What happened? Has there been an accident?" – "Murder. The doctor's been shot by one of his patients." – "No, it was on the second floor." – "The Russian, you mean?" – "No, some other man, dead. Two ex-officers, a duel without witnesses. The Russian was wounded." – "Let me through, I live here!" – "Move along there!"

"Yes," said Vittorin, "if I'm not out in half an hour you can come and fetch me."

And he shook hands with his brother more warmly than he had ever done before.

The stairwell was dark. A faint sense of apprehension stole over him as he ascended the steep stairs. He had a sudden feeling that he was not alone. The gloom seemed alive with movement – there were shadowy figures and silent footsteps all around him. The dead had come too, eager to witness the culmination of the battle in which they had perished. Baron Pistolkors, leaning against the banisters in his cherry-red dressing-gown, gave a welcoming nod. "Killed in battle," said a voice, and Vittorin had a momentary vision of Count Gagarin's laughing, boyish face. Artemyev addressed him out of the darkness in a whisper: "Is that you, comrade? I've been expecting you. Now show us what you're made of." Shuffling footsteps, groans and moans: they had come too, the Red soldiers whom he had led into a hail of shot and shell at Miropol. They stood at his back in serried ranks, ready to follow him once more.

Light slanting down from a landing window revealed the stairs, the worn banisters, the whitewashed walls. Slowly and laboriously, Vittorin climbed the last few steps. He was outside the apartment now.

The unfamiliar name on the door meant nothing to him. The sight of it jolted him like an electric shock: perhaps he was too late. "Herr Selyukov? He moved out yesterday. No, he left no forwarding address . . ." While he was still debating this possibility, he caught a whiff of something in the air, some faint and exotic fragrance emanating from behind the closed door. He knew it of old – he knew it from Siberia, from Chernavyensk Camp. It was the aroma of Chinese tobacco, the aroma of the cigarettes Selyukov used to smoke. Vittorin shut his eyes and breathed in the scent of bygone days with an ineffable sense of well-being.

Then he rang the bell. He knew it now: Selyukov was beyond that door.

Facing the door stood a bed with a striped counterpane. The space between the bed and the window was occupied by a peculiar piece of furniture, a kind of small table fitted with a treadle and two wheels. Screwed to the right-hand wall was a bookcase far too capacious for the few books it contained. Some of the remaining shelf space was taken up by a spirit lamp and a stoneware teapot. The wardrobe, the chest of drawers, the windowsill – every surface, every nook and cranny teemed with carved wooden figures: village musicians in colourful costumes, sabre-wielding Cossacks, carousing peasants, a troika, a village smithy, dancing bears, and, beside the ewer on the washstand, a multitude of little wooden pilgrims converging on a church with a blue onion dome.

The table in the middle of the room was a clutter of small knives with curved blades of different shapes, pots of paint, lengths of wood. Seated at the table was an unshaven, bespectacled man in a threadbare jacket, and that man was Selyukov.

Still holding the doorhandle, Vittorin surveyed the painted wooden figures, the torn counterpane, the bespectacled man, the chipped ewer. The room was cold, the cast-iron stove unlit.

Selyukov rose. His slippers were down-at-heel and his trousers had worn through at the knees. The table fitted with a treadle was a lathe.

"Do you remember me, Mikhail Mikhailovich?" Vittorin asked at length.

No, Selyukov didn't remember him. He took off his glasses and polished them. His eyes were inflamed.

"Lieutenant Vittorin, ex-prisoner of war, Hut 4, Chernavyensk Camp."

The man whose face resembled Selyukov's smiled and spoke in Selyukov's voice. "Chernavyensk! That was a long time ago. I was an officer in the service of Russia in those days."

"And now?"

"You can see for yourself. I get by. I make toys, and a comrade who used to be my orderly during the Great War peddles them in the street. Sometimes he sells a few, but sometimes he returns at nightfall empty-handed."

196

Vittorin dredged his memory for a word, but in vain. A great void yawned inside him. He stared out of the window at the buildings opposite. *Pashol* – wasn't that the word? *Pashol!* This man with the stubbly chin and worn-out slippers was Selyukov. Where was his St George's Cross? Where was his cigarette? He'd never seen Selyukov without a cigarette, so why was there no aroma of Chinese tobacco? All he could now smell was varnish, glue, and wet paint. He produced a packet of cigarettes.

"Do you smoke, Mikhail Mikhailovich?" he asked in a low voice.

"No. I used to, but I don't any more."

"But weren't you smoking just before I came in? Foreign tobacco?"

"No," said Selyukov. "I haven't smoked for a year, but if I may . . ."

He helped himself to one of Vittorin's cigarettes and lit up. Holding it in the old, inimitable way – clamped between two fingers of his left hand – he blew a succession of smoke rings. For a moment Vittorin felt that he was confronted by Staff Captain Selyukov of the haughty face, holder of the Cross of St George and the Order of Vladimir . . .

"How are you faring these days, Mikhail Mikhailovich?" he asked, and there was a cold, hard edge to his voice. "Are you content with life?"

"Content? You could even say I'm more than content. I've always been lucky. 'Selyukov has the luck of the devil,' my comrades used to say. 'He'd find a cool spot in hell itself.' I'm doing fine. Just to show you, I had a mistress in Moscow, an opera singer. Well, she's now in Vienna too, living in that house across the street. She doesn't know I'm here, though, nor is she going to find out. I don't want her to see me as I am today, but I can watch her from my window, sitting at the piano and singing. I see her every day. Sometimes a young man accompanies her. He isn't her lover, I've made inquiries – he's the singing coach from the opera house. Why shouldn't I be content with life?"

Vittorin said nothing. Without knowing it, he gave a little sigh.

"So you've done me the honour of calling on me," Selyukov said. "What can I do for you?"

Vittorin started. He had been far away in the snow-lashed Russian steppe, in the streets of Moscow, in open country with bullets whistling past his ears, in the isolation ward of a fever hospital, in a brilliantly lit Parisian hotel. A jazz band was blaring. The girl he loved had just said goodbye and walked off on someone else's arm, and now this ageing man had asked him a question: what did he want, why had he come . . .

"I wanted," Vittorin said haltingly, "I thought – I mean, someone told me there were Russian toys for sale here. I'm looking for some Russian toys – I'd like to buy some."

"By all means," said Selyukov, making no attempt to conceal his surprise and pleasure. "Buy as many as you like. They aren't expensive, but the materials, the paints, the incidentals – you understand, I'm sure. My assistant will deliver them to your home."

He produced a selection of garishly painted Cossacks, a white-bearded Orthodox priest, two hares with movable ears, a St Ivan, and a peasant woman carrying a pitcher of milk. Vittorin bought the entire set.

Grisha appeared in the hallway. He bowed low.

"*Sdravstvuy*, Grisha," said Vittorin, who had awoken from a kind of dream.

"My humble respects, Your Honour."

"I went to your village, Grisha – to Staromyena. I spoke with your mother. She's sitting at home, pining for you."

"So she'll laugh when I return," said Grisha, looking down at his hands, which were red and swollen with the cold.

"Your godfather Gavrila Shikulin is dead," Vittorin went on. "They've sent the blacksmith to prison."

"May a hundred bricks fall on his head there," muttered Grisha. "So he's dead, Gavrila Ivanich, and I'll never see him again. My godfather, he was. Well, God ordained it so. It was His holy will."

"The blacksmith sold some stolen horses. Your mother says to tell you she's being careful with money. She was all right for bread until March, but she doesn't have anyone to dig the garden for her."

"She should get hold of Katyusha, the tailor's daughter. She's only got one eye, Katyusha, but she's a sturdy creature and knows the work. Tell my mother to have a word with the tailor," said Grisha, looking at Vittorin as if it were a foregone conclusion that he would go straight back to Staromyena in the Government of Kharkov and advise the old woman accordingly.

"And here's your watch," said Vittorin. "Your mother asked me to give it to you."

Grisha took the watch and beamed all over his broad, flat face. He lovingly stroked its battered case, then wound it and held it to his ear.

"Dear little Mamushka," he cried. "She thinks of everything. Yes, this is my watch right enough. I knew she'd send it on – she promised she would."

Outside in the street the wind blew a cloud of snow into Vittorin's face, but the café was only just across the way. Oskar jumped up and came over as soon as he entered.

"Well?" he asked.

"That's that," said Vittorin. "What foul weather – I'm wet through. I might have picked a better day to come."

"What went on in there? What happened?"

"Nothing much – I really don't know why you're so worked up. I brought a Russian peasant greetings from his mother and passed on a few items of news about his village. Good lord, eleven o'clock already. I've wasted the whole morning."

And with one little gesture Vittorin wiped his life's slate clean of two years that had cast him in the role of adventurer, murderer, hero, coal-heaver, gambler, pimp, and vagrant – with one little, unrevealing gesture expressive of a wasted morning and a sodden overcoat.